PUFFIN BOOKS

UK | USA | Canada | Ireland | Australia
India | New Zealand | South Africa

Puffin Books is part of the Penguin Random House group of companies
whose addresses can be found at global.penguinrandomhouse.com.

www.penguin.co.uk
www.puffin.co.uk
www.ladybird.co.uk

First published 2024
001

Text design by Janene Spencer
Printed in Great Britain by Clays Ltd, Elcograf S.p.A.

The authorized representative in the EEA is Penguin Random House Ireland,
Morrison Chambers, 32 Nassau Street, Dublin D02 YH68

A CIP catalogue record for this book is available from the British Library

ISBN: 978-0-241-63130-0

All correspondence to:
Puffin Books
Penguin Random House Children's
One Embassy Gardens, 8 Viaduct Gardens, London SW11 7BW

For Jo

THE DAY MY DOG GOT FAMOUS

Jen Carney

PUFFIN

FRIDAY, TEN MINUTES UNTIL A FORTNIGHT OF FREEDOM

Drum roll, please!

Miss Grogan makes a final circuit of the display boards, then clip-clops back to her desk.

CLIP
CLOP

'You've made it *very* tricky for me, Year Five,' she says, her eyes twinkling. 'But I've made my decision. Drum roll, please!'

Some kids rap their knuckles on their tables. Others use pencils and rulers. Most also stamp their feet. Usually, I'd join in with this rare opportunity to make as much noise as physically possible in class. Today, I stay as still as I can, squeezing my thighs together to hold on to the nervous wee bubbling

1

inside me. If I'm to believe my classmates, my entry into the end-of-term art challenge has a high chance of winning. A wet patch on my pants would definitely ruin the moment.

I make the mistake of catching Destiny Dean's eye across the table. She flashes me a confident sneer, then flutters her eyelashes in Miss Grogan's direction, her right index finger placed firmly across her lips. Typical Destiny. As if our teacher's decision will be swayed by noticing who's pointing at their nostrils. Although, to be honest, Destiny's a regular winner of our class competitions. But we've never been set an art challenge before. And drawing's my thing.

My mum says I was born holding a felt-tip pen and announced my 'artistic genius' by drawing the intricate ring of leaves that circle her bellybutton.

I used to scrawl on anything I could lay my hands on when I was little – walls, floors, clothes, my own naked body(!) – so I totally didn't get this was a joke until I was about six and discovered what tattoos were. I'm *such* a doofus.

Nowadays, I stick to paper and my favourite things to draw are cartoons. That's what I've entered into the competition: a comic strip of my most popular character: **Astoundog**.

'It's got to be you, Ferris!' whispers Cal, my best mate, nudging me in my ribs as Miss Grogan makes a grand show of writing the winner's name on the certificate. He jerks his head to the display boards. 'That **Astoundog** cartoon you entered is brilliant.'

I smile. **Astoundog** is a regular feature of *The Hoot* – the monthly comic I make – and all my friends love him. For a moment, I let myself dream that Miss Grogan might love my genius super dog too.

3

'Without further ado,' announces Miss Grogan, 'the winner of the end-of-term art challenge is . . .' She flaps her hands up and down to silence the drum-rolling. Her eyes scan the classroom, stopping at my table. My stomach flips a somersault. A few of my friends turn to grin at me. Cal grips my knee. I cross my fingers and squirm in my seat. Miss Grogan picks up the certificate and smiles. 'DESTINY DEAN!'

ART CHALLENGE
★ Winner ★
Destiny Dean
Signed: Miss Grogan

A collective gasp sweeps the classroom. I feel my insides go cold. Destiny punches the air, then, to a ripple of unenthusiastic applause, skips to the front to collect her certificate. She sneers at me on her way back to her seat and, after checking Miss Grogan's not looking, whips her hand to her forehead and throws me the L for loser sign.

I shrug and pretend I'm not bothered. Inside, I'm reeling.

It's not that Destiny's entry was rubbish. She's a pretty good artist. Just like she's a good

5

writer, and a talented musician, and a fast runner.
Art's the *only* thing I'm any good at; I thought this
was my chance to finally beat her.

When the bell sounds for home time, I run to
the toilets as fast as my crossed legs will take me.
Two minutes later, I head to the cloakroom feeling
deflated, and not just because my bladder's empty.

'Told you I'd win, Ferris!' snipes Destiny, barging
past me to grab her glittery backpack from her peg.
'Cartoons are for babies.'

Jenson scowls at Destiny on my behalf. 'No,
they're not!' He turns to me and smiles. 'Hard luck,
Ferris. I thought your entry was best by MILES.'

'Me, too,' says Penny. 'I can't wait for the next
edition of *The Hoot* to come out.'

'Yeah!' adds Idris. 'When will it be ready? After
the holidays?'

'I hope so,' I say. That's my aim anyway.

Alfie thrusts his fist
towards me. 'Wicked!' he
shouts, as we bump knuckles.

'I'll save some of my spends!'

I smile. My friends are brilliant. Not just because they defend me against Destiny. They appreciate the work I put into my cartoons and not one of them complained when I started charging for *The Hoot*.

Creating ten pages of original content every month has been pretty full on. But boy, it's been worth it. So far, from four issues, I've made £76.50, one green yo-yo and three packets of chewing gum. I'm OK with swapsies; I know what it's like not to have money for the things you desperately want. It's the reason I had to stop giving my work away for free: I'm desperate for a d-TAB.

You probably already know this, but d-TABs are THE BEST drawing tablets money can buy. I've been dying for one since the day I watched a video of Clare-the-Flare, my comic-strip hero, using theirs to demonstrate how to draw Brainy Baz – the genius toddler that landed them a job as one of the chief content creators at KidToon, the biggest comic company in the world. Basically, d-TABs have EVERYTHING I need to take my cartooning to the next level: whizzy digital drawing software; tons of built-in pen styles; every colour in the world available at the tap of a button; unique animation features; and nifty functions that will make it mega quick and super easy to share my best work with comic companies, get my characters noticed and move a step closer to my dream of becoming a professional comic-strip artist. Ideally, I'd love a d-5000, but I'd be happy with a d-4000. Both come with a d-Pen.

The problem is, even the cheapest d-TABs cost five hundred pounds, and my mums are very particular about the difference between 'need' and 'want'. One of their favourite phrases is telling me that two pounds a week spending money is 'more than enough for a ten-year-old boy who has everything he really needs'.

As you can tell, it's a long time since my mums were ten. And, as far as I know, they've never been boys. What do *they* know?

'You were robbed, Ferris,' says Cal, jolting me from my thoughts. He manoeuvres his wheelchair over to me, claps me on the back, then turns to face Destiny. 'You only won because your entry was a portrait of Miss Grogan and it made her look twenty years younger than she is. Everyone knows Ferris is a better artist than you.'

I'm not. Not really. We just have different styles. But most people nod. No one likes Destiny when she's in one of her showy-offy mean moods, which, unfortunately, is more often than not these days.

Destiny waves her certificate so close to Cal's face his fringe wafts up and down. 'I think this proves otherwise, California!'

'Whatever,' says Cal. He rolls his eyes at me. 'Ignore her.'

I glance over my shoulder as though Destiny's invisible. 'Ignore who?'

As usual, Cal dissolves into a fit of giggles at my quick wit. 'Enjoy your holiday, Ferris. I hope you don't encounter that annoying neighbour of yours.'

Did I mention, not only is Destiny Dean my classmate, she's my next-door neighbour, too. Can you believe my luck? I literally have no escape.

As Cal wheels himself to After School Club, the scowl on Destiny's face is replaced with a sly smile.

'Face it, Ferris, I'm SO MUCH better at art than you.'

Grrr. If I had 50p for every time Destiny Dean told me she was SO MUCH better than me at something, or that she owned something that was SO MUCH better than mine, I'd be able to buy a d-TAB for everyone in Year Five. I bite my tongue to save myself getting into an argument, then grab my bookbag and pull out the only copy of *The Hoot*

I didn't manage to sell at afternoon break. 'Anyone want to buy this?' I ask no one in particular.

'Me, please!' says Destiny.

Wait, what?

Of all my classmates, Destiny's the only person who's never bought a copy of *The Hoot*. I frown. What's the catch? There's got to be a catch.

'Here you are!' she says, pulling a 50p piece from the front pocket of her backpack and thrusting it towards me.

After a moment of suspicious hesitation, I un-narrow my eyes, take the money and hand her my creation. 'Thanks,' I say. 'And well done on winning the art challenge. You deserved it.'

She didn't. Cal was right. Her entry was a suck-up. But it's the start of the spring holidays tomorrow and, like I mentioned, she's my next-door neighbour. There's no way I can avoid her for a whole fortnight. Playing nice is probably a good

11

call, especially as she's finally supporting my comic venture. Plus, I feel a bit sorry for her. Not a single person has congratulated her for winning the art challenge.

Destiny examines *The Hoot* and nods her head. 'Just as I thought. Flimsy! And the perfect size to put through Daddy's shredder. Harmony will love pooing on this.'

The cheek of her! *The Hoot* is a work of art. How dare she suggest all it's good for is hamster poop.

I've a mind to grab my comic back and tell her to stuff her money where the sun doesn't shine. But 50p's 50p at the end of the day, and I need every penny I can get.

Hmph. So much for playing nice.

Anyone for a Mr Whippy?

Across the playground, I spot Mum at the gate looking flustered. That's actually not an unusual look for Mum, but she doesn't usually attract such a crowd.

She waves when she spots me.

COME ON, SLOW COACH! I COULD USE AN EXTRA PAIR OF HANDS OVER HERE.

"*MB*"

I jog to the gate to see what's going on and stop dead when I see my dog, Aldo. It's not that he's panting like he's just completed a marathon that shocks me. Nor that his tongue is hanging from the side of his mouth like a slice of raw bacon. But because there's one leg of

13

a pair of pink tights dangling out of his bottom.

I know my dog isn't fussy about what he eats – he's saved me from a variety of leafy vegetables over the years – but even I'm surprised to discover he's taken to gobbling woollen underwear.

I bend to give him a kiss, and laugh, 'What have you done now, boy?'

After licking my face, Aldo regards his rear end with interest, then starts spinning in circles, trying to grab the material that's wafting about under his tail. When he realizes his neck isn't long enough, he scoots his bum across the ground, dragging Mum with him, then assumes his poo-squat. A little more of the tights emerge. It's like watching the weirdest, grossest Mr Whippy machine ever. The infants in the crowd erupt with laughter, stopping suddenly when Aldo lets out a low-pitched whine.

I glance at his bottom, then look at Mum.

'They're stuck!'

Mum slams her shoe on the section of the
tights that's made it to the ground, then
dips in her pocket and hands me half
a digestive. 'Take this and call him
to you, Ferris! They'll be out in
a jiffy.'

The crowd laughs again. Concealing my
embarrassment, I do as I'm told. I'd do anything to
help Aldo. He's my best friend, along with Cal. 'Aldo,
here boy!'

Aldo's brow furrows. His tail stills. He flops
his belly on to the pavement, his eyes bulging like
gobstoppers. Oh blimey. He's NEVER declined a
biscuit before. He must be in real pain.

'Here, sweetie,' says Mum, beckoning me back
to her. 'Don't panic. You hold his lead while I cover
my hand with a poo bag. I'm going to have to pull
them out.'

A collective 'Urgh!' comes from the crowd. This
is quickly followed by an 'Oooo!' that gets louder the

15

more material Mum releases, and ends with a cheer as she pulls the last threads of pink wool from Aldo's bottom with a pop.

As the crowd disperses, their afternoon entertainment over, Aldo nuzzles my leg. I kneel on the pavement and give him a cuddle for being brave. That's when I notice Destiny Dean staring at us from the passenger seat of her dad's flashy new car.

She lowers her window, holds up her copy of *The Hoot* and points at the drawing of **Astoundog** on the front cover. 'I know why you're always drawing this super dog, Ferris.' She glances at her dad to check he's still on his phone, then lowers her voice to a whisper. 'It's because your real-life dog's a loser, just like you.'

Before I have a chance to defend my best friend, the window is raised and the car zooms off up the road.

'Sorry, sweetie,' says Mum, returning from the poo bin. 'I was a bit sidetracked by that palaver.' She widens her eyes. 'How did you get on in the art challenge?'

I bite my lip and shake my head.

'Oh, sweetie. I'm sorry. I thought your comic strip was amazing.' She plasters my hair with kisses and takes my hand. 'Come on, let's go home. You're a winner in my eyes.'

It's only a ten-minute walk from school to our house. Even though I sometimes wish Mum would collect me in the car, sauntering along in the fresh air with Aldo improves my mood this afternoon. Especially when Mum asks me, as she always does, to tell her three good things that happened at school. I guess it's not been a completely terrible day: I sold every single copy of *The Hoot* I took into school; Cal gave me a finger of his Twix at lunchtime; and I rather enjoyed watching Mr Yee, our head teacher, trip over his own shoelace in assembly this morning!

By the time we round the corner of our street, my disappointment at losing to Destiny has subsided and I'm pleased to spot my three-year-old little sister, Keely, waiting to greet me on our driveway with Miz, my other mum. (In case you're interested, when I learned to talk, 'Miz' was what my expert vocal abilities made of 'Mummy Liz' and it's just stuck. Simples.) When we reach them, Keely throws her arms round my right leg, covering my trousers with whatever the goop is around her mouth.

My mums are foster carers, so Keely's actually my foster sister, but she's been with us for so long now I sometimes forget she's not my actual sister. She's a beautiful (often grubby-faced) rascal! I love her.

I tickle her ribs to release her from my leg, then lift her into a cuddle, deciding not to mention that Aldo's demolished her favourite pair of tights.

'Sorry, champ,' says Miz, cocking her head to one side and ruffling my hair.

I frown.

'The art challenge,' she says. 'Mum messaged me.'

Ah. I did wonder what Mum was up to when I was trying to distract Aldo from the discarded tray of chips outside the post office.

'Come on,' continues Miz. She grabs my hand and pulls me towards the front door. 'Miss Grogan might not have picked your entry as a winner, but I think it deserves a prize. In fact . . .' She winks at Mum. 'I have just the thing.'

Ooo, interesting.

We pile into the house and Miz dashes upstairs, returning a moment later with a parcel wrapped in brown paper. 'We've been saving this for your next birthday, but . . .'

Oh. My. Gosh.

The parcel is exactly the right shape to be a d-TAB!

Mums know how much I want one.

They've told me on more than one occasion how impressed they are with my efforts to raise some money myself.

They love my cartoons.

They've seen the light: I don't just WANT a d-TAB. I NEED one.

I throw my arms round Miz and take the parcel.

Eek! This is going to be the best school holiday ever! I know exactly which comic strip I'm going to digitize first. And I think the guys at KidToon will LOVE it.

My heart pounding, I fumble with the string. Will it be the 4000 or the 5000 model? Heck, at this point, even a second-hand 3000 would do.

Eventually managing to untie the knot, I tear the brown paper and reveal . . .

. . . a book about cartooning.

'Thanks, Mums,' I say, swallowing my disappointment. 'It's great.'

I run upstairs and lie on my bed, kicking myself

for getting my hopes up. Aldo comes to join me.
Completely over his tights trauma, he stays with
me until Miz shouts us down for tea. My mood
improves dramatically when I walk into the kitchen:
a takeaway pizza box is
sitting on the table.

It might not be a
d-TAB, but since I smelled
a vegetable stew on the boil
when I walked in the house earlier, I'd call
that a RESULT!

SATURDAY, THE FIRST DAY OF THE HOLIDAYS

A spot of wind

The next morning, Aldo has a terrible case of eggy trumps.

Mums blame me. They say it's because I snuck him the cabbage they piled beside my pizza last night. (Yep, my mums think a takeaway pizza, which, hello, is covered in TOMATO sauce, needs a healthy vegetable accompaniment. Welcome to my world.)

They're probably right, but I tell them they should be grateful I'm supplementing my best friend's meals with actual food so we don't have to install locks on our underwear drawers.

We usually eat breakfast late on Saturdays and today is no exception. So while Mum goes for a shower and Miz gets Keely dressed, I go back to bed with my sketchpad and start the holidays as I mean to continue them: making the next edition of *The Hoot* so good people will be tripping over themselves to buy a copy.

Aldo takes up his usual position under the duvet on my feet, letting off a particularly long and noisy guff as he gets himself comfortable. Not only does this make me laugh, it gives me a couple of ideas for an **Astoundog** strip.

PARRRP!

I'm wondering whether to add more motion lines when Miz walks into my room carrying one of her homemade candles.

'FERRIS!' she snaps, her free hand shooting to cover her nose. 'What have I said about Aldo sleeping in your bed?'

I avoid answering this question by asking one of my own. 'But he's my best friend. How would *you* feel if I said Mum had to sleep on the floor?'

Miz's left eyebrow rises so high it's in danger of developing altitude sickness.

IF MUM WAS A HAIRY BEAST WHO DROOLED AND MOULTED ALL OVER THE SHEETS AND COULDN'T CONTROL HER WIND, I'D AGREE LIKE A SHOT! NOW GET UP AND GET DRESSED.

She lights the candle, then dashes on to the landing as we hear Keely yell 'BANKIE?!' at the top of her voice.

'Bankie' is what Keely calls
the rainbow-coloured knitted
blanket she can't live
without, but which she
constantly chucks behind furniture. Go figure!

Five minutes later, despite my plan to spend my
pre-breakfast alone-time cartooning in bed, I realize
I'm going to have to relocate. My nostrils have pretty
much hardened to the smell of rotten eggs. Mixed
with the terrible smell of Miz's *Dandelion Delight*
candle, I'm in danger of suffocating.

Grabbing my sketchpad and pencil case, I throw
on some clothes and make my way to the front
step to do a spot of people-watching. Some of my
best ideas come to me when I observe real life.
They can be lucrative, too. My opposite neighbour,
Mrs O'Donnell, bought seven copies of Issue One of
The Hoot when I showed her 'The Vanishing Car' and
told her it was inspired by watching her husband
clean his Mini every day for a week.

26

I've barely stepped outside, however, when I wish I'd just found a peg for my nose. Destiny Dean is already out on her driveway next door.

Oh joy.

Oh poo(dle)

'Hello, Ferris!' shouts Destiny. 'SIT!'

I'm about to inform Destiny that Year Five seat-monitor duties don't stretch to our street, and certainly can't be enforced during the school holidays, when I spot the ball of fluff panting at her feet and realize she's talking to her poodle. Poor Princess Foo-Foo. I might not be able to avoid Destiny, but at least I get a fortnight's break from being bossed about.

I nod in their general direction, then sit on the doorstep and root through my pencil case for something I can fashion into earplugs. Listening to Destiny put her poodle through its paces gives me a headache. If you're ever in a similar situation, I have the following words of wisdom: a pair of metal compasses should only ever be used to draw perfect circles.

I'm still trying to wedge a rubber in my right lughole when a pair of fancy trainers with bright yellow laces appears under my nose. 'Look at my new Kickz, Ferris. They cost a hundred and eighty pounds.'

Unless I close my eyes, I have no choice.

'OK . . .' I mumble, wondering whether the laces are made out of gold.

Destiny points at my feet and sneers. 'How much were those things?'

'I'm not sure,' I say. Between you and me, if pushed, I'd hazard a guess at the £6 mark. I distinctly remember Mum whooping when she saw the sale sticker on them in the supermarket.

FOR MUMS WHO LIKE THINGS CHEAP!

ASDI

WHOOP!

I'm in the SALE

NOT AT ALL EMBARRASSING . . .

'Well, mine are SO MUCH better,' says Destiny.

'OK,' I repeat.

'Yes,' says Destiny, as though I've asked her a question. 'Daddy was so proud of me for winning the end-of-term art challenge. He ordered them online last night and they arrived this morning!'

I decide not to ask what a pair of expensive trainers has to do with winning an art competition. Hopefully, that's Destiny's Daily Boast out of the way and I can get on with cartooning in peace.

No such luck. As soon as I start to draw, the lead in my pencil snaps and she's off again. 'Paper and pencils are so last century, Ferris,' she snipes. 'Bet you wish you had a d-4000 like me, don't you?' She runs to her doorstep, picks up her tablet and returns to me, waving it dangerously close to my head.

I sigh. This isn't a new Destiny Daily Boast, but it's one I'm getting pretty tired of. Destiny knows very well I'm saving up for a d-TAB of my own. In fact, I'm almost certain she only asked her dad to buy her one to annoy me. That's how Destiny rolls.

I wouldn't mind, but she doesn't even use any of the cool stuff it can do properly! All she does is make YouStream videos of Princess Foo-Foo.

I glance over at the poodle, which hasn't moved a muscle since being ordered to sit. 'Don't you have a video to film or something, Destiny?' I say, forcing my mouth into a cheesy grin.

It's not that I want to encourage Destiny's driveway dog displays, but I do need her to get out of my face. The next issue of *The Hoot* won't create itself.

'No,' says Destiny. 'I've already posted today's clip. Wanna see it?'

Before I have the chance to decline this terrible, time-consuming offer, the d-4000 is on my knee, YouStream has been opened and a video starts to play.

To the soundtrack of 'Dance of the Sugar Plum Fairy', Princess Foo-Foo totters into the shot dressed in a pink tutu. I hear Destiny shout 'Twirl', at which point the poodle stands on one hind leg, raises its front paws as high as dogs can and performs a perfect pirouette.

As soon as the video ends, Destiny scrolls her finger down the screen, then thrusts it towards me. 'Look, Ferris!' she squeals. 'I only posted this ten minutes ago and it's got twenty-seven likes and eight comments already.'

I nod, then begin searching for my pencil sharpener. Hopefully, Destiny's need to reply to her 'fans' will be enough to divert her attention away from me.

Nope.

She prods my sketchpad. 'You've got to admit, Ferris, having a REAL-LIFE talented dog is SO MUCH better than having to draw one.'

Ignore her. Ignore her. Ignore her.

'I was right yesterday, wasn't I?' she continues. 'You only invented **Astoundog** because Aldo's such a useless mutt.'

Right. That's it. It's one thing being a show-off about beating me and having loads of fancy stuff, but I'm not going to let Destiny Dean keep insulting Aldo. He might be an embarrassing, tights-pooping wind machine at times, but he's still my best friend. Plus, he's far from useless. He's the best hugger ever. (And he makes an excellent footstool when I'm watching TV.)

My dog is far from useless . . .

'For your information, Destiny,' I say, sharpening my pencil to within an inch of its life, 'Aldo has a whole host of talents. *I* just never feel the need to be a massive show-off about it.'

Right then, Mum opens the front door. Unfortunately, before I can stop him, Aldo squeezes past her leg and waddles outside. Ignoring my request to sit, he shampoos my hair with frothy drool, treats me to an unrequested stinky-breathed kiss, then flops on to his belly and trumps.

Destiny sniggers.

'Hello, Destiny, flower,' says Mum.

PARRP!

33

'Would you like to join us for breakfast?'

Oh good grief, no.

Destiny glances at her dad's office window, then puts on the extra-polite voice she always seems to use around grown-ups. 'No, thanks, Mrs Foster. I've already eaten.'

Phew.

'We had an early breakfast because Dad had to jump on a call with Australia.'

Destiny's dad is always on video calls with far-flung countries. I don't know what he does for a living, but I sometimes wish *my* parents had jobs that entailed them leaving me to my own devices for most of every school holiday period. And paid them so much money that they could buy me expensive gifts every two minutes.

Mum cocks her head to one side. 'That's a shame,' she says. 'I've made some special muffins.'

34

My morning is going from bad to worse. When Mum adds the word 'special' to the title of her baked creations, it only ever means one thing: she's substituted sugar with vegetables. Yuk.

Pointing at my sketchpad, Mum laughs. 'Fantastic work as usual, sweetie-pie. Come on in now, though. It's breakfast time.'

As soon as Mum's out of earshot, Destiny drops the aren't-I-just-so-sweet act and jabs her finger in Aldo's direction. 'If this MUTT is suddenly so talented, Ferris, prove it! Show me his best trick. You know, as well as dancing, Princess Foo-Foo can –' she points at the fluff ball – 'STAND! SIT! GIVE A PAW! JUMP! LIE DOWN! ROLL OVER! PLAY DEAD!'

Good job she finished with play dead. The poor poodle looks like it needs a prolonged rest after performing that routine.

I peer at Aldo, wondering how I'm going to coax him indoors without heaving him by his collar, never mind get him to do something as whizzy as roll over. 'I'm not going to prove it right now, Destiny. As you've just heard, I have to go in for my breakfast.'

As I start to gather my belongings, Destiny crouches to pat Aldo's head. 'It's OK, Aldi-Waldi. Not all dogs are born to be online superstars.'

As you can tell, not only is Destiny Dean a massive show-off, she's completely deluded. And her patronizing tone riles me.

'Twenty-seven likes on a YouStream video and you think your dog is an online superstar?' I laugh. 'HA! I could film Aldo performing *any* of his party tricks and it'd be miles more popular than anything you could ever post.'

At that point, a sly smile creeps on to my neighbour's face. 'Challenge accepted!' she shouts.

Wait, what?

'Let me know when you've set up your

YouStream channel, Ferris. I can't wait to see what the world thinks of Aldo!'

Princess Foo-Foo at her heel, Destiny flounces towards her front door. 'Whoever's dog has the most likes by the last day of the holiday can choose a forfeit for the loser. Deal?'

I hold her gaze, thinking about all the work I need to do on *The Hoot*. Then I look at Aldo and stroke his head. He's beautiful and loving, but he's no **Astoundog**.

'Scared you'll lose, Ferris?' asks Destiny, as though she can read my mind.

When I don't reply, she pulls her 'I'm so much better than you' face. 'It's pretty obvious, Ferris. You think your dog is as useless as I do!'

'HE IS NOT USELESS!' I cover Aldo's ears before he has to listen to any more of Destiny's mean comments.

'Yes, he is!' says Destiny. 'He's a dozy dumpling who can't even sit. Pedigree dogs like Foo-Foo are SO MUCH better than mongrels!'

Right. That's definitely it! I've had enough. I can't let Destiny keep getting away with all her snarky comments. I've had enough of her boasting about all her stuff as though that makes her better than me. I'm sick of her beating me at everything, and I WILL NOT let her keep insulting Aldo.

'DEAL!' I yell.

Destiny raises her eyebrows and laughs. 'May the best dog win!' she sings as she skips inside her house.

'Yeah!' I shout, before the reality of what I've let myself in for dawns on me.

Oh no! It's...
ALDO

Aldo, sit!

Aldo! Roll over!

Aldo, stand!

Aldo, sleep!!

Deal-dodging dilemma

When I eventually persuade Aldo to follow me inside, Mum tells me I look a bit peaky.

Miz does that weird thing where she feels my forehead as though her palm is as effective as a medical thermometer, then suggests I go back to bed.

EVERY TIME A CHILD IS ILL . . .

Faking it!

Go for a little lie down.

Call an ambulance!

Have a glass of water.

Morning off school.

Missing out on the greeny-brown muffins I spy on the kitchen table doesn't bother me at all, so I agree. Besides, I need some alone time to think up a good excuse to get out of this deal with Destiny. One that doesn't involve admitting to her that she's right. Because the sad truth is, as usual, she is. Just as her gold-plated Kickz are better than my fabric trainers, Princess Foo-Foo is better than

Aldo when it comes to performing tricks. There's absolutely no way a video of him going about his average dog-ish life, or demonstrating how to act like the perfect hot water bottle, could get more likes than a performing poodle.

I fling myself on to my bed, stare at the stars Miz helped me paint on my ceiling and rack my brain for ideas.

My first brainwave involves trying to convince Destiny I shouted 'Delia!', not 'deal'. Hear me out – it's not as stupid as it sounds. Delia is the first name of the old lady with the mobility scooter who lives next door but one. I could pretend I'd been greeting our elderly neighbour!

It doesn't take me long to scrap that idea. Destiny's well aware I'd never shout 'Delia'. I wouldn't even shout 'Mrs Smythe'. Not since Aldo poisoned her peonies with his piddle and she yelled at me.

FERRIS!

Next, I wonder about asking Mums if we can scour the local dogs' homes until we find an exact replica of Aldo. Not to replace him. I'd never do that. But, if by some miracle Aldo's double exists, needs a new home and is able to perform an extraordinary feat, that'd be handy. It's unlikely, but not impossible.

I'm about to go downstairs to broach this idea when Aldo wanders into my room and paws my mattress. After I've removed a small broccoli tree and a sliver of onion from his muzzle, I thank the universe for the invention of the parental thermometer-hand and help him climb on to my bed.

He nuzzles my duvet and I lift it for him. When he's got himself comfortable, he resembles a particularly hairy baby snuggled up in a hooded bath towel. I grab my phone, snap a photo and another idea comes to me.

Maybe I could tell Destiny that Mums have banned me from posting videos of Aldo online! Being a foster family, we have to be careful about what we share publicly. I'm not entirely sure why. What I do know is that anyone who's not met Keely must think we're fostering a toddler with a huge smiley emoji for a face, the way Mums conceal her identity on their social media posts.

But Aldo's not a foster child. He's permanent like me, and Destiny knows it.

My brain aches. Maybe Cal will be able to help.

I'm halfway through typing *'How do you get out of a deal you've agreed to with an annoying show-off?'*, when my phone beeps with a message from an unknown number.

Hi Loser! Forgot to say. I have a new phone. Here's my number. Let me know when you're ready for your forfeit. I have lots of ideas. Most of them involve you wearing a tutu at school. Destiny (Dean).

43

Reading this message on my third-hand phone, something inside me snaps.

I'll never be able to beat Destiny at 'owning expensive stuff'. Her dad buys her whizzy gifts all the time. You should see the karaoke machine he got her after he missed our class's singing assembly last term. And the virtual reality headset he bought her when he couldn't attend 'Parents at School' day. Come to think of it, even the fluff ball was a present. Foo-Foo

Sorry I missed your assembly. Daddy x

Sing!

Sorry I didn't make it today. Dad x

Really looking forward to seeing the recording of your show! Dad x

arrived the day after he missed our Year Four Christmas play, *The Lamb Who Saved Christmas.*

But this – this is a challenge that doesn't rely on money. Maybe I need to stop thinking of excuses to get out of it and see it as an

44

opportunity. I've been so caught up with *The Hoot*, I haven't actually tried to teach Aldo anything new for a while. Maybe he really has developed a hidden talent. Perhaps, with enough dedication and plenty of cheesy treats, me and my best friend could win this. That'd certainly bring Destiny down a peg or two.

I pat the lump under my covers. 'What do you think, Sleepyhead? You up for a challenge?'

My duvet becomes a gas-wafting monster, as Aldo wrestles to escape. Once he's freed himself from the threads, he licks my face and thrums his tail on my mattress. I take that as a 'Yes'.

Replacing my half-composed message to Cal with the words: 'I need to train Aldo to do something amazing. Any suggestions?', I navigate to Google while I wait for a response.

Upcycled underpants

'How to teach an average dog a trick that will wow the world' generates more than a million hits. Most appear to be adverts for doggy obedience lessons. Now there's a thought. Getting someone else to put in the hard work with Aldo while I concentrate on *The Hoot* sounds right up my street.

EASY OPTION AVENUE

I click on the first link and a video begins to play. A man with a thin moustache introduces himself as 'The Mutt Magician'. He waves a twig like it's a wizard's wand, at which point, through the magic of video editing, his face morphs into a montage of performing dogs. The clip ends with a tantalizing message:

I CAN TRANSFORM EVEN THE DUMBEST OF DOGS IN EIGHT HOURS – GUARANTEED!

I immediately click the 'find out more' button and am redirected to a page of testimonials.

🐾   🐾

I'd tried everything, but Barbara, my bulldog, refused to fetch. After The Mutt Magician had done his thing, she was offered a job as the world's first ball-dog for international tennis tournaments. – Bob from Blackburn

I laugh. This is the stuff **Astoundog** is made of. I take a screen shot of Barbara and Bob and send the image to Cal. We both appreciate dogs who look like their owners!

The next review says:

Star pupil, Barbara (with owner, Bob)

🐾   *The Mutt Magician transformed my disobedient dachshund into the dog of my dreams. Not only does Lofty now fetch my slippers, he puts them on my feet! – Lucy from Letchworth*

I'm sold. If this guy can transform Aldo to be even a fraction as extraordinary as **Astoundog**, I'll be able to beat Destiny hands down. Excitement bubbling, I read on.

Eight hours with The Mutt Magician and my chihuahua went from terrorizing toddlers to becoming the mascot of our local nursery school. The investment was more than worth it. – Pei-yi from Perth

Investment? How much does this dog wizard charge exactly?

✳ ✳ ✳

'A thousand pounds!' gasps Mum, after refusing to up this week's spending money by £998 and leaving me with no choice but to explain my predicament. 'Don't be ridiculous, Ferris. Aldo is perfect as he is. Just film him playing in the garden.'

Miz is no help either. After telling me I shouldn't believe everything I see on the internet, she reaches for her sewing box. 'Maybe I could stitch a little costume to up Aldo's cute-factor? Grandpa gave me a bag for the charity shop yesterday – I'm sure I could fashion you something suitable. People love dressed-up animals.'

These responses illustrate perfectly why Mum and Miz are the inspiration behind 'Make-Do and Mend', another regular feature of *The Hoot*.

There's no way I'm going to post a video of Aldo napping on our lawn, or humiliate him by forcing him into a pair of upcycled Y-fronts – dressed-up dogs that aren't cartoon characters give me the heebie-jeebies.

There's only one thing for it. I'm going to have to transform him myself.

The way I see it, if a random guy can completely transform a dog he's never met in eight hours, how hard will it actually be for me to train my best friend to perform just one extraordinary trick in a whole fortnight?

Don't answer that. I've made my decision. The deal is on. Wish us luck.

SUNDAY
14 days till
D-DAY

The purple room

After Cal's apologized for not replying yesterday
(a dreaded screen-time ban) and stopped laughing
about my, in his words, task as impossible as getting
toothpaste back into its tube, he talks me through
how to set up a YouStream channel and wishes me
good luck. 'Sorry I can't come over and help you,
Ferris. We're off to our caravan for the holidays.'

I end our video call promising to let him know
how I get on.

I'm about to get down to business with Aldo
when Mum appears in my bedroom doorway, Keely
clamped to her side like a human koala. 'This

52

bedroom is a bombsite, Ferris! Tidy it before Tia
arrives, please.'

With that, she's gone.

I don't know what the grown-ups in your life
are like, but mine are prone to exaggeration. This is
a prime example. There are no demolished buildings
or casualties anywhere in sight.

To make Mum happy, I start to tidy up
my room. By which I mean hide my mess.
Transferring a few pairs of undies from
my carpet to my laundry basket and
kicking random balls of paper from
last night's doodling session under my
bed, I stop when I think about what
Mum said: *'Tidy it before Tia arrives . . .'*

Tia's the name of my new foster sister, who's
arriving today. But why would she be bothered what
state my room's in . . .?!

'MUM! Where will Tia be sleeping?' I yell in a
panic.

'In the purple room!' shouts Mum.

53

Phew.

I like Mums being foster carers, but I DO NOT want to share my bedroom with anyone.

The purple room has been unoccupied since AJ, a dinosaur-obsessed, pea-hating two-year-old, left us to go and live with his forever family last month.

This new girl is ten, like me.

I was a bit worried when Mums first talked to me about her coming to stay. My mums have been fostering babies and toddlers for as long as I can remember and, over the past ten years, I've had thirteen brothers and eight sisters. They've each stayed for different lengths of time, depending on what's going on for them, and usually it's fun. But we've never fostered anyone older than three before . . .

It should be fine. As long as she's NOTHING like Destiny. Can you imagine? With any luck, she might even be a fun friend to hang out with while Cal's away.

To be honest, I guess it doesn't really matter what she's like, as long as she doesn't get in the way of my plans for Aldo's transformation or prevent me from working on *The Hoot*. I doubt she will. According to Mums, she'll only be with us for a few nights while her nan goes into hospital to get a new lung. Or was it a hip? A knee? I can't remember. Something new anyway.

Mums are pretty good at keeping me informed. And I usually listen. Although I'm sure when Keely arrived they said she was staying for 'a night or two' and that was almost four years ago.

I hear a squeal from outside and stand to see what's going on. Destiny is in her back garden guiding Princess Foo-Foo through a range of fancy agility equipment she's set up on her lawn. The perfect pooch is currently navigating its way across a narrow beam. I wouldn't be surprised if it performs a triple backflip to dismount.

Our garden hasn't got the room for an agility set. It's big enough, but it's crammed with toys. We have three different-sized slides, a swing, a trampoline, four ride-on cars, a gazillion bubble machines, a sand pit, a water table and a mud kitchen. Mums like to cover all bases when it comes to foster children's interests.

I used to play with everything too, of course, but nowadays I prefer looking at the special plants and ornaments we've put in it to remember all the

children we've ever fostered. Like the sweet-smelling
yellow rose we planted when little Mo left us to live
with his aunty. And the delicate blue fairy ornament
we bought when Holly got adopted. And the huge
green orb I picked out last month after we'd said
goodbye to AJ, which will forever
remind me how much the little imp
enjoyed fork-catapulting his peas at
me. I miss AJ.

Our toddler's paradise
gives me my first genius idea.

Who wouldn't like a video of a dog on
a trampoline?

Astoundog inspiration

Once we're in the garden, I show Aldo one of my
older **Astoundog** comic strips so he understands
the kind of thing we're aiming for.

I can't spot any parachutists flailing around at the moment. And, don't worry, I'm well aware my real-life dog can neither hover nor sew. But I'm hopeful studying **Astoundog**'s antics will inspire Aldo to think big and act extraordinary.

He certainly appears interested. Especially in the final frame. Which may or may not be due to the blob of raspberry yoghurt Keely spilled on it five minutes ago.

Unfortunately, I encounter a small problem as soon as I try to get Aldo on to the trampoline.

I should have realized the little ladder would be a non-starter. Aldo's been terrified of ladders since the day our loft hatch broke. I get it. No one likes being roused from a nap on the landing by a bonk on the head from a length of clattering metal.

OK, plan B.

I put my arms around my best friend's belly and heave. His back arches a little, but his feet remain rooted to the ground. Hmmm. Either I need to gain some muscle or he needs to lose some weight. Neither of which are possible in a morning.

A quick scan of the garden is all it takes to formulate plan C. I'll fashion a sturdy staircase! Aldo loves stairs, especially if he's told NOT to climb them.

Keely's water table is the right height for a top step. My skateboard will work for the bottom. I just need something to bridge them.

I spot the solar-powered cube Miz likes staring at in the evenings. *Ooo, look Ferris. It's blue. Now it's red. Now green.* Recite this ten times for an hour and you'll understand how uninterested I usually am in the light-up cube. As a middle step, however, it'll be just the job.

I position it between the water table and the skateboard and, voilà, a staircase I have.

All I need to do now is tempt Aldo to climb it. Shouldn't be too difficult. All being well, I'll be done and dusted in the next ten minutes and be able to work on *The Hoot* before lunch.

I point at my creation, then glare at Aldo and put on my best stern voice. 'Do NOT climb these stairs!'

For the first time in his life, Aldo obeys this instruction.

Hmmm.

Digging into my pocket, I discover a cheesy cracker. It's the pre-licked one Keely gifted me last week. As you're aware, Aldo's not as fussy as me when it comes to what he puts in his mouth, so I wave it near his nose. His eyes widen, frothy slobber forms at his muzzle and his tail whizzes like the second hand of a time traveller's watch.

Perfect.

I chuck the cracker on to the trampoline and point at my amazing construction. 'Up!' I shout.

Aldo cocks his head to one side, raises his eyebrows, then lies down for a nap.

I don't blame him for being unimpressed. It's like the time Miz promised me a trip to McDonald's and only told me once we were in the car that we were bobbing to IKEA first. A trip to Ikea is never a bob. It's six hours minimum, and chicken nuggets are not really worth the wait.

Hmph. This is taking longer than I thought. I told Cal I'd call him back by eleven.

I'm wondering what to try next when I hear a snigger. 'That one of the party tricks you were referring to yesterday, Ferris? You say "up" and he goes down?!'

I turn and see Destiny's eye pushed up against the (not so) secret hole she made in the fence that separates our gardens last month so she could spy on us while we were enjoying AJ's goodbye party. Destiny enjoys spying on what's going on in our garden almost as much as she enjoys boasting.

I retrieve the manky cracker and give it to Aldo. 'Yes,' I shout. 'He's pretty much cracked the rules of Opposites.'

Destiny's eye disappears. The next thing I hear is her trampoline net being unzipped.

'Want to see what a REAL talented dog can do on a trampoline, Ferris?'

The copycat! Well, I bet I thought of trampolining first.

I'm not sure I do, but it's hard not to look when a ball of fluff with legs suddenly hurtles towards the clouds, then returns to earth like a graceful owl. Repeatedly.

When the dog descends from its fifth lofty leap, everything goes silent. I worry there's a poodle-shaped

crater under next door's trampoline until Destiny
shrieks, 'Ready for the trick now, Ferris?'

Wait, what? That wasn't the trick?

The pooch resumes jumping, only now it's
dressed in its tutu (ick). At the peak of its third
appearance, Destiny yells, 'Splits!'

Immediately spreading her four
legs, so they're perfectly parallel with
the ground, Princess Foo-Foo turns her
head towards me and literally grins.

My mouth falls open.

'CUT!' yells Destiny.

'Tia's here!' shouts Miz.

I'm doomed.

Not really

Tia looks a bit like an anime character, with her short, choppy hair and huge brown eyes. And she smells delicious – like she's just stepped out of a vat of strawberry smoothie. I know she's ten like me, but she looks about fourteen.

For the first time in my many years of being a foster brother, I feel a bit nervous. When we foster babies, I usually introduce myself by giving them lots of cuddles. When toddlers come to stay, I pull funny faces to make them laugh, then get them a biscuit, or show them all our toys and play with them. I'm not sure a cuddle would help Tia to relax. She's already refused a biscuit. And when I ask her if she'd like to play a game, she rolls her eyes at me and asks for the Wi-Fi password.

She'd better not be like Destiny Dean: all stuck

65

up and thinking she's better than me.

I tell her the password, then sit silently for a while, letting Keely stroke my hair while Mums waffle on about all the things Tia could do while she's with us to keep her mind off her nan's operation.

'Ferris will show you around, won't you, sweetie?' says Miz.

I don't say that I won't have time. But I think it. Although, from the expression on Tia's face, I don't think hanging out with me is something she'll be interested in.

'Why don't you start by giving Tia a tour of the house while I make lunch,' suggests Mum. 'I think she's had enough of listening to us two.'

I nod and offer to carry Tia's suitcase while I show her all the downstairs areas. Tia doesn't speak while she follows me round. She just raises her chin every time I tell her what a room is called, as though she can't work out for herself that the area with the oven and fridge is the kitchen. I'm *such* a doofus.

'Are you a foster kid, too?' asks Tia, breaking her

silence when I take her up to the purple room and mention that I sleep across the landing.

I tell Tia what I tell everyone who asks me that question. The truth. Apart from my last name being Foster (I know. The irony, right?), I'm not. I'm Mum and Miz's birth child. Born from Miz's tummy, but using one of Mum's eggs.

Tia nods as though she knows a million people who were born this way, then chucks her suitcase on to the bed and begins to unpack.

As well as a tracksuit similar to the one she's currently wearing, I spy two football shirts, a magazine about skateboarding and three pairs of trainers. My hopes rise when I also spot one of those colouring books with intricate patterns and a pack of felt tips. Maybe Tia is going to be more like me than I thought . . .

I point at the pens. 'Do you like drawing?'

'Not really,' says Tia, with a shrug.

Oh.

'I do,' I say, trying to keep the conversation going. Awkward silences are the worst. 'I make comics and sell them for fifty pence. I'm saving up for a d-TAB, you see.'

Tia raises her chin, then hooks her coat over the chair by the desk. Next, she pulls a phone from her pocket and places it on the bedside table.

I point at the phone. 'Do you use YouStream?'

Tia rolls her eyes. 'Not really,' she mutters.

Wow, she's not making this easy. 'Me neither,' I offer. 'But I really need to learn.'

Aldo pads in to see what we're up to. He sniffs Tia's trainers and she pats his head. I smile. Maybe this is the thing that'll get her talking.

'Do you like dogs?'

Tia sighs before sitting on the bed. 'Not really.'

Wow, great conversation.

I tell 'Not Really' to make herself at home, then leave her to it. So much for having a fun friend to hang out with while Cal's on holiday.

Sausages

Back in my bedroom, I call Cal.
I doodle a quick idea for a
comic strip about a boy whose
wheelchair can fly while I wait
for him to pick up. Which he

doesn't. Hey hum. I expect he used his screen-time
allowance on his journey to Wales. Or he's already
arrived and gone for a swim in the caravan
site's pool.

I end the call and open up YouStream.

Good grief! Destiny's trampoliney-splitsy video
has thirty-seven likes already. I really want to flesh
out this flying wheelchair idea for *The Hoot*, but I
think training Aldo is going to have to take priority.

I make my way downstairs to locate my furry
friend and am greeted by Mum carrying
a dish of sausages in one hand and a

plate of fairy buns in the other. Aldo's right behind her, a skipping rope of saliva trailing from his mouth to the carpet. I pat his head and laugh. Producing record-breaking lengths of drool at the faintest whiff of meat is probably his only real talent.

Would 'World's Longest Dog Drool!' attract a ton of YouStream likes? Nah, too gross.

'Can you tell Tia it's lunchtime, sweetie,' says Mum, heading into the garden. 'I've made a bit of a picnic. Grandpa's on his way over.'

My grandpa is a big part of our lives. Mums always say it's important that new foster children meet him, so they know they're going to be treated as part of the family. Whatever the reason, I'm glad he's coming over. He's wicked.

I return upstairs and knock on the door of the purple room. 'Tia . . .'

There's no reply, so I knock a bit louder and am told to go away. Well, she doesn't actually use the words 'go away', but I'm not allowed to swear.

'It's lunchtime,' I say.

'I'm not hungry.'

'My grandpa is coming over.'

'Big wow.'

'There are sausages.'

'Leave me alone!'

'And fairy cakes . . .'

The door flies open. 'How old are you, Ferris? Six? I don't care if there are balloons and party poppers and an inflatable dinosaur performing magic tricks. When I'm hungry, I'll make my own food. Now. Get. Lost.'

I feel a tap on my shoulder. It's Miz. 'You go down, Ferris.'

I do as I'm told and am just in time to greet Grandpa letting himself in our front door.

'Hello, champ!' he says. He draws me into a hug, then offers me a mint. 'How's tricks?'

72

'Is anyone coming to join this picnic?' shouts Mum from the garden before I can answer.

Grandpa and I share a smile. I lead him through to the patio doors, warning him to brace himself for meeting Tia. 'She swore at me!' I whisper.

Grandpa runs his finger and thumb over his beard. 'I expect she's nervous. Try to put yourself in her shoes, hey?'

While Keely throws her arms round Grandpa's leg, and Mum grabs him a garden chair, I decide Grandpa has a point. I should give Tia a chance. Lots of kids act up when they first arrive with us and I get it. Being in a strange house with new people, however nice they are, must be hard. Maybe even more awkward when you're ten. I'm not sure I'd like it. Pushing my worries that Tia is going to be a Destiny Dean clone to the back of my mind, I sit on the grass.

A moment later, Miz and Tia appear in the garden. 'Sorry for telling you to get lost, Ferris,' mumbles Tia, not looking at me.

I tell her it's fine and don't mention I can tell she's been crying.

'Where are all these sausages then?' asks Miz, throwing me a smile after Grandpa's introduced himself to Tia.

I point at the dish in the middle of the picnic blanket. It's only then that I realize it's now piled high with cherry tomatoes.

'Ah,' says Mum. 'We had a bit of an incident, didn't we, Keely?'

Keely points at Aldo.

Grandpa laughs. 'Did he steal them?'

Keely nods her head.

'Well, that's not the whole story,' says Mum. 'He *did* eat them. But only after Keely had thrown them in the sandpit.'

I turn to Keely and frown. She looks back at me, opens her mouth and screams, 'BANKIE!'

Tia almost jumps out of her skin.

'That's what Keely calls her comfort blanket,' Miz

explains to her, casting her eyes around the garden. 'Has anyone seen it?'

I shake my head, then turn to Tia. 'Be prepared,' I say. 'Keely shouts BANKIE a lot, particularly if she knows someone's not happy with her. It basically means she wants her blanket comforter and she'll be taking no more questions on the topic at hand.'

Tia tries to hide her smile. 'Clever tactic. I might try it sometime.'

'She's also fond of throwing,' I add, pointing at Tia's phone. 'I'd put that in your pocket if I were you.'

Miz crouches in front of Keely. 'I don't know where bankie is, sugar plum. How about you stroke Aldo's ears instead and we'll find it later?'

Keely nods. 'Dough's ee-ahs!'

Stroking soft materials is one of Keely's go-to activities if she's feeling anxious. When she can't immediately locate her blanket, Aldo is perfectly happy to offer his ears as an alternative. The only

75

problem is, Aldo's not always with us. The sooner we find the blanket, the better. I do not wish to be thrown off the 125 bus again.

BANKIE!

'So, what do you like doing, lovie?' asks Mum, trying
to help Tia relax when we've all finished eating. So
far, all she's really talked about is her nan.

Tia shrugs. 'Playing football.'

'Do you support a team?' asks Miz.

Tia unzips her tracksuit top and
points at her shirt.

Grandpa cheers. 'Good girl! The Wanderers are
my favourite team too!'

Tia smiles.

'Maybe we three could have a little kickabout
this afternoon, Ferris,' says Grandpa, rotating his
ankles in preparation for this awful-sounding idea.
Football's not my thing.

I offer Grandpa an apologetic smile. 'I actually
have plans. I need to teach Aldo a trick that will
wow the world.'

Miz looks at me, dips her chin and raises her eyebrows.

'Why does poor old Aldo need to "wow the world"?' Grandpa asks, looking confused.

'It's a silly game,' Mum says, shaking her head, then standing to tidy away what's left of the picnic, i.e. millions of cherry tomatoes. 'And something Ferris tried to get us to pay a thousand pounds towards yesterday!'

'It's not a silly game!' I argue, and quickly explain to Grandpa about Destiny's challenge and my plans for Aldo's transformation.

'A word to the wise, Ferris, lad,' says Grandpa. 'You can't teach an old dog new tricks.'

If the week I devoted to training Grandpa and his pal, Magic Alf, to Floss is anything to go by, he has a point. 'But Aldo's not old,' I protest. 'He's only eight and a half!'

At that point, Tia stands, walks over to Aldo, and looks him up and down. 'For a dog his size, that's equivalent to about sixty in human years,' she says. 'He's about the same age as my nan.'

That's a lot to know about dogs for someone who claims to 'not really' like them.

'I've already told him, Dad,' shouts Miz, chasing Keely away from Grandpa's glass of beer. 'Aldo is who he is. It's not about age. He's just not interested in learning fancy tricks.' She whisks Keely off her feet, settling her on Grandpa's knee so she can stroke his beard (another of my sister's bankie substitutes), then turns to face me. 'Imagine if we'd forced you to continue gymnastics club even though you hated it, pal. You'd have been miserable.'

That's a fair point. But kids like me aren't made to balance on upturned benches and contort our limbs into impossible positions. Aren't all dogs born to obey their masters?

'If you want people to like Aldo, Ferris, son,' says Grandpa, unwrapping a fresh packet of mints, 'you should bring him to my social club. The boys would love a furry friend to fuss over.'

I've met a couple of Grandpa's friends. It's a long time since they were 'boys', but they're pretty cool. I doubt they're YouStream fans, but maybe they could be. 'Do they go online?'

'On what?'

'Online. On the internet. Like, could we get them all to like a video I post on a website?'

Grandpa laughs. 'Oh, the interweb? No, I doubt it. We've had to leave our phones in a box at reception since the day Young Harold tried to sign us up for that inline dating malarkey. It got Magic Alf way too excited. You should have seen the size of this one young lady's –'

'DAD!' warns Miz, slicing her hand across her throat as Tia bursts out laughing.

'What's the matter, Elizabeth?' says Grandpa. 'I was going to say balloons.'

He winks at me. I'm not sure why. Magic Alf loves balloon modelling, so it makes sense he'd be enthusiastic about a woman with big balloons.

Maybe he winked because 'Young Harold' is actually about eighty-seven.

'No,' continues Grandpa. 'I'm talking about real-life likes – likes Aldo here would be interested in.' He pats Aldo's back and slips him a mint.

I sigh. 'That's no help, Grandpa. The challenge is who can get the most likes on online videos. I can't let Destiny beat me again.'

'Why not?' asks Tia.

I hesitate. I don't want to upset Mums by going into the whole 'because she always beats me when it comes to having better stuff' thing, and I'm not in the mood to tell Tia about how Destiny won the end-of-term art challenge.

'Because a deal is a deal,' I say. 'And I don't want to have to do a forfeit.'

Between you and me, that's actually the least of my worries. Picking up Princess Foo-Foo's brown business for a week would be easy. The poodle's only the size of a large rabbit. Shovelling Maltesers would be a doddle compared to Aldo's king-size Mars bars.

Tia frowns. 'Just tell her the deal's off and enjoy your time off school.'

'Excellent advice, Tia,' says Mum.

'Indeed,' agrees Miz. She prises Keely off Grandpa's lap. 'Come on, you. Let's wash your hands and find bankie.'

'BANKIE!' shouts Keely, grabbing Grandpa's hand and pulling him into the house.

Once we're on our own, Tia leans back on to her hands and shakes her head. 'So, let me get this straight. You're going to spend your whole school holiday training your dog to be more like the genius cartoon dog you draw, just so you can impress this show-off who lives next door? What, do you fancy her or something?'

I almost choke on my lemonade. 'No, I do not.'

Tia narrows her eyes at me, then makes to stand.

'You don't understand,' I say. 'You haven't met Destiny. It's not about impressing her. It's not even about the forfeit. It's about beating her.'

'Why's that so important?'

'I'm just sick of her insulting Aldo and thinking she's better than me at everything.' I turn to check Mums are not in earshot. 'Plus, she's a massive boaster who always beats me when it comes to having better stuff.'

'So what?'

'So, this is a challenge that doesn't rely on money. And there's a chance I could win it.'

Tia points at Aldo, her eyebrows raised. He's currently spinning in circles, trying to catch his own tail, hanging from which is a thread of what looks like a Cheestring. After about seven full circles, he's made himself so dizzy he face plants into the patio doors. She laughs. 'From what your mum said about this Foo-Foo dog, it sounds like you're wasting your time. Unless . . .' She dips her hand into her pocket and pulls out her phone. Opening her mouth to speak, she's interrupted by Miz's reappearance.

'There's a football in there, Tia love,' says Miz, pointing at the storage bench before making a circuit of the garden in search of Keely's blanket. 'Don't forget, what's ours is yours while you're here.'

'Unless what?' I ask. If Tia has an idea, I need to hear it.

'Oh nothing. It doesn't matter. I'm only here till Thursday. I'm not about to get involved in some babyish bet.'

She goes to get the football, turning to me as soon as she's found it. 'Unless you want a football in your face, I'd move if I were you.'

Charming.

Where are my pants?

Back in my bedroom, I call Cal.

After telling me all about finding a frog in his caravan's toilet (yuk), he listens to my problems. 'Maybe there's something else in your back catalogue of **Astoundog** you could try with Aldo, Ferris,' he says. 'You know, something a bit easier than saving a parachutist's life!?'

It's not bad as far as advice goes, so I spend the rest of the afternoon trying to convince Aldo to replicate one of his alter-ego's slightly more realistic, yet still quite amazing, feats.

It's a complete disaster:

● Every time I try to get him to step through Keely's hula-hoop, he acts like I've glued his paws to the ground, so I abort plans for making him leap through a ring of fire.

- He point-blank refuses to hold a paintbrush in his mouth, so getting him to produce a Picasso-style portrait is a non-starter.
- He's too wriggly to stay put on Keely's trike, so I don't even get round to introducing pedalling, never mind taking the front wheel off my bike to try unicycling.
- Even filming a boring old game of fetch on the back field ends in disaster. I mean, I know I was the klutz who threw his Frisbee into Mrs Smythe's hedgerow, but I was not expecting my furry friend to return with a pair of her knickers on his head.

By teatime, I'm out of ideas and not in the mood for everyone's comments about how I'm wasting my time (Tia). And how I should stop trying to change Aldo into something he's not (Mum). And how I need to clean up all the messes I've created (Miz).

By bedtime, I'm ready to throw in the towel.

I close my eyes and try to block the whole thing out of my mind.

It obviously works as, the next thing I know, the school holidays are over and I'm sauntering into the playground ready to start the new term. I'm distracted from considering where on earth the last two weeks went, when I pass a group of infants. They stare at me and collapse into a fit of giggles. I assume they're amused by the strips of coloured tape 'Make-Do' fixed my lunchbox with. Or the home-haircut 'Mend' gave me last night. Whatever. I ignore them and continue towards the junior yard in search of Cal.

Every single person I pass howls with laughter. Blimey, what's so funny? Have I put my trousers on back to front or something?

I look down to my legs and freeze.

87

Oh good grief! All I'm wearing is a pair of satin ballet pumps. Literally nothing else.

Concealing my privates as best I can with a taped-up, semi-transparent ex-ice-cream tub, I search for a place to hide. I spot the green plastic bin that looks like an overgrown frog with its mouth wide open and dash over to it. Only, when I get there, it's no longer a bin.

It's Destiny Dean. And she's shrieking with laughter. The sound echoes across the playground until . . .

HAHAHAHAHA!

. . . I wake up drenched in sweat, my heart beating so loudly I wonder if Mrs Smythe might come and complain about the noise.

Thank goodness that was only a nightmare. I know I said the forfeit was the least of my worries, but I CANNOT let something like this happen for real.

Unless what?

After a few deep breaths and a gulp of water, I turn on my phone and see that I have two notifications. One's a photo message from Cal; a selfie that makes him look like he has frog's eyes. The text says: **Help! Battery on 1% and I can't find my charger.** Typical Cal. The other's from YouStream, informing me that *@MyAmazingPoodle* has uploaded a video 'I may like'.

Presumptuous much! I doubt I'll like whatever Destiny has posted but click on the link anyway.

The video is of her and the fluff ball playing Connect 4 together and it's

89

got nineteen likes already. Added to the likes on the trampoline video, that brings her running total to fifty-nine. Good grief! I need to post something. Anything will do at this point (apart from dressing him up – I'm not *that* desperate . . . yet).

We don't have Connect 4. We used to, but Keely threw all the yellow pieces down the toilet.

I'm considering whether I could convince Aldo to hold the tweezers from Operation between his teeth if I smothered them in cheese sauce, when I remember what Tia said in the garden yesterday. 'Unless . . .'

I pull on my clothes and walk to the purple room. Wiping my sweaty palms on my trousers, I'm about to knock on the door when Mum and Keely walk out of the bathroom hand in hand. 'Hello, sleepyhead,' says Mum. 'Tia's out in the garden already. It's lovely that you were going to ask her to play, though. It'll take her mind off her nan's operation. I'm sure I heard her having a nightmare last night.'

I nod. Mum doesn't need to know that I wasn't going to ask Tia to play. Or that the screams she heard in the night were more likely mine.

Mum gestures to Keely. 'Would you mind taking this one out with you too? I'll be ten minutes. Keep her clean.' She smiles at Keely. 'We've got another party today, haven't we, munchkin?'

'BANKIE!' shouts Keely.

'And see if you can find her blanket, would you?'

Keely goes to lots of 'parties'. They're actually more like play-gatherings where people who want to adopt children get to meet those who need forever families. I went along to the last one and enjoyed all the activities, but I was glad none of the people who came to chat to us wanted to adopt Keely. They weren't nearly special enough.

I lift Keely into a cuddle. We head to the garden, where we find Tia practising keepie-uppies. Aldo's beside her, doing a super impression of a solar-powered nodding dog as he watches the ball going up and down . . . and up and down . . . and

up and down . . . and up and down . . . and . . .
blimey, is that thing on a string? I could be here
till tomorrow if I wait for the ball to drop; I'm
going to have to bite the bullet and hope I don't
put her off.

I pop Keely in the swing and take
a deep breath. 'Tia, what did you mean
yesterday when you said, "Unless . . ."?'

Tia boots the ball high into the air,
catches it on the back of her neck, then
shakes her head. 'I already said, nothing.'
The ball drops towards the grass, but she sticks
out her foot and it lands on her laces. She flicks it
towards me. 'Catch!'

Catching's not my strong point. The ball whacks
me in my belly before ricocheting towards Aldo. Aldo
tries to get his jaws around the ball, but it pings
away from him and lands at Tia's foot. Tia dribbles it
round Aldo, then taps it over my skateboard. After
a quick glance up at our basketball hoop, she volleys
the football straight through it.

Keely waggles her legs, giggling right up until this little show ends, at which point she realizes I've stopped pushing the swing and her laughter dissolves into tears.

Tia points at the swing, then forms a cylinder shape with her left hand. She pats the top of it with the flattened palm of her right. This impresses me even more than her ball skills. That's the Makaton sign for 'more', you see, and Mum only taught it her at teatime yesterday. Makaton is the sign language system we use with

Try it!

'MORE'

Keely. Not because she can't hear, but because she struggles to talk. Mums say that if we sign as much as we can, Keely will learn the signs she needs to be able to communicate better. I didn't mind the refresher lesson myself, to be honest. It was a good way to break the awkward silences we kept falling into at teatime.

Keely nods, squeals, then points at Tia.

'She wants *you* to push,' I say, despite that being obvious. I'm such a doofus.

I don't mind being sacked. I've just thought of something I could try with Aldo. And my skateboard . . .

He might not be up to executing an **Astoundog**-style rail-slide down a skyscraper's banister, but there's no harm in trying to get him to do a straightforward push and glide, is there?

Apparently, I'm welcome

Dropping to my hands and knees is enough to bring Aldo bounding over to me.

I immediately demonstrate how much fun can be had on a platform with wheels when you have four limbs. Between you and me, it's the only way I can ride the thing without falling off.

When I've moved back and forth across the grass a couple of times, I stand and point at the skateboard.

'Your turn!'

Aldo's tail stops wagging. He wanders over to his kennel for a lie-down.

Keely giggles.

'Maybe he needs to see something more aspirational!' says Tia. She picks up the football, flips my skateboard with her toe, jumps on the platform and proceeds to board between the swing and the trampoline, executing perfect headers all the while.

She's still performing this impossible feat when a voice comes from behind the fence. 'Is that new person a girl or a boy, Ferris?'

The question doesn't appear to bother Tia, so I follow her lead and ignore it.

Destiny doesn't like being ignored. 'I've not seen any content on your YouStream channel yet, Ferris. Ready to admit that my dog is SO MUCH better than yours?'

Tia catches her ball, stops skating and cocks her head towards the fence. 'Is that her? The show-off you're trying to beat?'

I nod.

Tia purses her lips, then jimmies herself up the fence. Leaning over into enemy territory, she says, 'Hi. I'm Tia. I'm a girl. Thanks for asking and not assuming. That's clever of you. Is that your poodle?

She's lovely. Ferris has been telling me how talented she is.'

Wait, what?

Judging by the eerie silence that follows, I assume Destiny's as confused as I am.

Tia jumps down from the fence and clocks my bewilderment. 'It's a way to deal with people who boast all the time,' she whispers. 'Compliment them and they don't know what to say. My nan always says people brag about stuff when they're insecure.'

'Insecure?'

'Yeah, or jealous.'

Destiny Dean jealous of *me*? Yeah, right!

I shake my head and copy Tia's whispered tone. 'There's nothing I have that she could be jealous of. Destiny's dad buys her stuff all the time.'

A throat-clearing cough comes from beyond the fence. 'Hello, Tia. Wanna come over and play? My house is SO MUCH better than Ferris's.'

Tia rolls her eyes. 'No. I'm good, thanks.' She lowers her voice to a whisper again. 'I'm telling you,

Ferris. This kid at my school used to constantly tell me all about having a Wanderers season ticket and a gazillion official kits. Nan said he was only boasting about things he knew we couldn't afford because he was jealous of my football skills. She was the one who taught me to surprise him with kindness. It worked, too. As soon as I started saying, "Oh, how lovely," and complimenting his strips, he had nothing to say back to me.'

I'm not convinced, but I have to admit Tia's approach has certainly silenced Destiny for now.

The same can't be said for Keely, who's currently screaming 'DOW-DOW-DOW!' at the top of her voice, letting us know she wants to get out of the swing. I get it, stationary swings are basically just elevated bottom cages.

I lift my sister out of the swing and she runs straight to Aldo's kennel. Aldo immediately shuffles sideways, letting her snuggle in beside him. I whip out my phone and press record. A dog who's willing to share his home with a toddler isn't extraordinary, but it's cute. Then I remember I'm supposed to be keeping Keely clean. And that I'm not allowed to post videos of her online.

I crouch in front of my sister so she can see me signing. 'Want to go on the trampoline?'

Keely responds with a high-pitched squeal. I know this means yes.

'That kid *still* not learned to talk?' shouts Destiny.

I'm wondering how on earth I'm supposed to kill this loaded comment with kindness when Mum appears at the patio door. She crouches with her arms outstretched, sticks out her

little fingers and thumbs, and waggles her hands. 'Come on, Keely! Party time.'

'BANKIE!' shouts Keely.

I give my little sister a squeeze. 'Have a good time!'

Keely whoops and says something *I* know means 'love you, Ferris!' but to anyone else sounds like 'Ruv-oo-Reh-wil', then runs inside with Mum.

I hear Destiny laugh. 'Shall we teach you how to talk next, Foo-Foo? Bet you'll be able to say more than Keely within a week! Wouldn't be hard though, would it?'

Tia stares at me, her mouth gaping. 'Let's go inside, Ferris. I see what you mean about your neighbour being braggy, mean and babyish.'

'I'm not babyish!' yells Destiny, in what I can only describe as a quite babyish whiny voice. (At least she knows she's braggy and mean.)

'Course you are,' says Tia. 'Setting a challenge for a forfeit? What are you, six?'

'I'm *eleven* actually. How old are you?'

'Fifteen,' lies Tia. 'That's old enough to know that if Ferris was going to spend all his school holidays filming his dog, he'd need a better reason than just to make you pick up Aldo's poo.'

After a moment of silence and some shuffling, Destiny yells, 'Fine! Forget the forfeit. If you win, I'll give you this!'

I look above the fence. Oh. My. Gosh. She's waving her d-4000 at me. What's the catch? There's got to be a catch.

'I don't need it any more. Not since Daddy bought me this . . .' The d-4000 disappears and is replaced with a brand-new d-5000. 'He said that now I've got so many more fans and followers I needed something better to film on. You should see the quality of the video recorder on this thing, Ferris. Bet you wish your mums were as rich as –'

'And what if *you* win?' interrupts Tia. 'What would you want?'

Ha! It doesn't matter what she wants. I'd give up ANYTHING to get my hands on that d-TAB.

'WHEN I win,' says Destiny, 'you give me this.' She holds up Keely's bankie. 'I'm sick of that kid throwing it over the fence. And besides, Princess Foo-Foo has taken quite a shine to it.' The blanket flies into our garden. 'Don't worry, Foo-Foo,' coos Destiny. 'It'll be back with us soon.'

Here! Take a kidney!

I grab bankie and run into the house, just catching Mum and Keely on their way out of the front door. My little sister will have a much better time at her party if she has it with her.

When I return to the garden, Tia's perched on the edge of the trampoline, grinning. 'You're welcome!'

'For what?'

'Isn't that the tablet you've been saving all your fifty pences up for?'

'Well, yes, but . . . Oh no, you didn't agree, did you?'

'I did.'

Nooooo!

'I can't give bankie to Destiny. Never mind that Keely can't live without it, it's sentimental too. It was the first thing Mums gave her when she arrived as a tiny baby. Plus, Granny Eileen knitted it for her.'

'Don't worry,' says Tia. 'You won't lose. Not now I'm involved. I lied when I said I didn't really use YouStream. I'm actually on it all the time. I know exactly the kind of videos people like. And, if the worst comes to the worst, your granny can knit another one, can't she?'

'I doubt it,' I say. 'She's been dead for two years.'

Tia's face drops. She jumps up and runs to the fence. 'Destiny!' she yells.

Destiny's eye immediately appears in her spy hole. 'Yes?' I can tell from her smug tone of voice that she's overheard my dilemma.

'Keely's blanket is more special than I realized,' says Tia.

'So what?'

'So it's worth a lot more than a d-4000,' I blurt out, blinking rapidly to prevent my tears from falling as I think about Keely's little face if bankie disappeared forever. 'This isn't a fair bet.'

'But your new big sister just agreed to the deal, so . . .'

'So, I made a mistake!' shouts Tia. 'But I have a solution.'

'Go on . . .'

'If Ferris wins, you give him the d-5000, not the d-4000.'

Oh blimey. As wonderful as that sounds, this is not a helpful suggestion.

Destiny doesn't speak for a moment. Tia looks at me, her eyes twinkling. I cross my fingers and hope Destiny will decline. That way, the deal will be off, bankie will be safe and I can get on with making issue five of *The Hoot*.

'What's the matter, Destiny?' shouts Tia. 'Scared you'll lose?'

'Stop,' I whisper. 'You're really not helping.'

My protests are too late. 'DEAL!' shouts Destiny. 'The d-5000 it is.'

TUESDAY
12 days till
D-DAY

Poo bags

I'm a fraction calmer today.

Tia spent all yesterday afternoon telling me everything she knows about YouStream. Turns out, that's loads! In fact, she admitted *all* the 'not really' comments she made on Sunday were fibs. She was just feeling upset about her nan and anxious about having to come to stay with a family she's never met. The truth is, she loves dogs, she doesn't mind drawing and she has her own YouStream channel where she posts snippets of herself performing football tricks. She showed me a fancy editing app on her phone that she

CUT-IT!

uses to make them. It can cut out boring parts, add text overlays and position funny stickers on bits you don't want people to see. Best of all, she's promised to use it to 'cut' a video of Aldo today that, in her words, will show Destiny who's boss.

I wouldn't say I'm feeling 100 per cent confident, but I'm certainly more pumped about the challenge. I mean, come on, if I can win a d-5000 AND beat Destiny Dean at her own game, how epic would that be?

'So, this park you said Aldo likes,' says Tia, after we've finished tidying our rooms. 'Do you think your mums will let us go on our own?'

'Probably,' I say. 'Keely's social worker is coming round, remember? They'll be glad we're going out so they don't have to whisper.'

Tia nods thoughtfully. After tea last night, we both overheard the hushed conversation Mums had about the party yesterday, and how Jo-Jo, Keely's social worker, is bobbing over today to 'discuss matters in person'.

Personally, I don't see what there is to discuss. If a couple who showed interest in adopting my sister changed their minds simply because she lobbed a plastic spoon at them, the only thing to say is that they certainly weren't the right forever family for her. Keely loves to throw. And if someone can't take a lightweight cutlery missile, they'd have no chance against an entire bowl of spaghetti.

I'm right about Mums wanting some privacy. After telling me and Aldo how lovely we are for showing Tia the local area, they hand us a wad of poo bags and practically push us out of the door.

We're still on the driveway giggling when Destiny and her dad pull up on to theirs in their fancy car. As Destiny climbs out of the passenger seat, I hear her ask her dad if he'll listen to her play her latest piano piece like he promised. Mr Dean, his phone pressed against his ear as usual, holds up his hand to silence Destiny, then marches inside.

This is not the first time I've seen Destiny being ignored by her dad. Despite her meanness, I start to feel a bit sorry for her. Until she spots me staring and asks me if I have 'some kind of problem', then points at Tia's clothes and turns up her nose.

Before the vein throbbing in Tia's neck has a chance to pop, I pull her off the driveway and, as Destiny runs into her house yelling 'Foo-Foo!', we set off.

We've barely got to the end of the street when my phone beeps with a message.

Remember not to talk to any strangers. Love you.
Mum. X. PS That goes for Tia too. X.

I roll my eyes and show the message to Tia.

She smiles. Then she frowns. 'I'm sorry I wasn't very nice to you on Sunday, Ferris,' she says. 'My head was all over the place. You know, with Nan and everything. Your mums are really nice.'

I tell Tia not to worry about it, then send Mum a thumbs-up emoji so she knows we've not been kidnapped in the two minutes since she set us free. I want to ask Tia what *her* mum was like, but don't want to upset her. When she was demonstrating her whizzy editing app last night, she showed me a couple of cool videos she'd created using clips and photos of her mum. After mentioning how it's almost three years since her mum died, she quickly changed the subject back to football and how her nan is her biggest fan.

'It sounds like your nan's nice too,' I say.

Tia grins. 'Yeah, Nan's great. We don't have much money, or a house as big as yours, but we have fun.'

I feel a bit silly when she says that. I know I get jealous of all Destiny's stuff, but I've never had to go without anything I actually need. And although Mums' 'Make-Do and Mend' behaviours frustrate me, I know they're just trying to do their bit to save the planet. I sometimes forget there are people in the world who have less stuff than me.

'Do you have a dad?' I ask, after a pause. That's a question *I* get asked occasionally. I don't mind

answering it – not everyone knows how my family was made – but I've no idea how Tia feels about sharing personal information.

Tia shakes her head. 'Not one I've ever met. It was always just me, Mum and Nan. Since Mum passed away, it's just been me and Nan. Nan used to have a budgie, but that died last year.' She bobs down to stroke Aldo. 'You're lucky. I'd love a dog, but we don't have a garden.'

Aldo immediately proves that owning a dog isn't always lucky by squatting to do his business. I pull my foot away in the nick of time, then hold out my hand like a doctor requesting a scalpel. 'Poo bag!'

Tia furnishes me with a couple, holding her nose as I dump the double-bagged load in a nearby bin. 'Your family should have shares in those things, the amount you use.'

She's probably right. It's a good job they're environmentally friendly ones because we don't even limit their use to poo-collection. Mum once packed my sandwiches in a non-fragranced variety for a whole term. And just this morning, before she went to nursery, Keely used some to gift everyone a bag of flowers, or 'wowas' as she says.

I don't know what happened to everyone else's, but my bag of soily-grass went straight in my 'Important Things' box, which is under my bed, next to my file of 'Not that good' cartoons.

That particular file is mostly stuffed with my old 'Average Aldo' comic strips – a series I scrapped for two reasons:

1. **Astoundog** is miles better. Everyone loves a super hero.

2. Mums couldn't stop raving about how good they were, and their opinions can't always be trusted when it comes to art. They told Keely the picture she brought home from nursery last week was a masterpiece fit for the National Gallery. It was literally a scribble of pink crayon next to a blob

of brown paint. Well, I hope it was paint. You never know.

Tia's obviously been thinking about Keely's poo-bag present too. 'Will you be upset when Keely gets adopted, Ferris?' she asks, as we walk through the ornate gates of Vickie Park.

I swallow the lump that forms in my throat. 'When the perfect family comes along, I'll be sad but happy.'

Tia nods and we walk in silence for a while. I don't know what Tia's thinking about, but all that's on my mind now is Keely. The thing is, even though we treat every single foster child who comes to stay with us as one of the family, Keely's the only one I sometimes forget is not my actual sister. The truth is, I'm dreading the day she has to leave us.

I glance at Tia. 'Keely came to live with us when she was one day old, you know. And she

115

was only supposed to be staying with us for a while. But she's nearly four now and . . .' I pause to compose myself. 'She deserves her forever family.'

Tia nods and smiles. 'What's it like for you, Ferris?' she asks after a moment. 'Having random kids coming in and out of your house all the time?'

No one's ever asked me that before. I'm not sure what to say. It's pretty cool having lots of brothers and sisters. In general, I like the chaos. (Although we once looked after a set of two-year-old triplets for a weekend and that was a bit too hectic even for me.) But saying goodbye (which I have to do a lot) can be tough. 'It's fine,' I say. 'I'd probably get bored and lonely if I was the only child in my house.' I realize what I've said. 'Sorry, I didn't mean –'

'It's OK,' says Tia, waving her hand. 'I don't get bored or lonely. Me and Nan are like best friends. When she's not working, we do loads of stuff together. She might be having a hip replacement, but she's not like those old nans with false teeth and stuff. I doubt she's much older than your mums.'

She stops talking and points at the play area just ahead of us. 'Right, enough of the serious talk. Let's get down to business. That looks like an excellent place to start!'

Opening the video recorder on her phone, Tia scans the play equipment then rubs her chin.

REMEMBER WHAT I SAID ABOUT SOME OF THE BEST YOUSTREAM VIDEOS BEING UNPLANNED? RELEASE THE BEAST!

Havoc

I unclip Aldo's lead from his collar, feeling both
nervous and excited. Usually when I come here with
Mums, we leave him tied to the railings. Watching
him dart around like a Hexbug in a shoebox, I think
I know why. And it's not just because of the 'No
Dogs Allowed' sign . . .

First, he bumps into a toddler at the
back of the queue for the slide.
The rest of them go
down like dominoes.

Next, he races towards the big basket swing.
After narrowly escaping being catapulted skyward
by a teenager's shoe, he darts towards the climbing
frame. Running under the monkey bars, he makes
like a bucking bronco as a small boy drops on to his
back, then bolts towards the roundabout. Careering
round it like a greyhound on the world's smallest

dog track, he soon makes himself so dizzy that he falls on to his side, knocking into a woman watching two girls on the seesaw. The contents of the woman's takeaway cup whoosh into the air and the cardboard receptacle lands on the head of a baby in a nearby pram.

The man with the cup-hatted baby glares at me, then points at the 'No Dogs Allowed' sign. 'GET THAT THING ON A LEAD AND OFF THE PLAYGROUND!'

To the sounds of crying, and tutting, and grown-ups mumbling phrases like 'Kids today, they can't even read!', I do.

'Well, that was terrible,' I say, as the three of us take refuge from the mob behind a copse of trees near the football pitches.

Tia stares at me, her eyebrows raised. 'Are you kidding? THAT was epic. Just what we needed, in fact.' She waves her phone at me. 'There'll be LOADS of stuff on here I can work with.'

'Really?'

'Yeah, look.' She brings her phone to life, looks at her screen and her face falls. 'Oh no . . .'

'What's up? Is it about your nan?'

Tia angles her screen towards me. I read the message flashing in red: STORAGE FULL. UNABLE TO SAVE VIDEO.

'Don't worry, Ferris,' she says. 'I'll free up some space and we can try again. Or we could use your phone.'

'Maybe,' I say. 'Not right now, though. I'm exhausted.' In truth, going back to the playground right now is the last thing I want to do. Angry adults who aren't my parents terrify me.

As Tia starts deleting a bunch of blurry selfies from her phone, I bring my phone to life and check if Cal's replied to any of my messages. Which he hasn't. Blimey, don't they have phone-charger shops in Wales?

Letting Aldo rest his chin on my lap, I check out Destiny's YouStream channel to pass time. Got to keep an eye on the competition, right?

Her latest video is entitled 'Poodle Virtuoso' and it has forty-three likes.

I click on it and see Foo-Foo seated on a posh velvet stool in front of an electric piano. Destiny's hand comes into shot and presses a few buttons, whereupon a tin whistle fanfare morphs into some speedy violin music. Soon keys start lighting up, which the poodle proceeds to press in perfect time, thereby performing the melody to a magnificent symphony. I tilt my phone towards Tia. 'How has she got a dog to do this? *I* couldn't even do this.'

'Shame her dad ignored her earlier,' says Tia, biting her bottom lip in thought. 'If he'd had time to listen to her perform, maybe she wouldn't have felt the need to teach Foo-Foo to play.'

Tia has a point. Maybe Braggy Von Dean does sometimes wish her dad paid her more attention . . . I have the opposite problem. My mums seem to want to know *everything* about my life!

After re-watching the video, Tia scratches her head, then looks over at a group of teenage boys playing penalty shoot-outs near the goalposts. 'Follow me!' she says. 'I have another idea.' With that, she sprints over to the boys.

I pull Aldo to his feet and we meander to the pitch's sideline. My foster sister is chatting to the teenagers as though they're not the scariest creatures on earth.

'Right,' she pants, returning to me a minute later with a twinkle in her eye. 'It's all set. Your job is to let Aldo off his lead and record what happens when I say NOW. Got it?'

I have no idea what's going on. 'Got it.'

Tia pelts back towards the goal, directs a few of the teenagers to stand in different places, puts the ball on the grass, then turns to me. 'NOW!'

I press record, unclip Aldo's lead and watch

as he bounds towards the unattended football.
He tries to grab it in his jaws and it pings away
from him. Tia points at a gangly lad wearing yellow
football boots. He immediately cuts in front of Aldo
and dribbles towards the goal. Aldo gives chase.
Suddenly, the lad veers off to the left,
causing Aldo to hurtle head first into
the football, which flies towards the net.
Next, Tia nips in to take the ball. Aldo gets back to
his feet to tail her. A couple of nifty touches later,
Tia pelts the ball into the net's top corner, leaving
the goalie face down in the mud. Aldo saunters over
to the keeper, licks his face,
then waddles to the upright of
the goalpost and cocks his leg
to wee.

   'CUT!' yells Tia. 'Thanks, lads!'
   She runs back to me with
Aldo. 'Did you get everything?'

   I nod (and continue to wonder what is going on).
Back at home, Tia downloads a free video-

editing app on to my phone and gets to work. Not long later, she shows me the finished clip.

Somehow, my clever foster sister has cut-up and fiddled with the footage so much it looks like my dozy dog has tackled a teenage footballer, scored a belting goal, then piddled on the keeper's goalpost. She's even added a twinkling star over Aldo's eye at the end of the clip that makes him look like he's winking.

'Isn't this cheating?' I ask.

Tia twists her lips to one side. 'The challenge is who can get the most likes, right?'

I nod.

'Then it doesn't matter *how* the footage is captured.' She pauses, steepling her fingers. 'I bet Destiny's doing this kind of stuff, you know.'

If I hadn't witnessed the poodle's trampolining skills with my own eyes, I'd be thinking the same. Still, four days into the holidays, and without a single video on my YouStream channel, I decide to agree and watch as Tia uploads the clip, adding a variety of hashtags she says will help it 'gain traction'. By which she means get likes.

She calls the video 'Amazing Footballing Dog Takes on Teenagers and Wins', and then we sit and wait for the likes to roll in.

WEDNESDAY
11 days till
D-DAY ☺

Non-stop filming

I have eighty-seven likes! That's only twelve off the number Destiny's got across all her videos.

If Tia can keep making clips like this football one, I could actually win. And I need to win. You should have heard the commotion Keely made this morning when Mum said bankie had had a little bath and would be dry in twenty minutes. I dread to think what she'd be like if bankie disappeared forever.

Plus, there's the d-5000, of course!

The problem is, it's Wednesday today, and Tia's due

to leave on Friday. She's not even here to help me now, as Mum's taken her to the hospital to visit her nan before her hip operation this evening. And she won't be able to come over to help me after she's gone home because she lives about fifteen miles away and her nan doesn't drive . . . and will be too busy recovering from her operation to catch two buses with her.

I have a plan, though. One I've already started actually. I'm filming Aldo's every move. Then, when Tia comes home, I'm going to ask her if she can do her stuff to cut something else amazing-seeming together, then teach me how to use the editing app, so I can maintain my lead.

As Miz has taken Keely to another 'party', and both my mums are insistent I'm not old enough to stay home alone with my dog – not even when I remind them he's actually almost sixty – Grandpa has come round to babysit me. He's in the living room reading, but he keeps giving me funny looks over the top of his glasses.

'What's happened to your hand?' he asks, as I pass him for the thirteenth time in half an hour. Aldo's often moochy when he can't find Keely.

I stop, frown and look at my hands. 'Nothing. Why?'

Grandpa closes his book and leans forward. 'For a minute there I thought it had changed into a phone!' He winks at me. 'Why are you hounding your best friend with that thing today, pal?'

I close the door to contain Aldo, then remind Grandpa about Destiny's challenge, being careful to avoid mentioning the possible loss of bankie. Pausing my video recorder to show him the football clip on YouStream, I'm delighted to discover it now has ninety-one likes! Eek. I can almost feel the d-5000 in my hands.

'Hmmm,' says Grandpa, closing his book as the microwave pings. 'After lunch, why not put your telephone down for ten minutes. Perhaps we could do some drawing together?'

'Maybe,' I say.

Part of me wants to say yes. We're into the fifth day of the holidays and I've hardly drawn a thing for the next issue of *The Hoot*. But I just don't have time. Not if I want to catch Aldo's every move before Tia gets back.

After lunch, I follow Aldo outside and sit on the storage bench watching him settle down for a nap in his kennel. Five minutes later, he's snoring and I'm bored. Propping my phone up against the bench, I leave it on record and return indoors, where I find Grandpa leafing through my sketchpad. 'Have you ever seen that cartoon?' he asks.

This is a classic Grandpa question. He always assumes I can read his mind. To be fair, I often can. He once asked me if I'd watched 'that programme', and I knew immediately he was talking about *The Great Knit-athon*. Although the photo of Granny

Eileen angled towards the TV on the seat beside him was a bit of a clue.

Anyway, I've seen a lot of cartoons. 'Maybe,' I say. 'What does it look like?'

Grandpa tears a page out of my sketchpad and talks as he draws. 'Some animals are sitting in front of a tree. I can't remember what they are. A fish, a monkey and an elephant, I think.'

It's a good job he's providing audio commentary – his 'elephant' resembles an overweight six-legged spider.

'And there's a judge pointing at them,' continues Grandpa, adding a stickman to his drawing.

I'm wondering what the purpose of Grandpa recreating this odd cartoon is, when he gives the stickman a speech bubble.

I frown. 'That's not fair. The monkey would win, obviously.'

Grandpa slaps his hand on to the table. 'Exactly! Does that mean a monkey is a better animal than an elephant who can carry a tree with its trunk? Or a fish that can swim the ocean?'

I shake my head. But I don't really understand what this has to do with anything. Hey hum. Grown-ups are weird.

Grandpa leans back in his chair and gestures to the back garden. 'I was thinking about what you said about Destiny's dog. And how you think you need to transform Aldo to win this daft challenge. And, well, here's my opinion, for what it's worth. Aldo's brilliant. He might not be able to dance, or play the piano, or, what was that other thing you said?'

'Do the splits in mid-air.'

'Or do the splits in mid-air. But he has plenty of other talents you could showcase without cheating.'

I'm wondering to which talents Grandpa's referring, when he points to the photo of me and

Aldo on the fridge door, the one Mum had printed out with the words 'BEST BUDS' across the top.

We're both much younger. I'm about five and Aldo's around three, but he's about the same size as he is now. He's got his paw on my shoulder and he's licking my face. Even though the picture was taken almost six years ago, I remember the moment well. A little girl called Marcy had just left us to go and live with her grandparents and I was so upset. Grandpa's right. Aldo's my best friend, and he's always there for me when I need him, but I'd hardly call that a talent. And it's definitely not something the YouStream community would be interested in.

I'm distracted from having to explain this point to Grandpa when we hear a terrific commotion coming from the back garden.

I run outside and am just in time to see Aldo dismount my skateboard.

Wait. WHAT?!

I grab my phone from the storage bench and rewind the footage.

Oh. My. Gosh.

My dozy dog has just executed a perfect backflip. On to my skateboard. And I've caught the whole thing on camera.

Flippin' heck!

I rewind and watch it again, just in case I'm hallucinating.

Good grief. I'm not. It's even better viewing the second time round.

You really need to watch it to appreciate it, but I'll describe what I'm seeing as best I can. Better yet, I'll draw it:

START

FINISH!!

Basically, Aldo wakes up with a start. There's an insect dancing on his nose, which he watches for a while, making himself go cross-eyed. Suddenly, the insect disappears and Aldo jumps to his feet. He paws his nose frantically. Then, in a wild frenzy, he whips his chin into the air with such force that his hind legs leave the ground. For a split second, his entire body is almost vertical. All of a sudden, he's up in the air, his back parallel with the lawn, four paws pointing to the sky. His wet nose seeks the safety of solid ground, then his front paws hit the skateboard. When his back legs join them, the momentum sends the skateboard whizzing forward, carrying my dog past my phone and out of shot.

I can't believe it.

Aldo's done something extraordinary! More than extraordinary, in fact. This is YouStream gold!

'Everything OK, Ferris?' shouts Grandpa. 'Aldo's just come inside looking a bit shell-shocked.'

'More than OK!' I shout.

I run up to my room and upload the exciting

135

part of the clip to YouStream. It's less than five seconds long, but amazing nonetheless. Entitling the post 'Genius Acrobatic Dog You DO NOT WANT TO MISS!', I run downstairs to wait for Tia to come home.

Mum pulls up on the drive ten minutes later and I drag Tia upstairs before she's even had time to remove her coat.

'What is it?' she says.

'How's your nan?' I ask, remembering my manners.

'She's good. She asked me if you'd –'

'ALDO DID A BACKFLIP!' I shout.

'Yeah, right.'

'He did! Look!'

I show Tia the video, which, oh my gosh, has thirty-eight likes already.

'WHAT?' she exclaims. 'How . . .? When . . .? That's EPIC!'

We watch the video about fifty-six more times before Mum shouts me down to say goodbye to Grandpa.

'Remember what I said,' says Grandpa, as I hug him goodbye. 'Talents come in all shapes and sizes. Oh, and tell your mum I think Aldo might be coming down with a cold. He's been sneezing like a good 'un for the past half an hour.'

WHOOP!

It's the morning after Aldo's feat of accidental extraordinariness.

I turn on my phone to check the time and think I must be dreaming. Not because I've slept until after ten, although that's this holiday's record, but because I have 396 notifications from YouStream!

I hold my breath and navigate to my channel.

Oh. My. Gosh.

My video of Aldo performing his backflip now has 123 comments and 273 likes!

138

I think I'm going to faint.

Aldo wobbles across my mattress to lick my face. It's nice he's concerned about me hyperventilating, but his morning breath doesn't help at all. I push him away and begin to scroll through the comments.

@Here4laffs: Brilliant. Post more!

@Jumpz: Get that dog signed up for the Olympics.

@SecretPineapple: Awesome trick. How did you train him to do that?

@Bernardsmyname: Great moves. Can he do anything else?

@BillyUG: Cool. What else can he do?

@Izzy&RoRo: WOW! Can't wait to see more!

@ChumpUK_Ian: SHARE TO: @PollyW_PGT. Check out this dog, Pol. He'd be perfect.

I'm so excited, I only stop reading when I hear my name being shouted through what I can only

assume is a microphone attached to
the world's biggest amplifier.

FERRRRRRRRRRRRRRRRIS!

Tia waves her phone at me, as
she barges into my room. 'HAVE YOU SEEN –'

'I KNOW!' I shout. I get out of bed and we jump
around my room like toddlers in a party room filled
with free cake. Aldo tries to join us but is hit by a
sudden sneezing fit. We both look at him and laugh.

'We need to check how many likes Destiny has,'
says Tia.

I pat Aldo's head, then sit down to catch my
breath and navigate to Destiny's channel. When I
add the likes on her latest video, 'My Poodle Can
Read', to her previous likes, it comes to 340.

'You have 364!' says Tia. 'You're in the lead!'

We roll back on to my bed, giggling.
After a moment, Tia sits up and
starts counting her fingers. 'Only by
twenty-four likes, though. Here, give me

140

your phone. I know what we can do to keep up the momentum.'

She taps away for a few minutes, then hands my phone back to me to show how she's replied to some of the messages.

@Here4laffs: Brilliant. Post more!

@Ferris_F_UK: Thanks @Here4laffs! Don't worry, I plan to! Watch this space for more ASTOUNDING dog tricks.

@Bernardsmyname: Great moves. Can he do anything else?

@Ferris_F_UK: Hi @Bernardsmyname. Thanks. Yes, loads more. SUBSCRIBE to my channel so you won't miss his next trick!

@ChumpUK_Ian: SHARE TO: @PollyW_PGT. Check out this dog, Pol. He'd be perfect.

@Ferris_F_UK: Keep sharing @ChumpUK_Ian! This is just a tiny glimpse of what my dog can do.

 Eek. I'm not sure about this. It's a good job Cal's phone's dead. He'd definitely be calling me out as a liar.

'Don't look so worried,' says Tia, pointing at my face and laughing. 'We're talking to a bunch of faceless strangers. No one really knows Aldo. The more comments you can get, and the more you interact with people, the more likes will come. Trust me.'

I need to trust her on this. After all, twenty-four is a narrow margin, and there's still over a week left of the school holiday.

'I'll cut some more videos for you before I go home. You can post them a day at a time until the end of the school holidays. That should put you in an excellent position to win the challenge.'

Tia's going home tomorrow, so I appreciate that offer. 'Brilliant! Thanks, Tia.'

'Maybe we can start with something involving your basketball ring. Make it look like Aldo can get

the football through the hoop with
a flick of his tail?'

I laugh. 'Sounds good to me.'

'For now, though . . .' Tia peers
around my room. 'Just post a video of anything to
keep your fans happy.'

'My fans?'

'Yeah, a clip that'll make people keep checking
your channel.'

She grabs a sketchpad off my desk. 'I know.
Give me your phone.'

I do as I'm told, thinking how lucky I am to
have a YouStream expert staying with us right when
I need it.

Tia hands me my sketchpad. 'Flip through all
these **Astoundog** cartoons while I film you.'

Again, I do what she says.

When I get my phone back, I have another
video on my channel. As my hand flicks through page
after page of **Astoundog** up to his usual genius
tricks, colourful text flashes up on the screen:

COMMENT BELOW IF YOU SPOT ANYTHING YOU'D LIKE TO SEE ALDO DOING IRL!

'Right,' says Tia. 'Next, breakfast!'

And . . . relax!

After breakfast, Tia and I take Aldo into the back garden to relax in the sun for a bit before making a start on her basketball idea.

'Ahhh,' says Tia, lying beside Aldo on the grass. Her elbows out, she crosses her hands behind her head and closes her eyes. 'This is going to be a good day. The sun is shining. The birds are singing. You're on track to beat Destiny and win yourself a d-TAB into the bargain, and I'm going home tomorrow.'

'GOOD!' comes a voice from beyond the fence, completely ruining our vibe. 'It'll be SO MUCH better only having one ten-year-old loser living next door.'

Me, a loser? Ha! I guess Destiny's not been online yet this morning. Odd that.

I'm about to break the news that will silence my braggy neighbour when Miz walks outside, a worried expression on her face. 'Tia, can we have a little chat? Ferris, will you come and sit with Keely for a minute?'

I do as I've been asked. Miz and Mum take Tia into the kitchen.

After five minutes, my curiosity gets the better of me. Leaving Aldo to supervise Keely, I walk to the kitchen, stopping at the door when I hear Tia crying. I don't know what's happened, but I know a way to find out. I put my ear to the kitchen door . . .

Miz: I'm so sorry, love. I know how much you were looking forward to going home tomorrow.

Tia: (sniffling)

Mum: Don't worry, you can stay with us until your nan gets a stairlift installed. Then you'll both be able to go home.

Tia: (sobbing)

Mum: Oh, love, come here.

SILENCE (I assume they're having a group hug.)

Miz: It won't be too much longer, you'll see.

Tia: How much do stairlifts cost?

SILENCE, FOLLOWED BY THE SOUND OF MUM
TURNING ON HER TABLET, FOLLOWED BY
A PAUSE, FOLLOWED BY A GASP.

Tia: Let me see. OMG! It'll take weeks for Nan to
        save up that much money – months, even, if
        she can't go back to work.

Mum: Well, that's only one company's website. Here,
        let me check eBay. Someone might be selling
        one second-hand.

Miz: Good idea. And, in the meantime, maybe
        we can help you raise a bit of cash. A few
        driveway sales, perhaps? I could make some
        of my natural air fresheners. They were a
        great hit at Ferris's last summer fair.

Mum: Try not to worry, sweetheart. We'll do
        everything we can to help you and –

The kitchen door swings open. Tia barges past me, runs upstairs and slams her bedroom door.

I rub my nose and stare at Mums. 'How much do stairlifts cost?'

Mum angles the screen of her tablet towards me. The website of a stairlift company is open. 'About three thousand pounds.'

Eek.

I'm wondering whether I should go upstairs to offer Tia some sympathy when my phone beeps with a message.

> What are the dimensions of that rainbow blanket, loser? I'm thinking of asking Daddy to buy Foo-Foo a new bed for it. DD

Considering I was ahead of Destiny on the YouStream likes front about an hour ago, this message confuses me. Until I click on the link to her channel she's pasted below it.

Entitled 'Behold! My Tumbling Princess!', she's

posted a video of the perfect pooch performing multiple cartwheels along the back of her living-room couch. It has 278 likes already. Now 279. Now 280.

How can a day that started so well have turned so bad so quickly?

Help wanted

'I told you yesterday, I can't help you, Ferris,'
snaps Tia, pushing my phone back towards me.
'I need to make some money. Nan and I need
every penny we can get if we're going to afford
a stairlift. Do you think any of your neighbours
might want their cars washing?'

I shrug and look back at my phone.

Although I'm sad for Tia that she can't go home
yet, a selfish part of me thought that'd mean she'd
have time to help me film some more videos. Nope.
Yesterday was a complete write-off. Tia barely left
her room, and the only thing I managed to film

Aldo doing was drool over a packet of frozen sausages. I couldn't even upload that to YouStream because Keely kept walking into the shot screaming 'BANKIE!'. It was rubbish anyway.

'Washing cars is an excellent idea, Tia,' says Mum. 'I'll make a batch of cakes for you to sell as well, if you like?'

'Thanks, Mrs Foster,' says Tia. 'That'd be great.'

My foster sister hasn't got enough experience of Mum's cakes to know otherwise. 'No problem,' says Mum. 'I'll make a start as soon as I've emailed some more recent photos of Keely over to Jo-Jo.' She taps her tablet and glances at Miz. 'For the new profile she's putting together for potential adopters.'

I try to ignore the funny feeling this comment brings to my tummy and focus on my phone. As things stand on the likes front, the score is 402 to

641. I must post another video today or I'll have no chance of catching up with Destiny. Looks like I'm on my own, though.

I click on the video of me flicking through my **Astoundog** strips. As Tia anticipated, it's generated quite a few comments. Seems like a lot of people want to see Aldo wake-boarding. Hmmm. That could be tricky.

'I've promised Keely an hour in the paddling pool,' says Miz, glancing at Tia with an apologetic smile. Keely squeals and waves her cereal spoon around. A blob of Weetabix lands on my shoulder. There's no way Miz can get out of that then. 'But, later, I'll give your social worker a call, Tia. Maybe Shazza will know about grants you can get for this type of thing?' I feel a tap on my shoulder. 'You'll help Tia wash cars, though, won't you, Ferris?'

I'm about to tell Miz I also have something quite pressing on, but change my mind when I see the

look in her eye. Miz's 'Fosters Help
When They Can' glare is not to
be ignored.

I figure I can bring Aldo
car-washing with us. If I can
persuade him to hold a wet sponge
in his jaws and make it look like he's assisting, that
could get me a few extra likes. I could say he's
raising money for charity too. Ooo, it might even
bring in a few donations for the stairlift as well.
'Sure,' I say, with a smile.

Water, water, everywhere

'How much do you think people round here will pay for a car wash?' asks Tia, as we begin filling buckets from the water butt Miz constructed from a wheelie bin she found in a skip.

'I'm not sure,' I say. 'Maybe five pounds?'

Tia's face drops. 'That's going to mean a lot of cars to be anywhere near enough money. We'll just have to ask for more.'

'But you know what?' I add. 'Miz will probably have found you one on eBay for 70p or something by this time tomorrow. Or even bagged you a free one from Freecycle. You should see her when she's bargain-hunting. She's like a kid on a treasure trail!'

Tia scratches her head. 'If we try for twelve pounds per car, and get through five cars this morning, that'd be sixty pounds. Then, if we sell twenty of your mum's cakes at two pounds a pop this afternoon, we'd have made a hundred pounds by this evening.'

I don't tell Tia there's no way anyone round my area would pay twelve pounds for an amateur car wash. Or that most of our neighbours have tasted Mum's veg-filled cakes before and would probably, therefore, need paying to eat them. Because, right then, a familiar snigger that's about as welcome as a fart in a lift comes from over the fence. Just what we need. A Destiny intervention.

We close off the tap and hear something being dragged along the floor. A moment later, my neighbour's smug face pops up above the fence, her lips curved into a smirk. 'Bet you wish your mums were as generous as my dad, don't you, Ferris?

Then you wouldn't have to resort to sad giveaway websites every time you wanted something!'

'Ignore her,' says Tia, flicking water in Destiny's face.

Destiny's hands fly to her hair. 'Watch it, loser girl. This hairband cost thirty pounds.'

Tia laughs. 'Thirty pounds for a hairband? You were robbed.'

Destiny points at Tia's hair and grimaces. 'What would you know about the price of hairbands?' She fiddles with something behind her ear and the bows

affixed to the band start to flash red, then orange, then green. 'Not laughing now, are you, Tia?'

She is. Destiny looks like a traffic light.

'Was there anything else you wanted, Destiny?' asks Tia, picking up her bucket. 'If not, why don't you run along? My good friend Ferris and I have things to do.'

Destiny's eyes narrow. Her nostrils flare. If looks

could kill, Tia would be a goner. 'Why are YOU still here anyway? I thought you were going home today.' She shifts her evil smirk from Tia to me. 'Oh, is that why you need money, Ferris? To buy her a new family? I thought you'd realized that, just like the end-of-term art competition, there's no way you're winning the YouStream challenge, so you need to find a way to buy your own d-TAB!'

I'm trying to think of a smart reply when my phone buzzes with a YouStream notification. It's yet another request for a live re-enaction of **Astoundog**'s wake-boarding adventure. This new commenter says they'd pay good money to see Aldo skimming across water at high speed on a single piece of plastic. Interesting. If people would be willing to pay money to watch this kind of video, it could work in both our interests – more likes for me and money for Tia. I pull Tia away from the fence and show her the comment. 'We need to post something new,' I whisper.

Tia thrusts her sponge in my chest. '*You*, not *we*, Ferris. I know Destiny is awful, and that you really want to beat her, but I've got more important things to worry about today.' She storms towards the front of the house, muttering under her breath, before I have a chance to explain my point.

I glance up at the fence to see if Destiny's been earwigging. Thankfully, I don't think she has. Her eyes are focused on the other side of my garden and she's smiling. I follow her gaze and realize she's watching Keely, Miz and Aldo playing in our paddling pool. Well, only Keely's in it. Miz is kneeling on the grass singing some daft song about a turtle going POP! And Aldo's pouncing around the perimeter attempting to catch every splash of water before it hits the lawn. Although Destiny's smiling, her eyes are sad – like she'd love nothing more than to join in with the fun. I suddenly feel kind of sorry for her always being on her own.

But in an instant my nice feelings fade, as

Destiny clocks I'm watching her and her smile morphs into a scowl. 'I'm so glad Daddy's ordered us a new pool. Aren't you, Foo-Foo? It'll be SO MUCH better than those rubbish little inflatable ones *some* people still have.'

As Destiny jumps down from whatever she was standing on, I stick my tongue out at the fence, then turn to catch up with Tia. Well, I try to. What actually happens is that I trip on my skateboard, face plant into the grass and add another gallon of water to the paddling pool as my bucket flies out of my hand.

'Gen! Gen!' shouts Keely, kicking her legs and jolting the extended first and second fingers of her right hand up and down – the Makaton sign for 'again'.

Aldo jogs over to lick me better, followed closely by Miz, who helps me up. 'Now do you understand why I'm always asking you to put your toys away when

159

you've finished with them? You could have really hurt yourself. Or Keely.'

I nod and pick up my skateboard. I'm about to replace it in the storage bench when an idea comes to me.

I have a skateboard in my hands. Aldo's here. From the way he's panting under the heat of the sun, I think he might enjoy a quick dip . . .

Once we've washed a few cars, could Tia work her editing magic to make the paddling pool look like a lake and the skateboard resemble a wake-board? Maybe she could even play about with Aldo's limbs! Make it look like he's standing on one leg and being towed by a speedboat? That'd certainly up my chances of getting more likes than Destiny.

Crouching beside the pool, I hit record on my phone, then tickle the water with my fingers. Aldo cocks his head at me. I suspect he might be warning me that the water has been diluted by my little sister's wee. I replace my hand with the skateboard. Aldo wags his tail. 'Come on, then,'

I say. I pat the surface of the board, cock my head towards it and widen my eyes. 'You know you want to!'

Aldo immediately leaps forward. Unfortunately, without enough thrust. Or lift. The inflatable edge of our paddling pool hasn't got a chance under his weight. Almost all the water whooshes on to the lawn. Keely is picked up in the current. Ending up in a flower bed, she points at me and screams, 'BANKIE!'

'Is this something to do with that YouStream challenge, Ferris?' snaps Miz, picking up my now filthy and distraught sister and stepping away from Aldo, as he shakes his body from tail to nose. 'Will you please leave Aldo alone and give it a rest.'

I nod and make my escape before Miz sees the state of the ex-flowers I've just spotted near her feet.

My drowned-rat dog follows me to the front street, where I find Tia stomping towards our house, her face like thunder.

'No one said yes,' she yells at me. 'It's because they don't know who I am. If you'd have come with me, Ferris, things would have been different. Thanks a bunch!' She storms indoors before I have chance to respond.

I follow her into the kitchen to explain my delay. Unfortunately, I make the mistake of wrinkling my nose at the sight of Mum chopping radishes into tiny cubes, ready to pour them in her cake batter.

And, with that, I've scored four out of four: upsetting every person in my family within the space of fifteen minutes.

I whistle for my best friend and take him upstairs to keep me company while I do the only thing I can think of that might calm me down: cartooning.

BEEPETY-BEEP DING!

When I turn on my phone the next day, along with the regular notification noises I've grown semi-used to, a weird BEEPETY-BEEP DING! blasts out.

I investigate and discover it means I've received a private message on YouStream. It's from someone with the handle *@PollyW_PGT* and it says:

Hi @Ferris_F_UK!

My name is Polly Whitewell. I'm a talent agent. Specifically, I represent talented animals.

I'm currently looking for a dog for a commercial I'm casting and, oh my gosh, I think Aldo would be perfect.

I know this is extremely short notice, but I'm holding auditions tomorrow. Would you be interested in bringing Aldo along?

If Aldo secures the role, the fee would be a one-off payment of £2,500, and the commercial would be used as a pre-clip advert on video apps like YouStream.

If you're keen, let me know and I'll send you the address.

Best wishes,

Polly Whitewell (aka @PollyW_PGT) Specialist Dog Agent at Pets Got Talent Limited

PS. I'm not sure how old you are, but if you're under eighteen, you'll need to bring an adult with you.

I read the message three times, scarcely able to believe it's real. My heart beating faster than a hummingbird's wing, I run to Tia's room to show her.

'This is the answer to all our problems!' I say. 'Aldo featuring in an online advert would pretty much guarantee me a million likes. A million likes would secure me certain victory in the YouStream challenge. Victory in the YouStream challenge would prevent me from having to give Keely's bankie away. And two and a half thousand pounds will be almost enough to buy your nan a stairlift!'

Tia doesn't speak for a moment. Her eyes brim with tears and she turns away from me, embarrassed. 'You'd give all the money to me?'

'Of course!' I say. 'When I win the challenge,

I'll get Destiny's d-5000. That's the only thing I've been saving up for anyway.'

Tia wipes her sleeve across her face then turns, throws her arms round me and squeezes me half to death. 'Thank you!' She releases me from her grip and looks at the floor. 'Sorry I was off with you yesterday. I just –'

'Forget yesterday,' I pant. 'We need to think about tomorrow!'

Tia takes my phone and re-reads the message. 'There's just one thing you're forgetting, Ferris.' She points at Aldo. Judging by the way his ears are pricked, he's been listening to our conversation intently. 'Aldo's not actually talented.'

I crouch to pat my dog's head and he licks my eyeball. 'But you're beautiful, aren't you? What do you think, boy? Up for a day out?'

Aldo sneezes, then wags his tail.

That's settled, then.

I message the agent immediately: *Definitely interested. Please send the address.*

Now all I need is a willing adult to take us. Grandpa would be my best bet, but he goes to his club on Sundays. Hmmm . . . I wonder if a permission slip from Mums will do?

SUNDAY
7 days till
D-DAY

Destination reached

Aldo is as calm as a yoga master lying on the floor between our feet as we travel on the bus into the

city. Either the day off I gave
him yesterday has helped him
to relax, or the vibration of the

engine and the heater under his belly has sent him into a deep, dreamless, sneeze-free sleep.

I feel good, too. And not just because my dog's behaving himself. This could be the first day of the rest of my life. My life as the owner of a real-life canine superstar (and a d-5000).

The same can't be said for Tia. She keeps

moving her football from one hand to the other and taking deep breaths as though she's going to speak, but changing her mind.

'You do realize they might ask him to DO something,' she eventually blurts out, as the bus stops to let more passengers on. 'It might be nothing to do with the way he looks.'

I glance at Aldo. He's been roused from his nap by the arrival of a shopping bag under the seat in front of us. It smells of pasties. Well, I think that's where the smell is coming from. Packed buses often have that sweet-potato-pie aroma. The one Miz says she can smell when I need a shower. 'We'll be fine,' I say.

To be honest, my main worry is that Mum doesn't check my location on her family safety app. I told her we were going to the park. I doubt she will. She had enough on this morning trying to get something I suspect might have been a glob of Aldo's snot out of Keely's bankie without putting it in a hot wash and taking it out of action for half a

day. Writing and signing a letter
of permission on her behalf was
basically my way of saving her
another job . . .

Dear Polly the
pet agent,
Ferris has my
permission to
bring Aldo to your
audition.
Signed: Emma
(Ferris's Mum)

For the rest of the journey,
Tia jabbers on about how her nan sometimes brings
her to the city to mooch in the charity shops. I nod
along, not really listening. I can't get Keely and her
beloved bankie out of my mind. The more I think
about how my sister would feel if I had to give
bankie to Destiny, the more my stomach lurches. I
mean, I'm 90 per cent sure that's what's causing the
wobbly sensation in my tummy. Ten per cent of me
blames taking a twisty bus ride after being force-
fed vegetable stew last night. Either way, the feeling
makes me determined not to let this opportunity go
to waste. Aldo HAS to be chosen to be the star of
this commercial, so I can use his fame to boost my
YouStream likes and save my little sister's lifeline.

When we arrive at the bus stop nearest
to the address Polly the pet agent sent me,

we use Tia's phone to navigate through a few busy streets. It takes longer than expected. I guess satnav apps don't account for you having a dog who needs to stop and sniff every single bench leg and lamp post he passes.

Eventually hearing 'Destination Reached!', we stop and crane our necks upwards. The audition venue is a massive old tower block. And Polly's message says: *Top Floor*.

After dragging Aldo up a gazillion stairs, we're met by a youngish man holding a clipboard. 'Dog's name?' he says.

'Aldo Foster,' says Tia, the only one of us not completely out of puff.

The man puts a tick next to something on his clipboard, then peers over our shoulders. 'Is there an adult with you?'

I finger the forged letter of permission in my pocket and my mouth goes dry. I hate lying.

'My nan is waiting downstairs,' says Tia, obviously sensing the inner battle going on inside me.

'You should consider where you hold your auditions in future. This place is not disabled-friendly at all. There's not even a lift.'

The man shrugs, then directs us through a door to his left.

'Nice one,' I say, as we enter what I assume is a waiting room.

There are three other dogs here, sitting quietly with their owners. To prevent Aldo instigating 'operation bum sniff', I hook the looped handle of his lead round the leg of a chair and sit on it to secure him.

I've barely caught my breath when a woman dressed in rainbow-patterned dungarees walks into the room. 'Aldo Foster?' she shouts.

Recognizing his name, Aldo bounds over to the woman. The chair, with me still upon it, is pulled along with him. I brush this embarrassing moment

off with a laugh. 'He's excited to meet you.' I unhook the lead from the chair leg and Aldo immediately starts sniffing the crotch of the woman's dungarees – proving my point perfectly. 'Sorry,' I say, feeling my face start to burn as I pull him away. 'He loves rainbows.'

'It's fairly common with his breed,' adds Tia.

'What breed is he?' asks the woman, gesturing that we should follow her down a corridor.

'A Bitlike,' says Tia, without hesitation.

The woman frowns. I glance at Tia and raise my eyebrows in question.

'Well, he's a "bit like" lots of dog breeds, isn't he?' she whispers. 'Gentle like a whippet, greedy like a Labrador, friendly like a spaniel, and daft like a boxer.'

I laugh, then take in our new surroundings.

The space we've arrived in is so bright I wish I'd brought my sunglasses. A dozen spotlights illuminate a rectangular area that's been marked out with masking tape. I gulp.

174

'I recognize this guy!' someone squeals.

I squint to see who's talking and spot a woman with red-framed glasses and short purple hair approaching us. She crouches to tickle Aldo's chin, then wipes her hand on her tummy. 'Does he always drool like this?' she asks.

'Only when he can smell food, really,' I say.

'Noted,' says the woman. 'I'm Polly. Which one of you guys is Ferris?'

'He is,' says Tia. She holds out her hand like a confident businesswoman. 'How do you do? I'm Tia, Aldo's assistant trainer.'

Polly shakes Tia's hand, then looks at me. 'Did you bring an adult with you?'

Tia laughs. 'Oh, Polly, you tease!'

Polly looks as confused as I feel.

'I'm nineteen next month,' continues Tia, her chin held high. 'After Aldo's done his audition, I can tell you about the anti-wrinkle face cream I use if you like. It's practically magic.'

Tia's worryingly good at fibbing.

175

Polly narrows her eyes at Tia, then points to the other end of the room. 'Right, then. Let's get down to business, shall we? Those two people down there are Ian and Marnie. They're the owners of Chump, the dog food company looking for a star for their next campaign.'

I squint towards where she's indicating and can just about make out a couple of figures hunched over a monitor. I've no idea if they can see me, but I wave politely. First impressions count, right?

'Between you and me,' says Polly, lowering her voice, 'they've hinted Aldo's exactly the look they're after: an everyday family dog. It was Ian who shared one of your YouStream videos with me, actually.'

I glance at Tia and we share a smile.

'Now,' says Polly. 'All Ian and Marnie want to see today is that Aldo is capable of following instructions. OK?'

I nod, feeling a little tension build in my neck.

'So,' she continues, 'I'll go and sit with them and give you the word when we're ready. Just run him through a few basic commands and we'll take it from there. OK?'

'Great!' says Tia, when she sees my mouth is open but no words are coming out.

As Polly walks away, she points at a man in a woolly hat aiming a camera at us. 'That's Beano. Our cameraman for the day.'

I wave at Beano. He throws me the peace sign back.

Tia and I share a wide-eyed stare. 'What are we going to do?' I whisper.

'Right, Ferris,' comes a shout. 'Take Aldo's lead off now. We're ready for you.'

The importance of eating breakfast

I wipe the drool from around Aldo's muzzle, unclip his lead from his collar . . . and stand there like a pudding as my dog immediately darts to the front of the room.

Beano laughs and dashes after him.

I chase after Aldo, who, I quickly realize, is headed for a table near the window. A buffet table. The table he's obviously been drooling over since we entered this room. It's loaded with food.

Uh-oh.

Before I can catch up with him, my dog's front paws are up on the edge of the table and his slobbery chops are all over a plate of pastries. Losing his balance, he tries to steady himself and catches a shallow dish. It flips into the air and

a selection of pies ends up on the floor.
Pleased with this achievement, Aldo gets
down and starts to tuck in, his tail whizzing
like the blade of an electric fan.

I pounce on him, trying to grasp his collar.
Suddenly an expert dodger, Aldo darts under the
table. I scramble after him, but I'm too late. His
paws are now up on the other side of the table.
And he's lapping up a dish of something
green and goopy.

'ALDO!' shouts Tia. She throws her ball
to divert my dog's attention from the glorious grub
he thinks has been laid on just for him.

The ball bounces on an unopened tub of
coleslaw, then lands with a plop in a
trifle. Much to Aldo's delight, the
cream splatters everywhere, including
all over the cheeseboard . . .

Cream AND cheese: it's Aldo's idea of heaven. He
scrambles towards the cheeseboard with
such enthusiasm that, a millisecond later,

almost all the delicious-looking platters are on the floor. My dog, his front paws nestled in a plate of triangular sandwiches, begins munching through a bowl of cocktail sausages.

 I yank him away and shout towards the guys at the monitor, who look like they're almost peeing themselves with laughter. 'Sorry! We were in such a rush to get here on time, he's not had his breakfast.'

Polly marches over to me, a look of fury on her face.

'He'll be more focused now,' I say. 'You know what it's like when you're hungry.' I grab a few wedges of cheese from the floor before it's all cleaned away and, in Polly's words, we reset. Which is, I discover, a fancy way of saying try again.

During a quick conflab, Tia points out that if I stand at one side of the masked-out rectangle with the cheese, and she stands at the other with her (still quite creamy) ball, not only will we have more chance of containing Aldo, but we'll be able to show his recall skills.

'ACTION!' shouts Polly.

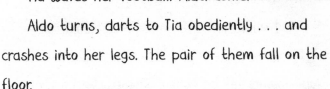

Tia waves her football. 'Aldo! Come!'

Aldo turns, darts to Tia obediently . . . and crashes into her legs. The pair of them fall on the floor.

'Sorry!' I shout. 'He's not used to shiny floors. We have carpet at home.'

'There's a rug in reception,' says Beano helpfully.

'I'll get it!' yells Polly. 'RESET!'

I glance at Tia, panic rising inside me like water in a fast-running bath. Tia's face does nothing to reassure me; her forehead is wrinkled in doubt. We both inhale deeply as the rug is laid before us.

'Right, Ferris!' shouts Polly, using the same voice my teacher employs when she's pretending she's calm. 'One more time. If you could just get Aldo to sit, then lie down, please, that would be super.'

Crouching, I put my nose against Aldo's.

'It's a thing they do,' shouts Tia, faking

confidence again. 'Ferris is like a dog whisperer.'

I stare into Aldo's eyes. 'I really need you to sit,' I whisper. 'Can you do that for me, boy? Please. When I say now. OK?'

I stand. Aldo gazes at me with adoring eyes. 'Now!' I shout.

Aldo lowers his bottom. I almost cheer until I realize that it's his poo-squat . . .

Oh, good grief.

'It's because the carpet's green!' I shout. 'It's exactly the same colour as the piece of artificial grass he uses as a kind of litter tray in my garden. He's brilliant at using it. He's not pooed on the lawn for months.'

Polly walks over while I'm still talking. 'I think we've seen enough, Ferris.' She hands me a poo bag, then turns to look at the Chump owners behind the desk, who are engaged in a whispered conversation. 'I'm not sure Aldo is quite what we're looking for.'

'He's just excited and nervous and not used to

all the lights,' says Tia, her voice wobbling as though she might cry.

Polly shakes her head. 'Close the door on your way out.' As she walks away, I hear her mutter under her breath: 'That'll teach me for believing everything I see on the internet.'

Flippin' great

My eyes itch and my head aches. I barely slept
last night. When Aldo wasn't sneezing, or pawing
my face, or sticking his tongue in my ear, which I
know he was doing to try to comfort me but I just
found annoying, I was tossing and turning with
weird dreams. Most of them involved me feeling like
a prize rat, handing bankie to Destiny Dean and
watching Keely's little
face crumple.

I don't think Tia got
much rest either. When
I took Mr Sneezy
down for a wee in the

early hours, I saw her light was on and could hear her sniffling.

Tiptoeing to the purple room, I knock on the door, pushing it open when I hear a quiet, 'Come in.' Tia's leaning on her pillow, looking at her phone. Her eyes are puffy and red. I go to perch beside her and see a photo of her and her nan on the screen.

I hesitate, then put my arm round her shoulder. 'You'll be together again soon.'

A tear plops on to the old football top Tia wears as pyjamas. 'I know. Ignore my waterworks, Ferris. It's just that you'd promised me that money from the filming for the stairlift and that's never going to happen now, is it?'

'Probably not,' I say, swallowing the lump in my throat. 'Don't worry, though. We'll think of a new way to get you your money.'

The problem is, I also need to think of a way to boost my YouStream likes. And quickly. You should

185

see what Destiny posted yesterday. While my crotch-sniffing, sausage-stealing, carpet-spoiling dog was behaving like a complete reprobate, the fluff ball next door was perfecting her synchronized swimming skills. Destiny's latest offering to YouStream is entitled 'Behold! My Magnificent MerDog'. Diving into a paddling pool the size of my bedroom, Foo-Foo swims over to Destiny. The pair of them tread water for a few seconds, disappear beneath the surface, then, in perfect synchronization, raise a leg skyward and spin 360 degrees.

The likes score now stands at 713 to 444.

So, while I do want to help Tia, if I don't post something new pronto, I'll never get the d-TAB, Keely's bankie will be a goner and Destiny will have boasting rights forever.

Leaving Tia to get dressed, I return to my own room and spend ten minutes making the final frame from **Astoundog**'s Wake-board Adventure into a flip book. I record myself flipping through it, then type: *When my channel has 1,000 likes, I'll post the live show.*

Desperate times call for desperate lies. And maybe this will buy me a bit of time.

Next, I brainstorm new ways to help Tia make some money.

I guess we could give the car washing another go? Tia was right that my neighbours would probably be more inclined to part with their cash if I'm with her.

Or we could go further afield, somewhere people haven't yet been treated to Mum's veggie delights, and try to flog Friday's unsold radish cakes. We could attach Mum's wheely shopping basket to Aldo's back and get him to pull along my remaining copies of issue four of *The Hoot* as well.

Or perhaps we could go back to the playground at Vickie Park (without Aldo and maybe in disguise) and offer to push toddlers on the swings for a pound per minute. Most parents and grandparents love having their hands free so they can look at their phones. Oh, I could even tell them to check out my YouStream channel while they're at it.

Or maybe we could –

BEEPETY-BEEP

DING!

There's that sound again. The one that means I have a private message on YouStream.

Urgh. It's a message from Polly the pet agent. I open it, fully expecting to read some kind of rant about how disappointed she was yesterday. Or maybe a message to let me know that, although Ian and Marmite from Chump found Aldo's antics utterly hilarious, they've cast the bow-tie-wearing Rottweiler we passed as we fled down the stairs yesterday.

All it says is:

Ferris, my clients didn't cast a dog yesterday.

The three dots flash while I'm reading. She's still typing.

For some reason, they really liked Aldo's energy and want to see him again on Friday.

Wait, WHAT? I knew Ian and Marmite found Aldo's antics entertaining, but I was NOT expecting that!

Can you make it? We'll remove the buffet, we'll bring a piece of neutral-coloured carpet, we'll turn down the lights . . . Think that'll help?

OMG! A second chance!

YES!!! I type. And I'm so sorry about yesterday. Now Aldo's seen the audition room and met everyone, he'll be miles better. What time?

The three dots flash again.

Same Time. Same place. Ian and Marnie have been looking again at your YouStream channel. They've come up with an idea that they could get a voiceover artist to say, 'Buy Chump. It's

Flippin' Great.' So be prepared. If Aldo can perform his backflip for us on camera, the job's yours.

I send a thumbs-up emoji, then pull Aldo to Tia's room to share the good news.

Smells and sneezes

Tia howls with laughter. 'Have you completely lost your mind, Ferris? There's no way we're going to be able to train Aldo to do a backflip on purpose in four days. We wouldn't even be able to do it in four hundred.'

'But think of the money, Tia! It would mean you and your nan could be back together.' I don't add that having a famous dog would probably also boost my YouStream likes, help me beat Destiny, save bankie and gain a d-5000, but Tia's not daft. I widen my eyes and clasp my hands, as if I'm praying. 'It's got to be worth a try, hasn't it? If Aldo did it once, surely he can do it again?'

Tia purses her lips. 'I guess.'

I look at Aldo. He stares back at me with his trusting eyes. 'What do you think, boy?

Ready to give backflipping another go?'

Aldo wags his tail, then sneezes so violently
a trump escapes at the same time. He turns to
stare at his rear end, then slowly moves his gaze to
Tia, as though she's to blame for the terrible smell
that's now wafting up our noses.

I laugh.

'That slow-motion accusation has given me an
idea,' says Tia. 'Send me the original backflip video.'

I do as I'm asked and watch as Tia receives it,
uploads it to her fancy video-editing app, fiddles
with a few controls and slows the footage right
down.

Watching Aldo perform a backflip in ultra-slow
motion is amazing, but I'm not sure this is a good
use of our time. 'Care to explain?'

'We need to identify exactly what caused Aldo's
moment of athleticism. If we can see that, maybe
we can replicate it?'

Ah.

We rewind and watch the beginning of the clip

over and over. The slow motion is helpful, but the zoom-in function isn't great. Although it's hard to see *exactly* what happened, the catalyst to Aldo's backflip appears to have been a bee tickling his nostrils.

'All we need,' says Tia, putting my phone on her bed and looking out of her bedroom window, 'is a bee!'

Hmmm. I'm not a massive fan of bees. I mean, I get their necessity for the future of the planet and all that, but I don't relish the idea of going outside to invite one in to dance on my dog's nose.

'Or something that can act a bit like one?' I suggest.

Tia scratches her head. 'A wasp?'

'NO! Something that can tickle Aldo's nose, but that doesn't have a venomous sting. Hang on. Back in a sec.'

Leaving Tia with Aldo, I run downstairs to see

193

what bee-like alternative I can lay my hands on.

Wielding a long-handled feather duster, I head
back upstairs like a knight with a comedy jousting

stick. I enter Tia's room and wave it
around near Aldo's nostrils.

Unfortunately, he doesn't perform a
backflip. He just sneezes again.

Unimpressed, as I guess you would be
if your best friend shoved a bunch of pink
feathers on a pole up your nose, Aldo furrows his
brow and pads on to the landing.

I follow him. Tia follows me.

In a warranted stroke of bad karma, our
own nostrils are immediately attacked. By another
terrible smell.

I assume Keely's had an early morning bout of
diarrhoea when I see Miz dashing in and out of
my little sister's bedroom with disinfectant-soaked
cloths. My suspicions are confirmed when Mum's
rendition of 'Poo Poo, Bum Bum, Wee Wee' comes
to a stop and the bathroom door inches open.

'Just watch Keely for a sec, will you, Ferris, sweetie? I need to grab some toilet rolls from the downstairs loo. She's got the runs.'

Oh, joy.

I hold my nose, prop the door open with one foot and ignore Tia's laughter. Aldo squeezes past my leg to lie on the cold bathroom tiles, as though he's the 'sweetie' who's been asked to guard my sister while she sits on the toilet and intervene if she tries to escape, or falls into the bowl. Trust me, where Keely's concerned, both are distinct possibilities.

I crane my neck to see if there's an air freshener within easy reach. There's not. But there is a tub of Miz's homemade talc next to the sink. Interesting. Maybe a little fragrant powder would work both as a smell-masker AND a nose-tickling backflip inducer.

To avoid getting too close to Keely and her brown business, I stretch my arm from the doorway and reach for the tub of talc. I fumble and it falls on Aldo's head. A tiny puff of powder escapes. Aldo screws up his face. One of his eyes closes. His head whips upwards . . . Is this it? Is he about to backflip again?

Nope.

His entire skull shakes, as it slams downwards with another sneeze.

ACHOO!

Keely giggles.

Aldo sneezes again. And again. And again.

I don't know why she finds the onset of dog flu so funny, but Keely chuckles so much a series of tiny trumps escape at the same time. I bend double with laughter and Tia pokes her head round the door to see what's going on.

Relishing the attention, Aldo wags his tail and clamps the talc tub between his jaws. This time, a large cloud of white smoke erupts from the holes in its lid. Surely this will be nose-tickly enough to make my dog perform his infamous backflip.

Nope. It induces another series of comedy

sneezes that make him pounce around in circles, but at no point does he turn upside down.

'GEN! GEN!' squeals Keely, bouncing up and down on the toilet and signing 'again' as though her life depends on it.

Tia points at my back pocket, where my phone is nestled. 'Shame you weren't filming then, Ferris. THAT was both hilarious and educational. Dogs are so funny when they sneeze. And did you see that Makaton sign language was trending on YouStream the other day?'

I slow-blink. 'I am not about to film a video of my sister sitting on the toilet.'

Tia nods. 'Fair point.'

'Plus, we don't want funny or educational. We need another backflip.'

'Oh yeah,' says Tia.

Soon, Mum rushes upstairs with six toilet rolls and Keely's bankie. 'Good news, Keely!' she says. 'Bankie's all clean now.'

That is good news.

Better news, possibly, is the backflip-inducing brainwave the emergency inflatable mattress I've just spotted Miz taking into Keely's room has given me.

Forget nose-tickling. This idea is SO MUCH better!

Dog-apult

Sadly, Miz, who can be a right fun-thief after dealing with diarrhoea, scuppers my genius plan by refusing to let me put the blow-up mattress on the damp grass.

Hey hum.

Not on your nelly!

I take Aldo down to the garden anyway and return to my metaphorical drawing board. I wish I was at my real drawing board. This dog-training business is sooooo time-consuming.

'It'll all be worth it in the end,' I say, patting Aldo's head as I remind myself why I'm doing this: to beat Destiny, to make sure I don't lose bankie, to help Tia get her nan a stairlift . . . to gain a d-5000 . . .

Come on, brain! Think!

I scan the garden and my eyes rest upon

AJ's green orb. I smile as I remember the cheeky monkey's pea-catapulting behaviour. Hang on . . . I feel the twinkling of a brainwave. A catapult could work. Or should I say a DOG-apult . . .

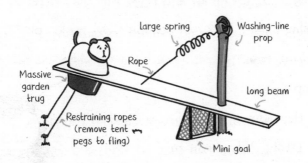

I know it sounds ridiculous, but I'm certain if I can just get Aldo to remember how super performing a backflip *felt*, he'll be more receptive to trying one on his own again.

The only long beam I can spy is a wide length of thick Perspex covering the tomatoes Mum is cultivating in the raised flower bed.

Hmm . . . dare I?

Probably not. Mum can get a bit funny about other people interfering with her weird 'Make-Do' garden maintenance creations. And I never know what she considers off limits. I once used a few plastic bottles I found scattered around the lawn for a game of ten-pin bowling. Turned out they hadn't been lobbed over our back fence by an odd litter bug who filled bottles with water and pierced them with holes for fun. They were intentional 'soil moisteners'.

Out of ideas, I'm just messaging Cal to ask for his input – in case he finds a way to recharge his phone in the next few days – when Tia arrives in the garden with Keely.

'You feeling better, Keels?' I ask. I raise my eyebrows, swipe my palms up my chest and stick up both my thumbs before pushing my hands away from my body. (The Makaton sign for 'How are you?')

Try it!

'HOW ARE YOU?'

Keely nods. She tries to copy my thumbs-up sign but, as usual, manages to swear with her fingers. While

I giggle like the child that I am, Tia clasps Keely's hand and they join me and Aldo on the lawn.

I squeeze my neck into my spine, then glance at Tia. 'What can we do?'

Tia shrugs.

Keely makes the sign for 'TV'. Ha! She obviously thinks I'm seeking an activity for us all to do together. I laugh. Then, after checking her hands aren't grubby, tap on my phone's video gallery and hand it to my little sister. She smiles, signs 'thank you', then snuggles up beside Aldo, stroking his ears while Tia and I discuss our next move.

Tia's not impressed with my 'dog-apult' idea. In fact, she seems to want to give the whole thing a rest.

'I know you want to beat Destiny, Ferris,' she

says. 'I'm just not sure trying to get Aldo to repeat a move that was obviously a one-off is the right way.' She points at Aldo and sighs. 'Let's face it, he's just not destined to be the star of the Chump advert.'

'But Tia!' I plead. 'It's not *just* about beating Destiny. I mean, of course that'd be epic, and, sure, I'd love a d-TAB, but . . .' I sit more upright to look her in the eye and lower my voice so my sister can't hear me. 'At this point, it's more about saving Keely's bankie and getting YOU money for your stairlift.'

I'm not fibbing. Those two things suddenly seem so much more important than proving to Destiny that she can't beat me at everything.

Tia sighs. 'I know you're trying to help me, Ferris. And I appreciate that, but, trust me on this.' She points at Aldo. Watching videos with Keely, he looks as content as a sleeping sloth. 'He's never going to be able to backflip.' She jerks her head in the direction of Destiny's garden. 'I was thinking maybe I could go round to that little old lady's house next door-but-one to ask if she needs any odd jobs doing.'

'Please,' I beg. 'Fifteen more minutes of brainstorming and then I'll come with you.' I'm comfortable offering this; I saw scary Mrs Smythe whizz out on her mobility scooter earlier.

As Tia sighs, Keely shouts: 'GEN! GEN!' She thrusts my phone towards me and I see that she's just watched the OG video of Aldo backflipping.

I restart it so she can watch it 'again' and she giggles her little socks off. 'GEN! GEN!' she repeats, waggling her first two fingers up and down.

I take my phone and hold it in front of Aldo's nose. 'Remember doing this?' I ask, stroking his soft head as he joins Keely in watching the video for a third time. 'It was epic. You think you could do that again, boy?'

'Gen! Gen!' squeals Keely. She jumps to her feet

and points at Aldo, excited at the prospect of witnessing the live show.

If only it was that simple.

'I guess I could demo,' says Tia, standing and bending her knees.

'You can backflip?' I ask, although this new information doesn't surprise me.

'Yeah.'

'Hang on,' I say. 'I have an idea.'

Broken

Leaving Tia to watch Keely, I run indoors, grab
a block of cheese from the fridge, then
head back into the garden.

Breaking off a chunk, I hold it in
front of Tia. 'Go with me on this,' I say
before staring at her with a stern expression and
channelling my inner sergeant major. 'SIT!'

After looking at me as though I'm a particularly
difficult maths problem, Tia plops her bottom on the
grass like a dog. I pat her hair and stuff the cheese
into her mouth. Keely giggles. Aldo wags his tail. Tia
rolls her eyes.

I break off another piece of cheese and hold it
near Tia's nose. Glancing at Aldo through the corner
of my eye to check he's still watching, I command
Tia to: 'lie down!'

Like an obedient dog, Tia does. And so does Aldo!

He presses his belly into the lawn and wags his tail
so much his bottom moves from side to side too.

Excellent!

I reward them both with a bit of cheese.
Aldo takes it with far more enthusiasm and much
more grace than Tia, who looks like she'd rather be
doing anything else, especially when, right at that
moment, a snigger comes from the other side of
the fence. Great. Destiny's spying on us again. Just
what we need.

Ignoring the eye twinkling at me through the
spy hole in the fence, I break off two more chunks
of cheese and hold them towards Tia and Aldo.
'Stand up!' I order.

They do. Yes, both of them. Ha! Take that,

Destiny Dean. I'm getting somewhere at last.

I should have thought of this sooner. Aldo's always been brilliant at copying. You should see the way he imitates me when I'm sad. Like when baby Maximillian left us to go to live with his new dads when I was seven; we lay on my bed together for a good hour after that goodbye, both our heads under one pillow.

'Come on!' says Tia, with a huff. 'I see where this is going. Just try it.'

She's right. I can reminisce any time.

I hold out two extra large chunks of cheese. 'FLIP!' I shout.

Tia bends her knees, swings her arms behind her, then whips her legs over her head, landing on her feet. A perfect backflip.

Aldo, on the other hand, nuzzles my leg, then starts to bark.

Destiny sniggers again. 'Come on, Foo-Foo!' she says. 'Let's go and get your bed ready for your new . . .' She raises her voice. 'BANKIE!'

Her assured tone, and obvious attempt to wind up Keely, riles me.

'FLIP!' I yell, holding the cheese near Aldo's little nose.

Tia glares at me, her brow furrowed. 'Calm down, Ferris! No one likes being yelled at.'

She's right. 'Sorry, boy,' I say, ruffling Aldo's neck as he gets to his feet.

I slump into a garden chair, my head in my hands, only raising my chin when I hear Aldo barking. But he's not just barking. He's pouncing his front paws forward. He's trying to lift them off the grass at the same time. Oh my gosh. I think he understands what I need him to do.

'Go on!' I say, more calmly. 'Flip!' I make the sign for 'tumble'.

Aldo stares at me. He thrusts his body forward and . . .

Yelps, then wobbles and falls on to his side.

'Stop it, Ferris! He's trying so hard to please you, but it's hurting him,' yells Tia. She bends to kiss his head.

'Boo-Boo!' shouts Keely, throwing herself on top of her buddy.

I waft the girls away and bend to stroke my dog. 'He's fine. You're fine, aren't you, boy?' Aldo whimpers and hobbles to his feet. Limping indoors, he collapses on to the carpet.

He's not fine.

Later on, my best friend won't eat his tea. He's not interested in the dollop of carrot mush I slip under the kitchen table when we're all having ours. He can't walk without limping. He doesn't come up to my room at bedtime.

What have I done?

I've broken my dog. My beautiful, trusting dog.

TUESDAY
5 days till
D-DAY

Shaken and teary

The next day, Aldo won't get up off his bed. Not even when I add a sneaky slice of sandwich ham to his breakfast.

Miz and Mum decide he needs immediate medical attention and my stomach flips a somersault.

My eyes keep welling up with tears on our way to the vet's. Aldo's tail is uncharacteristically still. Keely doesn't lob her sippy cup at the window once. Tia keeps throwing me glances that make the already massive guilty ache in my heart increase. And, most worryingly of all, Mums are having one of those chats they engage in when they're trying to pretend everything's OK when it's actually not.

The last time I remember such a conversation was the day Granny Eileen was rushed into hospital.

When we arrive, Mums have to carry Aldo in. His body quivers from nose to tail as the smell of dog food and disinfectant hits him. I worry I've caused more problems than I thought, until I remember he always shakes like this when we visit the vet's. I guess I might be the same if all my past experiences of a building consisted of injections in my neck and thermometers being stuck up my bum.

A vet with curly hair and pink-rimmed glasses asks Mums to put Aldo on a table in a consulting room and starts to examine him.

My best friend yelps when the vet touches the wrist of his front paw. Keely can't stand seeing her best buddy being prodded by a stranger. She releases herself from Tia's grip, grabs the stethoscope from round the vet's neck and throws it across the room. The vet doesn't seem bothered, but Miz asks me and Tia

213

to take my little sister to sit in the reception area.
'Don't look so worried, pal,' she says, ruffling my
hair. 'I'm sure it's nothing serious.'

While we wait on the hard plastic seats, Tia
entertains Keely with an album on her phone's
camera roll. When Keely gets bored of looking at
pictures of footballs, I take her to the dog weighing
scale to distract her. Last time we were here, I
discovered my little sister was the 'ideal weight' for
a King Charles spaniel. I've just figured out she's
now more like a Staffordshire bull terrier when
Mums enter the waiting room
and tell us that Aldo's been taken
for an X-ray.

Over the next half hour, I
try to join in with all the small
talk Mums make with the owners of the creatures
we see coming and going, but all I can think about
is how my best friend is hurt and it's all my fault.

My mind drifts to the day Mums adopted Aldo.
We'd just said goodbye to Hassan – a little boy

we'd been fostering for a few months – and I was devastated. I guess, aged two and a half, I didn't understand fostering as well as I do now, and Mums were giving me a friend I'd never have to see leave with another family. Since then, Aldo's always been there for me, like a brother. I should have known he'd push himself too hard to try to please me. I'm the worst brother ever.

I'm jolted from my thoughts as the vet comes back to speak to us. Aldo's not with him and I burst into tears.

Nasal blockage

The vet puts his hand on my shoulder. 'Don't worry. He's going to be OK.' He removes his glasses and turns to Mums. 'We've done a couple of X-rays and it looks like Aldo's sprained his ankle. It's very common. It'll heal through rest.'

Tia lifts Keely into her arms for a cuddle. 'We can make sure he rests, can't we, Ferris?'

I nod and make a pact with myself to contact Polly as soon as we get home to cancel our arrangements for Friday. Aldo's well-being is miles more important than getting one over on Destiny.

The vet smiles, then reverts his attention to Mums and lowers his voice. 'A bit more concerning is that we've discovered a small blockage right at the back of Aldo's nasal passage.'

I glance at Tia, as the realization hits me. 'It might be a dead bee,'

I say, swallowing my nerves.

The vet's brow creases. I tell him all about the bee that was dancing on Aldo's nose just before he executed his accidental backflip. 'I think it might have gone up.'

'Why didn't you say something sooner, Ferris?' asks Miz, throwing me a stern glare. 'We all wondered why Aldo was sneezing so much.'

I stare at the floor. Admitting I had a stupid challenge against Destiny on my mind sounds so selfish now.

'OK,' says the vet. 'Thanks for the heads-up. That might explain why he's off his food.' He passes Mum a piece of green paper. 'We're going to sedate him and see what we can do by going up his nose before we consider operating. But, just in case, I need you to sign this.'

We have to leave Aldo at the vet's and I feel terrible. I miss him as soon as we get home and see his empty bed. I miss him at teatime, even though Mum orders in pizza. I miss him the most at bedtime. I'm not used to sleeping alone, and Aldo'll be so homesick staying all night in a place with strangers.

I reach under my bed to pull out my old 'Average Aldo' strips. I'm leafing through them, feeling sorry for myself, when my thoughts drift to Tia. She's been away from the most important person in her life for almost two weeks.

Tiptoeing across the landing, I tap on her door. She invites me in and I can see she's upset too.

'It's over, Ferris,' she says. 'I'm sorry you're not going to win the challenge.'

I sit on the end of her bed. 'And I'm sorry I won't be able to buy you a stairlift.'

We sit in silence for a while, me looking at my 'Average Aldo' cartoons, Tia scrolling through photos of her nan on her phone.

After a while, Tia shuffles down to sit

beside me and glances at my drawings. 'Try not to worry about Aldo, Ferris. He's a tough cookie. He'll be home before you know it. I'm sure of it.'

'Yeah,' I say, swallowing the lump in my throat. I return to my bedroom and pray that she's right.

WEDNESDAY
4 days till
D-DAY

Confession time

Thankfully, she is!

The vet rang this morning to inform us that the remnants of the dead nose-tickler have been extracted without having to perform surgery, and all Aldo needs is some TLC and forty-eight hours of bed rest. Basically, his idea of heaven.

Mum's gone to collect him. I'm at the kitchen table, making him some 'Welcome home' pictures.

Welcome home,
❦ALDO❦

First, I draw Aldo letting Keely stroke his ears.

Then I draw him as a nodding dog, watching Tia as she practises keepie-uppies.

220

My third drawing is of him snuggled on the settee with Miz. He's licking her salty cheeks as she cries at one of her 'Save the Planet' documentaries.

It's so good to be drawing again. I'm much calmer by the time I start my fourth picture: Aldo drooling while he watches Mum fry sausages.

I turn this one into a full-on comic strip. Mum slips on the drool and a sausage flies into Aldo's mouth. The end frame is Aldo winking as though this was his cunning plan from the start, and in no way was he merely trying to make a finger of pork teleport from the pan into his mouth by the power of a prolonged stare.

Lastly, I draw him in bed with me, his chin on my lap as he watches me draw. Happy just to be near me. And, of course, making my room smell like a sewer.

I've just zipped up my pencil case when I hear the car pull on to the drive. I run to the front door and throw my arms around Aldo. 'I'm so sorry, boy,'

I whisper. 'I promise I'll be a better best friend from now on.'

Aldo licks my tears away, his tail wagging. The perfect brother, he's not one to hold a grudge.

I take his lead and guide him through to his bed in the kitchen. Tia, Keely and Miz run in from the garden to join me. Together with Mum, we all sit with him, feeding him bits of cheese and stroking his ears.

Us three kids are still here an hour later when Grandpa arrives.

'I believe this one's not been too good?' says Grandpa, patting Aldo's head. 'Want to tell me all about it?'

I nod and feel my throat tighten, as I recount our trip to the vet's.

Grandpa's such a good listener, I end up telling him EVERYTHING.

I tell him all about Aldo's accidental backflip, and how guilty I feel for not realizing my best friend had a dead bee stuck up his nose; I tell him about all the lies I've told online; I tell him about our secret trip into town to meet Polly, and how we've been invited to return on Friday, and how Aldo's sprained ankle is all my fault because I was pressuring him to learn how to backflip for real before then.

I tell him about how I really wanted to help Tia raise some money for her nan's stairlift, but now I can't.

Last of all, I tell him about how terrible I feel. Not because I'm going to lose the YouStream challenge, but because I'm going to ruin Keely's life by giving her bankie to Destiny.

When I've finished speaking, I feel like I'm out of breath and burst into tears.

Tia hands me a tissue. 'Don't worry about the money, Ferris. I'll work something out.'

Keely strokes her bankie on my foot.

Aldo licks my tears away, then rests his

chin on my lap.

Grandpa's knees

crack as he crouches to comfort me.

'Sounds like you've got yourself in a

bit of a pickle.'

'A bit of a pickle?' exclaims Miz.

'They've met up with a stranger

they met online.'

I whip my head towards the

kitchen door and realize Mum and Miz

have heard everything too. Oh heck.

'Calm down, Elizabeth,' says

Grandpa, as Tia and I stand to face

the music. 'We all make mistakes

when we're young. You made plenty

of your own, remember?' He cocks

his chin to one side and raises his eyebrows.

'What kind of mistakes?' asks Tia, her eyes

twinkling.

'Never mind about that,' says Miz. 'All you need to know is that I tried my best to fix them.'

'Which is what you need to do, Ferris,' adds Mum. 'And you can start by contacting this Polly woman to let her know Aldo won't be visiting her to perform a backflip on Friday.'

'I'm going to,' I say.

Mum hands me a tissue, her tone softening. 'And let that be an end to this YouStream nonsense, yes?'

I nod. I've already made my peace with the fact that I'm going to lose the YouStream challenge. Even if I did want to try and film Aldo doing an amazing trick – which I don't any more – Destiny's last video was of Foo-Foo performing headers with multiple-sized balls, and her total likes are now at 952 compared to my 487. There's no way I could reach that before Sunday.

What I've not made my peace with is giving Keely's blanket away. I should have spent the last ten days learning how to knit. 'But what about Keely's bankie?'

Grandpa leans back against the kitchen worktop and folds his arms. 'Now *THAT* I can help with. I've got one of those at home.'

'WHAT?' shout Mum and Miz in unison.

'I think you'll find the word is *pardon*, ladies. I *said* I have one of those at home.' He points at Keely, who looks like she's in a trance, stroking Aldo's ears and her bankie simultaneously. 'Knitting those brightly coloured rainbow blankets took Eileen's mind off things towards the end, when she knew she was . . .' His voice breaks. He removes his glasses and wipes the corner of one eye. 'Now you mention it, I think she said I was supposed to pass it on to you, Elizabeth, for your little visitors.'

Mum looks at Miz and laughs. 'All that secret overnight washing and drying we've been doing, and all this time your dad had a spare at home!'

'I can't believe it!' says Miz, reaching for Grandpa's hand. 'I remember asking Mum if she could knit us another one, and then she got poorly and . . .'

Well, this is turning into a right family weep fest. Now Miz is crying too.

'Anyway,' says Grandpa, coughing to clear his throat. 'That's one of your problems solved, Ferris. The question is, how can we help you with your others?'

I glance at Tia. 'I'm not sure you can, unless you've got a spare three thousand pounds knocking about.'

Grandpa shakes his head. 'Unfortunately not.' He rubs Tia's arm. 'Sorry, lovie.'

'It's OK,' says Tia. 'I've set up alerts on Freecycle, GiveAway and LovedOnce. A stairlift that's the right size, and not hundreds of miles away, will turn up soon, I'm sure.'

Mum squeezes Tia's shoulder and smiles. 'I'm keeping my eye on eBay too.'

'But what about all those lies you've told on the interweb, Ferris?' says Grandpa. 'You know what I

always say. Honesty is the best policy. Lies have
a habit of coming back and
biting you on the bum.'

'Agreed,' says Mum.

'Indeed,' adds Miz.

I look to Tia for help. 'You know what, Ferris?'
she says, fingering the pictures of Aldo I drew
earlier and nodding her head. 'I think they're right.
Follow me, everyone. Ferris has one last YouStream
video to make and he's going to need our help.'

The moment of truth

Grandpa holds my phone. Aldo lies with his chin on my lap, drooling over the Cheestring Keely is waving around just out of shot.

'Three, two, one . . .' Tia points at me. 'Action!'

Take 1

I take a deep breath and look into the camera lens. I'm not 100 per cent sure Tia's idea will get me any likes, but I'm ready to tell the world the truth. 'My name is Ferris. This is my dog, Aldo. He can't do any extraordinary tricks, but –' I hold up the BEST BUDS photo I pulled off the fridge – 'he's my best friend and I love him.'

Tia comes to sit beside me. 'This is Aldo. When I first came to be fostered, he helped me settle in by playing football with me.' She holds up the picture I drew of the pair of them and ruffles Aldo's fur.

'If I was lucky enough to have a dog, I'd want one just like this guy.'

Holding up her cartoon, Mum joins us on the floor. 'This is the real Aldo. He's constantly slobbering all over my kitchen floor. But he keeps me company while I'm cooking and is the first to welcome me home when I've been food shopping.'

Miz crouches beside Mum. She strokes Aldo's head as she holds up her picture. 'This is Aldo. He trumps like a trooper and makes our furniture look like it's made out of dog hair, but he's always there to lick away our tears whenever we're upset.'

Grandpa zooms in on Aldo, whose drool has reached a record length. 'This is Aldo,' he says. 'He's an average family dog. He can't do any extraordinary tricks. But, to us, he's perfect.'

After a group hug, I upload the video to YouStream, along with a comment explaining the truth behind his backflip and an apology for lying. Ending the message with #AverageAldo, I hit the 'post now' button before I can change my mind.

Then, after a lecture about not keeping secrets and the dangers of arranging to meet online strangers, I message Polly the pet agent to explain everything and to let her know I won't be attending Friday's audition.

Even though I'm sad I won't be able to help Tia, and disappointed I'm going to lose the YouStream challenge, I feel a huge weight lift from my chest.

At bedtime, I put my phone on silent, help Aldo climb under my duvet and sleep like a log until . . .

#AverageAldo

. . . Tia runs into my room ten hours later.

'FERRRRRRRRRRRRRRRRRRIS! Have you looked at your phone?'

I roll over to face the door and shake my head.

'You really should . . .'

Rubbing my eyes, I reach towards my bedside table, but Tia can't hold in her excitement. 'THE NEW VIDEO HAS OVER A HUNDRED THOUSAND LIKES!'

Wait. WHAT?

'And hashtag Average Aldo is TRENDING!' She thrusts her phone under my nose.

Oh. My. Gosh.

It's not a dream.

Yesterday's honest upload has 123,216 likes! Not only that, it's been shared by thousands of people from across the globe. And #AverageAldo is indeed trending.

Some YouStream users have even responded with photos and videos of their own average but lovable dogs. I scooch myself into a sitting position and scroll through the first few comments.

@ordinaryjoss: So refreshing to see content like this on YouStream. #KeepingItReal #AverageAldo

This is accompanied by a photo of a whopping great dog whose folds of fur look too big for its body.

@ValleyVoo: SHARE TO: @Neville-N-Bobby. Yay! I feel the same about my gorgeous Meggy-Moo. #HonestPostAlert #AverageAldo

Beneath this, there's a photo of a black whippet-like dog sleeping with her impossibly long tongue dangling out of the side of her mouth, all four legs in the air.

@Harry-Bow: Big up the average dogs of the world. My Derek can't do any tricks either. He's brill. #AverageAldo #AverageDerek

Under this comment is a short video of Derek, a scruffy terrier, watching football on TV.

@BillieUG: SHARE TO: @DaleRrrrrrr @LaylaDixon @JaneyMcSplitz. Ferris! Your dog is gorgeous. My dog, Mr Paws, would love to meet him one day. PS LOVE your drawings!

A photo of a wild-haired, wide-smiled girl and her befuddled-looking Frenchie accompanies this one.

@PollyW_PGT: Sent you a PM. The guys from Chump still want Aldo. Please respond ASAP.

Wait, what?

Giddy with excitement, I grab my own phone, turn it on, open YouStream and navigate to my private messages folder.

Ferris,

Thanks for your message. I admire your honesty.

I LOVE your new video. More to the point, so do the guys from Chump. They still want Aldo. They've scrapped the backflipping idea. They're thinking of getting their voiceover artist to say something along the lines of 'Mouth-wateringly good'. Reckon you can get Aldo to drool in front of a bowl of dog food tomorrow? Same fee. Let me know ASAP.

Polly

Oh. My. Gosh. Drooling is Aldo's superpower!

BEST DROOLER EVER

I turn to show the message to Tia. 'I can't believe it. Not only is the YouStream challenge almost certainly in the bag now, I'll be able to pay for your nan's stairlift after all!'

I begin to reply to Polly's message, but Tia pulls my hand away from my phone. 'You promised your mums you'd let Aldo rest his ankle for the next two days.'

I shake my head. 'Drooling in front of a bowl of dog food won't put any pressure on Aldo's ankle.'

'But what about all those steps he'd have to climb up to the audition room?'

Drat.

Tia takes my phone off me. 'We should talk to your mums before you reply.'

Unfortunately, I think she's right . . .

Accidental Avenger

After a while of umming and erring, Mums decide
they're so proud I'm going to give all Aldo's fee to
Tia, they offer me a compromise and suggest I ask
Polly if the filming can be done at our house.

Which I have done. But now I'm waiting for
a reply.

'We should celebrate anyway,' says Tia. 'It's not
every day your dog becomes an online sensation!'

No one can argue with that, so we spend all
morning in the garden.

After a few party games, Mum makes a picnic.
Along with a variety of 'special' treats for the
humans, she brings out a bowl of sausages doused
in cheese sauce for Aldo. He wolfs them down before
Keely has a chance to lob them into her mud kitchen,
then flops beside my little sister for an ear massage.

After lunch, Miz and Tia construct a giant

bubble-maker out of two sticks, a long piece of string and a bucket of soapy water. Keely races around the garden, mesmerized by the beautiful rainbow spheres glistening in the sun, and I get out my phone to record her. I catch a brilliant clip of her giggling as a bubble lands on Aldo's unsuspecting nose and smile. I'm so glad I don't have to think before I film, now YouStream is not on my mind. I watch the video and wonder who could not want to adopt this little beauty?

I lie back on to the grass, trying not to think about the day I'll have to say goodbye to my little sister, and spot Destiny spying on us from her bedroom window. Her arms wrapped around her body, she looks positively depressed. As soon as she clocks I've spotted her, she backs away. A few minutes later, I overhear her shout to her dad, asking him if he'll play Hide-and-Seek with her and Foo-Foo. I hear Mr Dean's reply too: 'Not now, sweetheart. I'm working.'

I chew my lip for a moment, wondering if Destiny's dad ever takes a break from his job, then, while Mum reads Keely a story, and Miz plays football with Tia, I fetch my sketchpad and get to work on *The Hoot*.

Soon, the ball lands on my lap. 'Sorry, Ferris!' shouts Miz, as Tia comes to retrieve it. 'My bad!'

I hand the ball to Tia and she glances at my drawings. 'You know, Ferris,' she says, pointing at my sketches. 'That **Astoundog** character you draw is good, but the cartoons you draw based on real life are better. Especially the ones you draw of Aldo. You should draw more of those. They're funnier. More relatable.'

Mums nod. They've always said I should make Aldo a feature of *The Hoot*.

'You've got loads of material you could use,' says Tia. 'I'll never forget that story you told me about him pooping a pair of Keely's tights like a Mr Whippy machine!'

'And what about that time he got himself wedged in that bench outside the library!' adds Miz. 'It was like a re-enactment of *The Enormous Turnip* that day, with about nine of us trying to pull him out.'

We all laugh.

'Remember last week at the park?' adds Tia. 'I can just imagine a comic strip of Aldo accidentally giving a load of odd hats to babies, as he crashes around a play area!'

'And that time he picked up that massive branch in Dickie Forest!' says Mum. 'And wouldn't let it go. He took down at least six hikers by their ankles that day!'

'Yes, but then he tripped up that shoplifter running out of the cafe, remember?' says Miz. 'The police called him an accidental hero.'

Do you know what? They might be on to something. Average Aldo: Accidental Avenger. It has a good ring to it.

Family time

Twenty minutes later, I'm still jotting down ideas when my phone goes BEEPETY-BEEP DING!

The guys at Chump said yes. Send me your address. We'll be there at 9 a.m tomorrow. Polly :)

We all get a bit giddy then.

Tia and I run a few victory laps round the garden.

Miz whisks Keely into the air and whizzes her around, making her laugh so much I worry she'll wee.

Mum starts rambling about baking more 'special' treats for when the film crew arrives, then dashes inside to check what vegetables we have left.

And Aldo lets off a few comedy trumps as he watches us all behave as

though we've just won the lottery.

'A film crew at our house!' exclaims Miz. 'I better go and tidy up. Keep your eye on Keely for a bit, would you, guys?'

I nod and put Keely in the swing.

Tia grabs the football. 'Keepie-uppie challenge?'

'Go on, then,' I say. Since Tia's been here, my keepie-uppie skills have improved. I can now do two.

Tia goes first. Aldo assumes his nodding-dog position and I help Keely to keep count. By the time we've reached sixty-nine, Aldo's dizzy and Keely's bored. Tia clocks this and kicks the ball to me. 'Your turn!'

I drop the ball on to my foot; it bounces upwards. I knee it. It pings away at an odd angle, bounces on Aldo's head and comes back to me. I tip it with my toe and it flies over the fence.

'I did three!' I exclaim.

'I'll get it,' says Tia, laughing

before scaling the fence and disappearing into enemy territory.

'Oh, sorry, Destiny,' I hear her say. 'I didn't know you were there. Are you OK? Why are you crying?'

I bet I can guess why Destiny's crying. She knows I've beaten her. Well, I think I have. I mean, I presume I'm soon going to be the owner of a d-5000, but I probably shouldn't count my chickens. A lot can happen in four days, as well I know.

The next voice I hear is Destiny's. 'It's against the law to trespass. Don't they teach you that where you're from?'

Tia doesn't answer this question. 'What's the matter, Destiny?' she asks. 'Have you hurt yourself? Do you want me to go and get your dad for you?'

'No!' shouts Destiny. 'He's busy.'

No surprise there, then.

'It must get a bit lonely for you always being on your own in the school holidays,' says Tia.

I guess she's right about that.

Not according to Destiny: 'No, it doesn't. I have Foo-Foo and all my stuff. Look at this new electric scooter Dad bought me yesterday. Bet you wish you had one of these, don't you?'

Here we go . . .

'Not really,' says Tia. 'It looks good, though. Ah, there's our ball. Thanks.'

I hear Tia approach the fence. I'm expecting her face to pop over it when Destiny shouts, 'Why are you still here anyway? Have your real family decided they're better off without you?'

Tia's reply is much calmer than I expect. 'No, I should be going home this weekend, but even if I

had to stay here for longer, I'd be OK. Ferris
and his family are lovely. But then you know that,
don't you?'

Destiny starts crying again then.

'You know, Destiny,' says Tia, her voice a little
softer now. 'If you weren't so mean to him all the
time, I bet Ferris would love to invite you round
to play.'

Whoa, whoa, WHOA! There's no need to be rash.
Although, thinking about it, Tia's probably right.

Tia clambers back over the fence. 'I told you,
Ferris,' she whispers. 'It's what I've been saying since
the day I met her. She brags and makes fun of you
because she's jealous.'

Huh?

'She's jealous of the one thing you get that no
amount of money can buy: family time.'

The more I think about this, the more it makes
sense to me. Destiny's dad might spoil her with tons
of expensive stuff, but I've not seen him play out in
the garden with her once this holiday.

'You should try to make friends with her,
Ferris. She's lonely.' Tia throws her ball in my chest
and laughs. 'And when I've gone, you might be
lonely too.'

FRIDAY
2 days till
D-DAY

Lights! Camera! Action!

'And that's a wrap!' shouts Ian from Chump. He grins and crouches to scratch Aldo's head. 'Well done, fella. That was perfect!'

'One-take wonder!' adds Beano, who's been filming again.

'Just what we wanted!' says Marnie. 'It'll be online in about a week.'

'Well done, Aldo,' says Polly. She looks more than a little relieved that my best friend was perfectly able to sit and drool when a large bowl of dog food was placed in front of him. Turning to Mum, she adds, 'Could I pay you by bank transfer, Mrs Foster?'

Mum nods and they exchange details.

Half an hour later, the film crew

have gone.

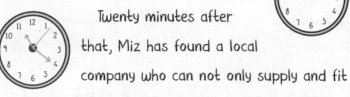

Twenty minutes after

that, Miz has found a local

company who can not only supply and fit

a stairlift for £2,499, but are available to

install it this afternoon!

Fifteen minutes after that, Mum

has called Tia's social worker, Shazza.

Ten minutes later, Shazza

calls back to say she's spoken

to the hospital and that the doctors

have agreed Tia's nan can be discharged

tomorrow.

Five minutes after that, Mum has

arranged to pick up a key for Tia's

house so she can let in and supervise

the stairlift fitters.

Thirty seconds after that, Tia's in

floods of tears. 'I can't believe this. I can

go home tomorrow? You guys are just . . . THE BEST.'

I'm so pleased we could help Tia. But I'm going to miss her. And goodbyes suck.

Ta-ta, Tia

First Tia gives Keely a hug. 'Keep being you, squirt,' she says.

Keely puts both her palms on her chest. 'Ruv-Oo-Ear,' she says.

Tia mirrors Keely's sign for 'love', then pretends she has something in her eye and crouches to cuddle Aldo. 'Bye bye, you.' Aldo licks her tears before sitting beside Keely on the step.

Next Miz throws her arms round Tia. 'It's been a pleasure having you here, sweetie. Follow your dreams. You'll be a Lioness one day, I'm certain of it.'

'Thanks, Miz,' says Tia. Well, I think that's what that muffled noise was. Miz is a very tight squeezer. 'I couldn't have asked for a better family to stay with. Nan would love you guys. She likes to make-do and mend too.' Tia throws me a wink.

Mum's next. She hands Tia a box filled with suspicious-looking baked goods. 'Just a little something for after your tea.'

I raise my eyebrows and stifle a laugh. Tia takes the box. 'Thanks, Mrs Foster. You shouldn't have. And thanks for having me. And for sorting everything out with Nan and the social workers yesterday. I didn't think I'd make it home before school started again. But you pulled out all the stops.'

Homemade
with love x

'Don't mention it,' says Mum. 'I know how important family is.'

Then it's my turn. It's always hard saying goodbye when children we foster move on, but

there's something about what me and Tia have
been through over the past fortnight that makes
this goodbye even harder. 'So, you'll ask your nan if
you can come round when the advert is due to go
online?'

We've already agreed we'll keep in touch, but I
want Tia to know I mean it. Sometimes people say
they'll keep in touch and never do. We haven't heard
a word from AJ's new parents since they took him
to live in Scotland. I'm sure he's fine. They were
a fun couple. But I'd love to know how the pea-
catapulter is getting on.

Tia nods and waves her phone at me. 'And I'll
bug you with messages every day until then.'

Shazza, Tia's social worker, opens the passenger
door of her car. 'Come on, Tia. Your nan will be
wondering where you are.'

Picking up her suitcase, Tia turns
to me again, her face more serious.
'I can't thank you enough, Ferris. I
don't know anyone else in the world who would

give £2,500 to someone they'd known for less than two weeks.'

'Don't mention it,' I say. 'Family is tons more important than stuff.'

We hear a window close and look towards the sound. Destiny jumps away from her spying place a little too late to miss Tia wave goodbye.

As Shazza's car pulls away, Mum turns to me. 'I can't tell you how proud I am of you, Ferris.'

'Me too,' says Miz, lifting Keely into her arms.

I'm drawn into a group hug and I know I've done the right thing. Who needs money? I have everything I need right here. Well, I will have by tomorrow.

Eek, I can't wait to test out my d-5000.

D(5000)-Day

It's the last day of the spring holidays and I've come to the front step to draw. Aldo's beside me. We agreed that avoiding the BIG CLEAN Mums are doing in preparation for our next arrival was a good plan.

I'm busy playing around with the title frame for my fabulously funny new comic strip, 'Average Aldo', when my phone buzzes. It's a video message from Tia.

After a close-up of her left nostril, I hear the sound of a motor. The camera pans to a smiley-

faced, brightly dressed woman with the same
big eyes as Tia, ascending a staircase on her
newly installed stairlift. She's holding
a sign that reads, 'Thank you, Ferris
and Aldo!'

I feel a rush in my stomach and
ruffle my best friend's fur proudly.
'You bought that, boy!'

Tia turns the camera back on
to herself. 'It's like the slowest roller coaster ever,
Ferris,' she squeals. 'You'll have to come over to try
it. Bring Keely and your mums. And Aldo, of course!'
Her voice lowers. 'And remember what we talked
about.' She points her index finger at the screen.
'Don't gloat when Destiny gives you her d-5000. Well,
not for too long anyway!'

I pocket my phone and look towards my next-
door neighbour's front door. What Destiny's managed
to get her poodle to do over the past fortnight
has been nothing short of astounding, but her
YouStream likes are still way off the viral levels of

my #AverageAldo video. There's no disputing I've won the challenge, but there's still the small matter of claiming my prize.

Right on cue, Destiny exits her house. Princess Foo-Foo at her heel, she approaches me. 'Here!' she says, thrusting her d-5000 into my hands. 'You win. I don't care. Daddy will buy me another one.'

'Thanks,' I say.

As Destiny starts to walk back to her house, I remember the conversation I had with Tia on Thursday after we'd heard her crying. Could it be true that Destiny brags about her dad's money because she's jealous of me? Does she wish he'd play with her instead of buying her whizzy gifts? The story Tia told me about that boy who always bragged about his season tickets and football strips, but stopped when she started complimenting him, comes into my head.

'You know what, Destiny?' I say, as she reaches her front door. 'You're SO MUCH better than me when it comes to gadgets. Fancy giving me a quick lesson?'

Destiny frowns.

I wave my new d-PEN at her
and smile.

After a long pause, she clears her throat, taps
her hip and says, 'Foo-Foo, come!' The pair of them
make their way over to join me and Aldo on the
step.

We shuffle sideways, Aldo in excitement at
having a new bum to sniff (Foo-Foo's, not Destiny's);
me hoping I've not made a mistake.

I've not.

Destiny might say, 'You know, the d-4000 is
actually a lot better,' a few times, and she can't
resist reminding me that she beat me in the end-
of-term art challenge, but she's great at showing
me how to use all the tools and features of the
d-5000. She even gives me a genuine smile when I
tell her how good I think she is at dog training, as
she demonstrates the video recorder. And then, most
unbelievably of all, after she's finished her lesson,
she leans over to Aldo and gives his belly a proper

good scratch. 'How does it feel to be an online superstar, hey?'

Aldo's back leg jerks involuntarily as she catches his tickly spot.

I laugh. 'He's taking it in his stride.'

In all honesty, Aldo's no idea he's the canine celebrity of the moment. He's just happy I'm no longer trying to force him to perform. Even after I left him with a bee stuck up his nose for nearly a week, and pressured him so much that he almost broke his leg, he never once stopped loving me. I guess Mums were right all along. I don't know what I was thinking trying to change him.

'I'm sorry for calling him a useless mutt,' says Destiny, wiping her drooly hand on her skirt and not even grimacing.

'It's OK,' I say. 'And you know what? You were right about one thing. I *did* invent **Astoundog** because I was too embarrassed to draw Aldo. But I'm not any more. Look!' I open my sketchpad and proudly show her my 'Average Aldo' sketches.

Destiny flicks through the first few pages. She even laughs a couple of times. 'You could make so much money from *The Hoot* now Aldo's famous.'

Cal said the same to me this morning. He phoned me the minute he got home from his caravan and plugged in his phone. To say he was gobsmacked when I told him everything that's been going on while he's been on holiday would be a huge understatement!

I lean back on my hands and repeat what I said to Cal: 'I'm not going to sell *The Hoot* any more actually.'

Destiny frowns.

'No,' I say, answering the question she didn't ask. 'I'm going to go back to giving it away for free. I want all the kids at school, even those who never have spare money, to know how proud I am of my best friend.'

I am too. He's the best pet in the world. I don't know how I ever forgot that.

'Plus,' I add, pointing at my wonderful new d-TAB, 'this was all I was saving for. Thank you for giving it to me.'

Destiny smiles. 'You're welcome.'

OK, this is getting a bit weird now. And, you know what, it's about to get weirder. 'Wait there,' I say. 'I have something for you.'

I run inside, grab the spare rainbow blanket Grandpa gave us, return to the front step and hand it to Destiny.

'This is for you. And Foo-Foo, of course. You both deserve a reward for all the work you've done over the holidays. It's a spare one my grandpa gave us.'

I figure Mums won't mind too much. Speed-washing original bankie is part of their routine, they've been doing it for so long now.

Destiny glances at the spare blanket. Then she points at Keely's bedroom window, hanging from which is OG bankie, dangerously close to flying away. 'Thanks, but I think your mums might appreciate the spare.' She pauses. 'And little Keely, of course.'

Well, that's a turn-up for the books. Destiny's never been kind to Keely before.

'I never really wanted it anyway,' she adds. 'I just wanted to make sure you didn't give up on the challenge.' She pauses, clearing her throat as she returns the blanket. 'You know, so you'd be in your garden more often.'

I don't ask her why. Admitting she gets lonely is a massive step for Destiny.

It all goes a bit quiet and awkward until Mum

opens the door. 'It's lunchtime, Ferris. Oh, hello, Destiny, flower. Would you like to join us? I can text your dad to ask.'

As Destiny glances up at her dad's office window, I think about what Tia said about how Destiny craves family time. I remember all the school events her dad has missed since he started working from home. And, despite their frequent embarrassing ways, how I'd feel if Make-Do and Mend never made time for me. I look at Mum. 'As well as asking Mr Dean if Destiny can come over, why not ask if he'd like to join us too? We could eat in the garden and all play a game together afterwards maybe. You're always saying "the more the merrier" and I bet Destiny's dad needs a break from his work. It's Sunday, after all.'

'Why not indeed,' says Mum, with a wide smile. 'Good idea, Ferris. In fact, blow texting, I'll knock on the door.'

While Mum chats with a frazzled-looking Mr Dean at

263

Destiny's door, I ask Destiny more about his job. At first she bangs on about how he's some kind of president of a mega-important computer company, but she goes all quiet and thoughtful when I ask her if she wishes he had more time for her.

'You need to tell him how you feel,' I say, when she eventually nods. 'Maybe mention that you'd love to go to the park next time he offers to buy you a present or something?'

Would you like me to buy you a pony, my darling?

No, thanks. I'd like a walk in the park with you instead.

Destiny doesn't comment on that suggestion as, just then, Mr Dean and Mum walk towards us. 'I'm so sorry, sweetheart,' says Mr Dean, his shoulders slumped as he crouches in front of Destiny. 'Mrs Foster here is right. I've been so busy dealing with work problems over the past few months that I've forgotten to pay attention to the most important thing in my life.' He stands and offers Destiny his hand. 'Would you care to join me for lunch with The Fosters?'

Good old Mum!

An hour later, as Destiny and her dad get their jackets from our utility, I overhear Mr Dean suggest they go for 'a stroll and a proper chat' before they go home. I mean, it could be an excuse – being in an open space would be a good opportunity for him to release the crazy amount of wind he must be holding on to after guzzling the three pints of homemade 'ginger and beetroot fizz' Miz supplied him with – but a family walk is definitely a step in the right direction for the Deans.

I say goodbye, feeling genuinely happy that Destiny has her dad's attention. Who knows, maybe this will bring an end to her bragging even more than my victory in the YouStream challenge has? I guess only time will tell.

ONE WEEK LATER

Premiere party

Ten of us are squished into the living room, our personal devices on our knees. It's nine minutes until the Chump advert is due to go online.

'How do you feel, Aldo?' I say, curling my arm around his neck.

He closes his eyes, lets off a silent-but-deadly, then resumes his nap. Some things never change.

'This is so exciting,' says Tia. She jiggles her knees up and down and shares a big grin with her nan. 'Our hero's big day!'

'Can't we get it up on the big telly, Michael?' says Grandpa, squinting at the phone Miz has lent him, before glancing at Destiny's dad.

Since Destiny and her dad, Michael, came for lunch last week, Mr Dean has been a frequent visitor to our house. He fixed our dodgy Wi-Fi in exchange for a crop of Mum's tomatoes on Tuesday evening, and helped Miz set up her own website on Friday as a thank-you for mending the fence.

One of these good turns works in my favour: better Wi-Fi and fewer tomatoes.

The other, not so much: a website that my mum intends to use to share her money-saving, planet-protecting tips may involve too much Making-Do and Mending for me . . .

Mr Dean picks up our remote control, presses a few buttons and, within minutes, Chump's home page is on the screen.

Can I just borrow you, Ferris? I need a model for my T-SHIRTS FROM T-TOWELS invention.

www.chump.co.uk

'I didn't know our telly could do that!' gasps Miz.

'My dad's brilliant with

technology, isn't he?' says Destiny, brimming with pride.

I nod.

Destiny and I have been getting on . . . OK. Things aren't perfect by any means, but I'm helping her to rein in her 'SO MUCH better' comments by getting in first. 'Yes,' I say. 'He's SO MUCH better than my mums!'

A million presses of the refresh button later, the video appears and we all whoop as Aldo walks into the shot, stopping when a finger points at him.

'That's *my* finger, you know, Michael!' says Mum, nudging Mr Dean, who's squashed between her and Miz, 'enjoying' a 'special'  muffin. Mum leans over him and squeals at Miz. 'I have a famous finger!'

Back on screen, as Mum's hand places an enormous bowl of dog food on our freshly mopped kitchen floor, Aldo sits.

'Look how shiny our floor is!' shouts Miz. 'Lemon juice and hot water, that!'

'Shush, Elizabeth,' says Grandpa, making Tia's nan giggle.

The camera zooms in on Aldo. Performing his role perfectly, his drool has reached the kitchen tiles and is starting to puddle at his feet. Keely giggles and runs to touch the TV screen. 'Boo-Boo!'

'I can't believe this is going to pop up before hundreds of YouStream videos from tomorrow!' says Cal, as 'the Finger' gestures to the bowl. 'I hope I see it in the wild!'

'Great pointing, Mum!' I say.

The next shot is of Aldo wolfing down the bowl of Chump while wagging his tail so fast it looks like it's in danger of flying off.

Mr Dean leans forward. 'Do you think they've sped that up?'

Those of us who know Aldo well laugh and shake our heads.

The final image shows Aldo drooling again.

Next to him is a large sack of Chump. The voiceover artist says, 'For your best friend, choose Chump. It's mouth-wateringly good.'

We all clap and cheer, then watch it again, and again, and again, and again, and again . . .

In memory of my 'brother',
Ben – the original tights-pooper

ACKNOWLEDGEMENTS

Just as it takes a village to raise a child,
it takes a team to bring a book
to publication, so I'd love to use these
pages to say some great big thank yous!

Firstly, to my agent, Chloe Seager,
whose support and encouragement has,
as always, been stellar. Chloe, I'm so
pleased I have you in my corner. Thank you.

To Jane Griffiths, my editor at Puffin, whose
inciteful suggestions made this story TONS better
than it was to start with. Hats off to
you, Jane.

To Emily Smyth who, amongst
many other things, designed the cover of this book,
and to Janene Spencer for all her artistic
and graphic design input. Ladies, you're
brilliant. Thank you.

 To my managing editor, Philippa Neville, and her team, and to the wider Puffin and Penguin teams who I know, after these acknowledgements have been written, will work to get this book into hands like yours. I might never know your name, but I appreciate every single one of you.

And last, but by no means least, to my sister, Jo – a wonderful foster carer, a huge inspiration for this series, and an all-round marvellous human being. Jo, I love you.

About the author

Jen Carney lives in Lancashire with her wife and three children. She loves writing and illustrating contemporary, laugh out loud children's books that celebrate diversity and modern families.

For more information please vist www.jen-carney.com

Jen can be found on social media as follows:

Twitter: @jennycarney

Facebook: /AuthorJenCarney

TikTok: @jencarney

Instagram: @jencarney76

DON'T MISS
THE NEXT HILARIOUS
FERRIS FOSTER STORY

THE DAY
MY SCHOOL
EXPLODED!

PUBLISHING
SPRING 2025!

HAVE YOU READ
JEN CARNEY'S B.U.G. SERIES?

'Perfect for fans
of *Wimpy Kid*'

Daily Mail

'Warm and funny'

Louie Stowell, author of *Loki*

A POCKET GUIDE

THE
WELSH LANGUAGE

JANET DAVIES

UNIVERSITY OF WALES PRESS
WESTERN MAIL
1999

© Janet Davies, 1999

First published 1999
Reprinted 2000

Published by the University of Wales Press and The Western Mail.

British Library Cataloguing in Publication Data
A catalogue record for this book is available from the British
Library.

ISBN 0-7083-1516-X

Front cover: *Y Wyddor* (*The Alphabet*) by T. C. Evans, *c.*1900.
Reproduced by permission of the National Museum of Wales.

Cover design by Chris Neale
Typeset and printed in Britain by Dinefwr Press, Llandybïe

Contents

Acknowledgements

I am greatly indebted to John Davies for his advice and assistance, and to Ruth Dennis-Jones and Liz Powell of the University of Wales Press for their co-operation and help.

Illustrations in this book are included by kind permission of the following:

Professors J. W. Aitchison and H. Carter, pp. 70, 72, 74, 76, 77 (these maps were published in *A Geography of the Welsh Language 1961–1991*, J. W. Aitchison and H. Carter, 1993, University of Wales Press); Brith Gof: p. 91; Books Council of Wales: p. 89; Cardiff Central Library: p. 12; Mary Giles: p. 104; Museum of Welsh Life (National Museums and Galleries of Wales): cover illustration; Nant Gwrtheyrn Language Centre and Utgorn Public Relations: p. 86; National Library of Wales: pp. 24, 26, 30, 38, 40, 41, 47, 51, 60, 66, 101; Angela Price: pp. 3, 8, 16, 112, 123, 124 (the maps on pp. 123 and 124 are based on maps in *The Linguistic Geography of Wales*, Alan Thomas, 1973, University of Wales Press); Sianel Pedwar Cymru: pp. 96, 106; University of Wales Centre for Advanced Welsh and Celtic Studies: p. 34 (published in *The Welsh Language before the Industrial Revolution*, ed. Geraint H. Jenkins, University of Wales Press, 1997).

The Welsh Language – a Personal Perspective

For many people in Wales, the Welsh language is the essence of Welsh identity. Yet, for the majority of the people of Wales, the language has only a marginal impact upon their lives. That was my experience as a child. I was brought up on the borders of Breconshire and Monmouthshire, a district where a considerable number of the inhabitants had a knowledge of Welsh a hundred years ago. By the 1950s, however, none of the native inhabitants could put together a sentence in the language. A few incomers were Welsh-speakers, a fact that sometimes impinged upon us. Our parish church was Llanelli, magnificently sited above the Usk valley. Its vicar was Daniel Parry-Jones, a native of Carmarthen-shire, and the first Welsh I ever heard came from his lips as he proffered the communion cup to the distinguished Irishwoman, Dr Noëlle French. Welsh, I came to the conclusion, was a liturgical language, rather like Latin among Roman Catholics. There were Welsh lessons at school, but it was difficult to imagine that any-one of my age could weave together the words we learned and turn them into intelligible and effortless speech. That some of my contemporaries could do so was something I discovered when pupils from Bryn-mawr met pupils from Ystradgynlais, at that time in the same county. Thus I became dimly aware that somewhere over the hills, in the upper Swansea valley, in Carmarthenshire, and also, according to some, in Anglesey, there were people who not only spoke Welsh effortlessly, but did so all the time. It seemed very odd indeed.

Yet although Welsh was rarely heard in our community, it existed all around us. There was hardly an English place-name within miles. Indeed, Welsh names continued well over the border with England; on the train journey to Hereford, it was noticeable that the first station after passing the border was Pontrilas. Living in a land of *llan* and *aber*, *dôl* and *cwm*, *pant* and *maes* – the building blocks of place-names throughout Wales – it was impossible to escape the fact that a language unspoken by my community was legible throughout that community. And although purists might think that some of the place-names were pronounced in a rather cavalier fashion (we did dreadful things to Maesygwartha), on the whole we managed them well enough. We did so because an instinct for the correct pronunciation of Welsh was built into the way we spoke English. When I eventually came to learn Welsh, I found that the pronunciation presented no problems at all. Neither did many aspects of word-order, for the syntax of our ordinary speech – the much-derided Wenglish – preserved patterns it had inherited from Welsh.

In no sense did the lack of knowledge of the language make us feel less Welsh. The traditions of the community included Brychan and his saintly progeny, the hidden city under Llangors Lake, and De Breos, the wicked Marcher Lord. We played on the banks of the canal and around the foundries and the tramroads of the early industrial age; we visited Crawshay Bailey's round houses and the caves of the Chartists; we knew of Lady Llanover; we learned of Bryn-mawr's unhappy reputation as the blackest of the black spots of the depression years; we eagerly read the serialized versions of Cordell's novels. All these things made us fully aware that we were in the mainstream of the traditions and the history of Wales. Many years later, when giving birth at Llandovery Cottage Hospital, I was totally baffled when I heard the woman in the next bed to me referring to me as 'y Saesnes sy'n dysgu Cymraeg' (the Englishwoman who's learning Welsh). The Welsh-speaking Welsh, I came to the conclusion, use words in a different way. That seemed even odder.

The oddities of the Welsh situation intrigued me. Over the years, through meeting Basques and Catalans and Bretons and Frisians, I came to realize that these oddities are by no means unique. I should have been glad, when I first began to think about them, if there had been a brief guide to the origins and nature of Welsh, to the use that had been made of the language over the centuries, its present condition, and the parallels which can be drawn between its history and the history of others among the languages of Europe. Wanting to read a book is the best possible reason for writing one. This book was written primarily for those people in Wales – the great majority – whose childhood experiences were similar to mine. I should also like to think that it will be of interest to those visitors to Wales who begin to ask questions when they first encounter *llan* and *aber* and *dôl* and *cwm*.

1 The Origins of Welsh

The Indo-European family of languages

The Welsh language, like most of the languages of Europe, and many of those of Asia, has evolved from what linguists term Indo-European. Indo-European was spoken about 6,000 years ago (4,000 BC) by a semi-nomadic people who lived in the steppe

COGNATE INDO-EUROPEAN WORDS			
WELSH	LATIN	ENGLISH	SANSKRIT
ieuanc	juvenis	young	yuvan-
dant	dens	tooth	danta-
tenau	tenuis	thin	tanas
gweddw	vidua	widow	mi vidhava
tri	tres	three	trayas

region of southern Russia. Speakers of the language migrated eastwards and westwards; they had reached the Danube valley by 3,500 BC and India by 2,000 BC. The dialects of Indo-European became much differentiated, chiefly because of migration, and evolved into separate languages. So great was the variety among them that it was not until 1786 that the idea was put forward that a family of Indo-European languages actually exists. In the twentieth century, Indo-European languages are spoken in a wide arc from Bengal to Portugal, as well as in countries as distant as New Zealand and Canada, to which they have been carried by more recent emigrants. The Indo-European family is generally considered to consist of nine different branches, which in turn gave rise to daughter languages. Welsh evolved from the Celtic branch, as did its sister languages – Breton, Cornish, Irish, Scots Gaelic and Manx.

1

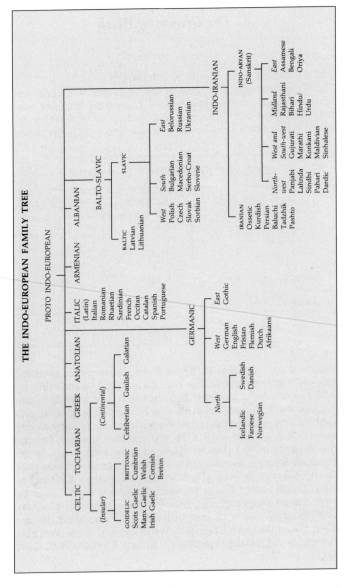

THE INDO-EUROPEAN FAMILY TREE

PROTO INDO-EUROPEAN

CELTIC   TOCHARIAN   GREEK   ANATOLIAN   ITALIC   ARMENIAN   ALBANIAN   BALTO-SLAVIC   INDO-IRANIAN

(Insular)

GOIDELIC
Scots Gaelic
Manx Gaelic
Irish Gaelic

BRITTONIC
Cumbrian
Welsh
Cornish
Breton

(Continental)
Celtiberian   Gaulish   Galatian

ITALIC
(Latin)
Italian
Romanian
Rhaetian
Sardinian
French
Occitan
Catalan
Spanish
Portuguese

GERMANIC

North
Icelandic
Faroese
Norwegian
Swedish
Danish

West
German
English
Frisian
Flemish
Dutch
Afrikaans

East
Gothic

BALTO-SLAVIC

BALTIC
Latvian
Lithuanian

SLAVIC

West
Polish
Czech
Slovak
Sorbian

South
Bulgarian
Macedonian
Serbo-Croat
Slovene

East
Belorussian
Russian
Ukranian

INDO-IRANIAN

IRANIAN
Ossetic
Kurdish
Persian
Baluchi
Tadzhik
Pashto

INDO-ARYAN
(Sanskrit)

North-west
Panjabi
Lahnda
Sindhi
Pahari
Dardic

West and South-west
Gujurati
Marathi
Konkani
Maldivian
Sinhalese

Midland
Rajasthani
Bihari
Hindu/
Urdu

East
Assamese
Bengali
Oriya

2

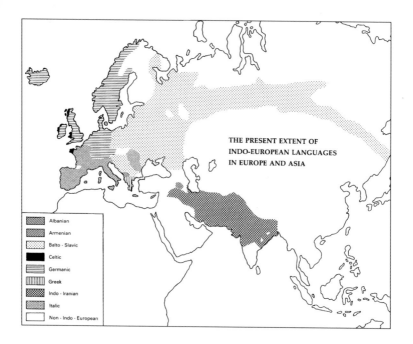

THE PRESENT EXTENT OF
INDO-EUROPEAN LANGUAGES
IN EUROPE AND ASIA

	Albanian
	Armenian
	Balto - Slavic
	Celtic
	Germanic
	Greek
	Indo - Iranian
	Italic
	Non - Indo - European

The Celts

The Celts were probably the first Indo-European people to spread
across Europe. They appear to have emerged as a distinct group-
ing in central Europe; from there they spread eastwards to the
Balkans and Turkey, southwards to northern Italy and westwards
to France, Spain and Britain. They left their mark upon the place-
names of Europe. The names of the rivers Rhône, Rhine and Danube
are Celtic, as are those of the cities of London, Paris and Vienna.
Gallipoli on the shores of the Dardanelles is the city of the Gauls
or the Celts, and there is a town called Bala (a Celtic word
meaning the efflux of a river from a lake) in the heart of Anatolia
in modern Turkey. Linguists identify three forms of Celtic
spoken on the European mainland and in Asia Minor in the last
centuries of the pre-Christian era – the Galatian of central Anatolia,
the Celtiberian of Spain and the Gaulish of France and northern
Italy.

COGNATE CELTIC WORDS			
WELSH	BRETON	IRISH	GAELIC
tŷ (house)	ti	teach	tigh
ci (dog)	ki	cu	cu
du (black)	du	dubh	dubh
cadair (chair)	kador	cathaoir	cathair
gwin (wine)	gwin	fion	fion

The Brittonic language

The language introduced into Britain was similar to that spoken in Gaul; indeed, the Celtic speech of Gaul and Britain at the dawn of the historic era can be considered as one language, frequently referred to as Gallo-Brittonic. A different form of Celtic – Goidelic – became dominant in Ireland and, in later centuries, in Scotland and the Isle of Man. Goidelic, the ancestor of Irish, Scots Gaelic and Manx, is known as Q-Celtic, because it retained the *kw* sound of Indo-European, writing it as *q* and later as *c*. In Gallo-Brittonic, the ancestor of Welsh, Breton and Cornish, the *kw* developed into *p*, and Gallo-Brittonic is therefore known as P-Celtic. The distinction is apparent in the Irish *ceann* and Welsh *pen* (head). The distinguished Irish historian Myles Dillon argued that Celtic-speakers reached Britain and Ireland as early as 2,000 BC, but the most generally held opinion tends to date their arrival to the centuries following 600 BC. Of the forms of Celtic outside Britain and Ireland, Galatian had been supplanted by others of the languages of Anatolia by the beginning of the Christian era, and Celtiberian succumbed to Latin at much the same time. Gaulish proved more resilient; by about AD 500, however, the Gaulish-speakers of eastern Gaul had been overwhelmed by German speakers and, over most of the rest of the country, Gaulish had been replaced by Latin. Some Gaulish influence may have survived in Brittany, but the existence of the Breton language is largely the result of migration to Brittany from Britain over a period extending from about AD 450 to about 650.

WORDS OF LATIN ORIGIN IN WELSH	
WELSH	LATIN
pont (bridge)	pons
eglwys (church)	ecclesia
lleng (legion)	legio
ystafell (room)	stabellum
trawst (joist)	transtrum
bresych (cabbage)	brassica

The impact of Rome

The Romans invaded Britain in AD 43 and by about AD 70 those parts of the island which were to be England, Wales and southern Scotland formed the Roman province of Britannia. Latin became the language of law and administration, but Brittonic continued to be spoken by the mass of the population. The cities of Britannia were bilingual communities and Brittonic absorbed a number of Latin words. The borrowings tended to be words for things unknown to the Britons before the coming of the Romans and they therefore throw light on the material as well as the lexical debt of the Britons to the Romans. Further borrowings from Latin were made as the Christian Church, which in the west used Latin as its official and liturgical language, consolidated its hold over the Britons.

Roman power in Britain had collapsed by AD 410 and Britannia ceased to be a part of the Empire. The Brittonic elements reasserted themselves and the following century was a period when it was possible to travel from Edinburgh to Cornwall in the certainty that Brittonic would be understood all along the way, and when Brittonic kingdoms were dominant in Britain. These kingdoms, however, were challenged from all points of the compass.

The influence of Irish

To the west lay Ireland, which had never experienced Roman occupation. Settlers from Ireland created colonies in western Britain even before the collapse of the Empire. They were numerous in north-west Wales; indeed, the name Gwynedd maybe of Irish origin. The Deisi of south-east Ireland established themselves in south-west Wales and are still commemorated in the name Dyfed. Irish settlers also penetrated further east, to form the kingdom of Brycheiniog, a name deriving from Brychan, the Irish Broccán. Other Irish place-names in Wales include Llŷn, Dinllaen and Mallaen, but the clearest evidence of the Irish presence in Wales is the existence of about thirty memorial stones bearing inscriptions in ogam, the script devised in south-western Ireland. Irish was extensively spoken in Wales in the century or two following the fall of the Roman Empire; the monastic community founded by St David (died *c.* 589) on the western tip of Dyfed may well have been partly Irish in speech. The Irish element in north-west Wales declined rapidly, perhaps as the result of a migration of Brittonic speakers from southern Scotland. That migration is linked with the name of Cunedda of Manaw Gododdin on the banks of the Firth of Forth; the royal house of Gwynedd (north-west Wales) claimed descent from Cunedda, a tradition which may contain mythological elements. Elsewhere also, the Brittonic elements won supremacy and Irish probably ceased to be a spoken language in Wales by about 650, although some Irish words survived in the speech of the inhabitants of Wales; the Welsh words *cadach* (rag), *cnwc* (hill), *talcen* (forehead), *codwm* (fall) and *cerbyd* (vehicle) are all of Irish origin.

The Anglo-Saxon kingdoms

Throughout the Roman occupation, Germans had been a major element in the imperial army in Britain and there is evidence of a Germano-Roman culture in eastern Britain by about 300. The collapse of the Empire led to a movement of people to the island from what later became the Netherlands and Germany. By 500, they had created in eastern Britain kingdoms in which their language – Anglo-Saxon or Old English – was dominant. Despite campaigns against them – possibly led by the semi-mythical Arthur – they had reached the Severn estuary by 577 and the Dee estuary by 616. It was once believed that the Brittonic-speaking people in those areas colonized by the English were either massacred or driven out, but it is now acknowledged that the great majority

BRITTONIC PLACE-NAMES IN ENGLAND	
Cognate with **mynydd** (mountain)	Cognate with **rhos** (moor)
Myndtown (Salop) The Mynde (Herefs) Mindrum (N'berland)	Ross (Herefs, N'berland) Roose (Lancs) Roos (Yorks)
Cognate with **dŵr** (water)	Cognate with **du** (black) + **glais** (stream)
Dover (Kent) Dovercourt (Essex) Andover (Hants)	Dawlish (Devon) Dowlish (Somerset) Douglas (Lancs)
There are six rivers Avon, from the Welsh **afon** (river).	

of them were assimilated by their conquerors. This would seem to be confirmed by the survival of place-names of Brittonic origin in virtually all parts of England. Many of those names, noted the historian F. M. Stenton, appear 'in forms implying that the English settlers who adopted them had more than a casual acquaintance with Brittonic speech'.

The varieties of Brittonic

The advance of the English caused wedges to be driven between the Brittonic-speaking kingdoms of the north, the west and the south-west. Three successor languages of British evolved: Cumbric in southern Scotland and north-west England, Welsh in Wales and Cornish in south-west Britain. The speakers of all three of them were known by their Anglo-Saxon neighbours as *Wealas*, or Welsh. The word is usually considered to mean foreigner, but it can also mean people who have been Romanized; versions of it exist in several parts of the marchlands of the Empire where Romanized people came into contact with Germanic speakers – the Walloons of Belgium, the Welsch of the Italian Tyrol and the Vlachs of Romania. To describe themselves, the Welsh and the Cumbric speakers adopted the name Cymry and called their language *Cymraeg. Cymry* comes from the Brittonic *Combrogi* (fellow countryman) and its adoption marks a deepening sense of identity.

7

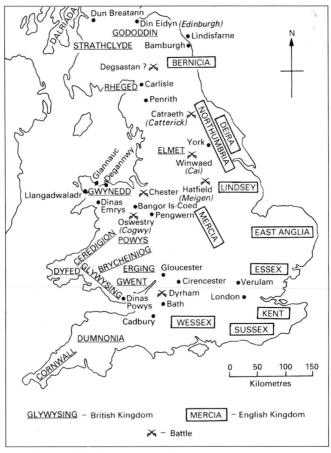

Map showing British and Saxon kingdoms during the period AD 500–700.

Of the versions of Brittonic which developed in Britain, Cumbric came under pressure from the English settlers in Northumbria and the Goidelic speakers who had migrated from Ireland to Argyll. However, the kingdom of Strathclyde, which absorbed much of north-west England in about 900, remained Cumbric-speaking until its collapse in about 1018. Place-names such as Ecclefechan and Penrith, as well as Cumbria itself, preserve a memory of Cumbric, as does the system of counting recorded among shepherds in parts of northern England. In south-western Britain, Devon fell to the English in about 710 and the kingdom of Cornwall came to an end in about 878. Cornish survived in Devon until around 950 and in Cornwall until the eighteenth century. Dorothy Pentreath, who died in 1777, is usually considered to be the last native speaker of Cornish, although a group of Cornish patriots is now actively promoting the revival of the language.

From Brittonic to Welsh

Wales is the only part of Britain where a version of Brittonic has had an unbroken history down to the twentieth century. Indeed, Welsh is one of the rare examples of an indigenous language of the Western Roman Empire continuing to be spoken today. Of the languages now spoken in Britain, Welsh has by far the oldest roots in the island; those roots go back at least 2,500 years and perhaps 4,000 years, compared with little more than 1,500 years in the cases of English and Scots Gaelic. As J. R. R. Tolkien put it, Welsh is 'the senior language of the men of Britain'.

The transition from Brittonic to Welsh took place somewhere between AD 400 and 700. The major problem in tracing this transition is the paucity of evidence. Not a sentence of Brittonic has survived. The language was almost certainly written down, but the writing materials used were probably perishable, the more highly esteemed Latin being used for permanent inscriptions. Brittonic, like Latin, was a synthetic language; that is, much of its meaning was conveyed by a change in the endings of words, as in Latin *puella* (girl), *puellae* (to the girl), *puellarum* (of the girls). In an analytic language, like Welsh, the relation of one word to another is conveyed by the use of prepositions or by the placing of the word in the sentence. It is difficult to date the change from synthetic to analytic, from Brittonic to Welsh, with any certainty. It is generally accepted that it had occurred by about AD 600 but it may have taken place in the spoken language much earlier. The most obvious sign of the change was the loss of the final syllables of nouns; when *bardos* (poet), *aratron* (plough) and *abona* (river) had become *bardd*, *aradr* and *afon*, Brittonic had become Welsh.

2 The Changing Fortunes of the Language

I Welsh in the Early British Kingdoms

Early and Old Welsh

Early Welsh, a phase in the history of the language extending from its beginnings to about 850, only survives in a few inscriptions and marginal notes or glosses. The most interesting of the inscriptions is that on a memorial in the parish church of Tywyn in Meirionnydd. It was carved in about 810 and consists of the words CINGEN CELEN TRICET NITANAM (the body of Cingen dwells beneath). Although the inscription appears incomprehensible to the Welsh-speaker of the present day, the words *celen*, *tricet* and *tan* (in *nitanam*) are related to the modern forms *celain* (corpse), *trigo* (dwells) and *dan* (beneath).

Old Welsh, the succeeding phase in the history of the language, extends from about 850 to 1100. Again the evidence is slight. Of the material that has indubitably survived unchanged from that period, there is little beyond marginal notes and a few brief texts and poems. An account of the settlement of a land dispute, written on the margin of an eighth-century gospel book and known as the Surrexit memorandum, is the earliest known example of written, syntactical Welsh. Two series of three-line poems written in about 880 are preserved as marginal notes on the Juvencus manuscript, now preserved in the Cambridge University Library and this manuscript is therefore the earliest surviving literary text in Welsh. Also in

The inscribed stone at Tywyn, Meirionnydd (*c.* 810).

the Cambridge University Library is the remarkable Computus Fragment, written in about 920. It is a prose work of twenty-three lines discussing the methods of recording the moon's course through the signs of the zodiac and provides evidence that Welsh was being used in the tenth century to discuss complex and abstruse topics.

The Cynfeirdd

Although there are very few literary manuscripts in Welsh before Old Welsh evolved into Middle Welsh in the years after 1100, a substantial body of literature was almost certainly composed in both Old and Early Welsh. A thirteenth-century manuscript known as the Book of Aneirin commemorates the attack of the Gododdin (the Votadini, who lived on the banks of the Firth of Forth) upon Catraeth (Catterick), an episode which it would be reasonable to date to around 595. Aneirin is mentioned in the *Historia Brittonum*, a mass of material put together in about 830, as is Taliesin, the reputed author of the Book of Taliesin. Taliesin sang to Urien, who was king of Rheged (Dumfries and Cumberland) in the years around 580. Aneirin and Taliesin are the first of the Cynfeirdd (the Early Poets), singing, as the scholar John Morris-Jones put it, 'the birth-song of a new speech'. They are considered to be the founders of the Welsh poetic tradition and it is ironic that they belonged not to Wales, but to Yr Hen Ogledd (The Old North). Indeed, if it is accepted that their work is contemporary with Urien and the attack upon Catraeth, it could be claimed that they wrote in Cumbric rather than Welsh, although it is doubtful if there was any great difference between the two languages at that time. On linguistic grounds, what has survived could have been written much later than the sixth century. However, it is generally agreed that the nucleus of the work of Aneirin and Taliesin was composed in that period, but that oral repetition over the centuries led to adaptation and modification. A later manuscript, the Red Book of Hergest, written about 1400, contains cycles of poems associated with Llywarch Hen and Heledd. The Llywarch poems, which were probably composed around 850, are considered to be verse passages in a saga of which the narrative has not survived. The Heledd poems lament the defeat of the royal house of Powys and, in their restrained passion, they are among the greatest glories of Welsh literature.

The defeat of Powys deprived that kingdom of the rich lands of the Severn valley and brought the English colonizers to the edges

A page from the Book of Aneirin. The last full sentence reads: 'Gwyr a aeth gatraeth oed fraeth eu llu. glasved eu hancwyn a gwenwyn vu.' (Men went to Catraeth; they were ready for battle. Fresh mead was their feast, but it was poison.)

of the uplands of Wales. Offa, king of Mercia (central England) from 757 to 796, sought to demarcate the boundary between the English and the Welsh. As Asser, King Alfred's biographer, put it: Offa 'ordered a great *vallum* to be made from sea to sea' between Wales and Mercia. Offa's Dyke, wrote F. M. Stenton, is 'an impressive suggestion of the power of command which belonged to the greater Anglo-Saxon kings'. It was that power which had by 800 caused Brittonic and its daughter languages to retreat from virtually the whole of England. The retreat was not universally considered to be irreversible. A remarkable poem, known as *Armes Prydein* (the prophecy of Britain), was written in about 930, probably at St David's. It foresees that the Welsh, in alliance with their fellow Celts of Cornwall, Ireland, Brittany and the Old North, and with the assistance of the Norsemen of Dublin, will arise and drive the English out of Britain and will thus reclaim the whole realm 'from Manaw Gododdin to Brittany, from Dyfed to Thanet'. *Armes Prydein* was a powerful example of the prophetic or vaticinatory verse which is a major element of Welsh medieval literature.

The influence of Norse
The prophecy of *Armes Prydein* was not fulfilled. Indeed, while it was being composed, Hywel Dda, the leading Welsh ruler, was co-operating with the rulers of England in resisting the attacks of the Norsemen. In some parts of Britain, Norse settlement was sufficiently extensive to introduce a new linguistic element. Many common English words – husband, rotten and ugly, for example – are borrowings from Scandinavian languages, and Scots Gaelic also has a considerable Scandinavian element. In Wales, however, the Norsemen made few permanent settlements. Only one Welsh word – *iarll*, from *jarl* (*earl*) – is indisputably a Norse borrowing. On the other hand, the English form of a number of place-names along the coast – Anglesey, Fishguard and Swansea, for example – are of Scandinavian origin.

The Law of Hywel
According to tradition, Hywel Dda's activities included the codification of the Law of Wales. No text survives of the original Law of Hywel, but forty-two texts written between 1230 and 1500 are extant. The surviving versions, six of which are in Latin, contain material which is much later than the age of Hywel, but some at least of their contents has a distinctly early flavour. Welsh was

the language of the Law; 'there can be no doubt', stated H. D. Emanuel, a leading authority on the Law, 'that the oral legal tradition was in the vernacular'. The Law of Hywel was central to the identity of the Welsh people in the medieval period and the need to defend it is frequently cited as a reason for resisting external aggression. The Welsh Lawbooks are proof of the rich legal vocabulary of the Welsh language, and because of their form and style they are works of literature as well as of law.

The Mabinogi

Even more impressive as literature is the collection of stories known as the *Mabinogi*. Though they are thought to have been written down some time between 1050 and 1170 – several dates have been suggested – the tales of Pwyll and Pryderi, of Branwen and Bendigeidfran are links with the remote Celtic past, for their heroes are lineal descendants of the old Celtic gods whose deeds had been celebrated by the *cyfarwydd*, the story-teller, over many centuries. The stories of the *Mabinogi*, to quote Gwyn Jones, 'are Wales's own distinctive contribution to medieval prose literature', and Thomas Parry claims that it is 'difficult to exaggerate the literary gifts of the man [*sic*] who gave the Mabinogi its final form'.

Thus, by the end of the eleventh century, Welsh was a rich, supple and versatile language. It had an oral literary tradition which was one of the longest in Europe. It had an enviable coherence, for the literary language was the same in all parts of

WELSH BORROWINGS	
from English before 1100	from Norman-French
capan (cap)	cwarel (windowpane)
sidan (silk)	palffrai (palfrey)
berfa (wheelbarrow)	ffiol (viol)
bwrdd (table)	barwn (baron)
llidiart (gate)	gwarant (warrant)

Wales. It was spoken throughout the land to the west of Offa's Dyke and in some communities to the east of it. It was deeply rooted in the territory of the people who spoke it. They had used it to name their churches and their settlements, their rivers and their hills. Although the language had borrowed words from Latin and from English (surprisingly little from English, compared with what was to come), it remained overwhelmingly Celtic in its vocabulary and syntax. Following the Battle of Hastings in 1066, it was to come face to face with the French of the Normans, the most powerful of the vernaculars of Europe.

II Welsh in the Middle Ages

The coming of the Normans and the conquest of Wales

The victory of William of Normandy led to the expropriation of the land of England by the new king and his followers. The English language, which had enjoyed high prestige and been the medium of a distinguished literature, fell upon hard times. With the conquest, French became the language of the English court, of the homes of the nobility and of high culture. As late as 1300, an English chronicler lamented that 'there is not a single country which does not hold to its own language save England alone'.

The Welsh language did not suffer the fate of English, although the Normans made their presence felt in Wales also. By the reign of Henry I (1100–35), much of the border and the southern coast-lands of the country was in their hands. They organized their territories into quasi-independent marcher lordships, each centred upon a castle and a borough. Thus Wales became divided into *Pura Wallia* and *Marchia Wallie*, a division which survived until the Act of Union of 1536. Norman French, the language of the leaders of the invaders, struck roots within the lordships. Fulk Fitzwarin, who died in about 1256, is celebrated in a French saga written on the borders of Wales. Native Welsh rulers such as Rhys ap Gruffudd of Deheubarth (died 1197) and Llywelyn ap Iorwerth of Gwynedd (died 1240) undoubtedly had a command of French, and Llywelyn Bren (died 1317), a nobleman of northern Glamorgan, owned a copy of the French poem *Roman de la Rose*. French words became assimilated into Welsh, and Welsh literature came to be influenced by French forms and conventions. A few places in Wales, such as Beaupré, Beaumaris, Grace Dieu and Hay (La Haie Taillée) were given French names,

Map showing *Pura Wallia* and *Marchia Wallie*. The shaded area shows the extent of *Pura Wallia* in the year 1200. The border on the right shows the extent of Wales today.

and Norman-French personal names – Richard, Robert and William, for example – eventually won popularity among the Welsh.

But while the leaders of the invasion were French-speaking, the humbler of their fellow-colonists were not. *Brut y Tywysogyon* (the Chronicle of the Princes) notes that in 1105 Henry I permitted a colony of Flemings to settle in the hundreds of Rhos and

Daugleddau in Dyfed. They were joined by English-speakers (English and Flemish would have been very similar in the twelfth century) and as a result the Welsh language was uprooted from what later became south Pembrokeshire. In addition, extensive English settlement took place in Gower, the Vale of Glamorgan and parts of Gwent and the north-east, though some of the areas Anglicized were re-Cymricized through later demographic movements. The towns planted by the Normans were also centres of English and French speech, thus giving rise in later centuries to the erroneous belief that urban life is alien to the Welsh people. As a result of these population movements, English has been the spoken language of some communities in Wales for at least 800 years. There was a further wave of English immigration following the defeat of Llywelyn ap Gruffudd, Prince of Wales, and the collapse of his principality in 1282–3. In particular, the chief garrison towns of Gwynedd – Caernarfon, Conwy and Beaumaris – became bastions of English influence.

Despite the influx of French and English speakers, Wales remained overwhelmingly Welsh-speaking throughout the Middle Ages and beyond. In most of the marcher lordships – Brecon and Abergavenny, for example – the vast majority of the population was monoglot Welsh and in lordships such as Knockin and Clun (now in Shropshire) and Huntingdon and Clifford (now in Herefordshire) the Welsh-speaking population was considerable. The spoken language had a variety of dialects and there are references to Gwyndodeg (the speech of Gwynedd) and Gwenhwyseg (the speech of Gwent). Giraldus Cambrensis (died 1223) believed that Welsh 'is more delicate and richer in north Wales, that country being less intermixed with foreigners', but he also recorded the opinion that 'the language of Ceredigion in south Wales, placed as it is in the middle and heart of Cambria, is the most refined'.

Welsh as a language of learning and literature

While there was a variety of dialects, there was only one literary language. The historian Llinos Smith notes that 'it is difficult to determine the geographical source of the different versions of *Brut y Tywysogyon* on the basis of the idioms in the text' – a marked contrast with English, Chaucer lamenting in about 1380 that there 'is so great diversity . . . in the writing of our tongue'. The texts of the *Brut* are translations from Latin and their existence shows that Welsh had won its place side by side with Latin as a language of learning and culture. Welsh also became an effective medium for religious literature, as the treatises on the Paternoster and the Creed and the translations of Biblical passages contained in manuscripts of about 1250 testify. Even with the collapse of Llywelyn's principality and Edward I's insistence that the Law of England should replace the Law of Wales in many spheres, Welsh continued to be extensively used in legal texts. In addition, it was used in works on medicine, heraldry and husbandry, and in a wealth of prose sagas and romances.

Above all, it was used in poetry. The poets who sang to the Welsh princes between 1100 and 1300 are known as Y Gogynfeirdd (the fairly early poets). They were a class of professional poets who expressed themselves in intricate forms and archaic diction, and their art reached its apex with the magnificent elegy of Gruffudd ab yr Ynad Coch for Llywelyn ap Gruffudd.

Pa beth y'n gedir i ohiriaw?
Nid oes le i cyrcher rhag carchar braw;
Nid oes le y triger: och o'r trigaw!
Nid oes na chyngor na chlo nac agor,
Unffordd i esgor brwyn gyngor braw.

What thing is left us that we linger here?
There is no place to flee from the prison of fear,
There is no place to abide in; alas, the abiding!
There is no counsel nor key nor open way
To cast from our souls the sad conflict of fear.

Lament for Llywelyn ap Gruffudd
by Gruffudd ab yr Ynad Coch

The extinction of the major Welsh dynasties in the 1280s robbed the poets of princely patrons, but they continued to practise their craft under the patronage of gentry families. The work of about 150 Beirdd yr Uchelwyr (Poets of the Gentry) has survived, extending from about 1300 to about 1600. The content of the poems is largely praise of the patron, his home and his hospitality, and the more accomplished the poet, the higher the social status of the family whose patronage he enjoyed. Their work, noted H. I.

18

Crefft ddigerydd fydd i ferch –
Cydgerdded coed â gordderch
Cadw wyneb, cydowenu,
Cydwerthin finfin a fu,
Cyd-ddigwyddaw garllaw'r llwyn,
Cydochel pobl, cydachwyn,
Cydfod mwyn, cydyfed medd,
Cydarwain serch, cydorwedd,
Cyd-ddaly cariad celadawy
Cywir, ni menegir mwy.

It is a blameless occupation for a girl
to wander through the forest with her lover,
together to keep face, together smile,
together laugh – and it was lip to lip –
together to lie down beside the grove,
together to shun folk, together to complain,
to live together kindly, drinking mead together,
to rest together and express our love,
maintaining true love in all secrecy:
there is no need to tell any more.

Dafydd ap Gwilym, 'Y Serch Lledrad'
(Love Kept Secret).

and David Bell, is 'linguistically one of the most difficult bodies of work in any European language . . . It aims at the maximum of force and compression . . . giving us not so much a meaning as clues to a meaning.' Some wrote in the *awdl* form, which dated back to Taliesin and Aneirin. By the later Middle Ages, the *awdl* had developed a fixed pattern and would generally include a number of *englynion*. The favourite metrical form of the Beirdd yr Uchelwyr, however, was the *cywydd*, which was devised in about 1350. *Awdl*, *englyn* and *cywydd* are written in *cynghanedd* (literally, harmony), an intricate system of sound-chiming which has characterized Welsh poetry from its beginnings. The greatest master of the *cywydd* – indeed, the greatest figure in the whole of Welsh literary history – was Dafydd ap Gwilym (*fl.* 1320–70), but there were others of great distinction. The Church attempted, as the historian Glanmor Williams put it, 'to impose its imprimatur on a poetic tradition which had in origin and early development been completely independent of it', but the existence in medieval Wales of a considerable body of exceedingly lewd verse suggests that its attempts were not always successful.

Among the patrons of Beirdd yr Uchelwyr were the Turbervilles and Stradlings in Glamorgan and the Salesburys and Pulestons in north-east Wales, a fact which suggests that gentry families of English origin were being assimilated into Welsh-language culture. There were similar developments in the rural areas which had been Anglicized during the Norman Conquest. Although the linguistic boundary or Landsker in Pembrokeshire proved remarkably stable, other areas, particularly in the Vale of Glamorgan, became increasingly Welsh-speaking in the later Middle Ages. The same was true of the towns, as migration from the countryside overwhelmed the English elements planted in earlier centuries.

The resurgence of English

If Welsh was making a comeback, so also was English. In the fifteenth century, English came to replace French and Latin in law, in administration and in the social life of the upper classes. By about 1390 the English were writing wills and letters in English, and by about 1450 land deeds in English were the norm. There was, in both Church and State, a tradition of using Welsh for official purposes. Determined efforts were made to ensure the appointment of senior clergy who were fluent in Welsh, and one of the demands of Owain Glyndŵr in his letter to the Avignon Pope, Benedict XIII, in 1406 was that the clergy 'should know our language'. Although the official documents which survive from independent Wales are in Latin, the lawcourts of the Welsh princes were held in Welsh. After the Conquest, it was found necessary to translate Edward I's Statute of Rhuddlan into Welsh, and there are examples of land deeds in Welsh in the fourteenth and fifteenth centuries. Nevertheless, as English law increasingly replaced Welsh law and as the task of framing official documents came to be undertaken by professional scribes, it became usual for official documents in Wales to imitate those of England in language as well as in content. As English came increasingly to be the medium of legal transactions, it is hardly surprising that Welsh gentry, even in the more remote parts of the country, came to feel a need to be fluent in the language. John Wynn (1553–1627), the choleric squire from the Conwy valley, notes that his great-grandfather, probably about 1470, went to

Caernarfon to gain a knowledge of English. Thus when Henry VII, a descendant of the Tudor family of Penmynydd, Anglesey, ascended the throne of England in 1485, English had already gained a role – indeed, a dominant role – in official life in Wales.

III From the Act of 'Union' to the Industrial Revolution

The Act of 'Union'

In 1536 the advisers of Henry VIII secured the passage through the English parliament of the so-called Act of Union. The Act incorporated Wales into England and made the inhabitants of Wales subjects of the English crown in the same way as were the inhabitants of England. It also laid down that English should be the language of the courts of Wales and that no person using Welsh should have public office. It may be doubted that Thomas Cromwell, the framer of the Act, was intent upon the obliteration of Welsh. What he sought was uniform administration and the deployment of the Welsh gentry as the agents of royal administration. The gentry became justices of the peace and members of parliament, positions for which a command of English was essential. Thus implicit in the Act was the creation of a Welsh

ALSO BE IT enacted by auctoritie aforesaid that all Justices Commissioners Shireves Coroners Eschetours Stewardes and their lieutenauntes and all other officers and ministers of the lawe shall proclayme and kepe the sessions courtes hundredes letes Shireves and all other courtes in the Englisshe Tonge and all others of officers iuries enquestes and all other affidavithes verdictes and Wagers of lawe to be geven and done in the Englisshe tonge. And also that frome hensforth no personne or personnes that use the Welsshe speche or langage shall have or enjoy any maner office or fees within the Realme of Englonde Wales or other the Kinges dominions upon peyn of forfaiting the same offices or fees onles he or they use and exercise the speche or langage of Englisshe.

The 'Language Clause' of the Act of Union, 1536.

ruling class proficient in English, a development assisted by the growing tendency of the Welsh gentry to send their sons to English public schools. The learning of English by the gentry did not necessarily mean that they abandoned Welsh. One of the leading noblemen of the reign of Elizabeth I, William Herbert, earl of Pembroke, was more at home in Welsh than in English, and in 1591 the parents of Edward Herbert of Cherbury 'thought fit to send me to some place where I might learn the Welsh tongue, as believing it necessary to enable me to treat with those of my friends and tenants who knew no other language'.

Nevertheless, as they became increasingly assimilated into the English ruling class through education, intermarriage and association, and as it came to be believed that the ability to speak polished English – the touchstone of gentility in later centuries – was marred by even a nodding acquaintance with Welsh, the gentry eventually abandoned the Welsh language. The chronology of abandonment varied according to locality and status. The first to cease to speak Welsh were the greater squires of the borderland, and the last were the lesser squires of the west. The process took at least 250 years and was virtually complete by the late eighteenth century. It had profound consequences. Linguistic difference reinforced class difference. Welsh culture, which had been essentially aristocratic, came into the guardianship of the peasantry and the 'middling sort of people' – craftsmen, artisans and the lower clergy. As the inhabitants of the gentry houses ceased to speak Welsh, the system of patronage which had maintained the Welsh poets over the centuries collapsed, and the standardized Welsh they had jealously defended came in peril of deteriorating into an assortment of mutually unintelligible dialects.

Personal names

Indicative of the growth of English influence was the adoption of fixed surnames, after the English pattern, instead of Welsh patronymics. Thus Richard ap Meurig ap Llywelyn of Bodorgan in Anglesey became Richard Meyrick, and John ap Rhys ap Gwilym of Brecon became John Price. Most of the new surnames were based upon the father's Christian name – Jones (John), Davies (David), Powell (ap Hywel), but some were based on a nickname – Lloyd (Llwyd – grey), Voyle (Moel – bald), an occupation – Gough (Gof – blacksmith), or a place-name – Trevor (Trefor), Lougher (Llwchwr). The change had occurred among the gentry by the mid-sixteenth century and was virtually complete among all classes by the late seventeenth century, but as late as the mid-nineteenth century there are examples of a son taking his father's Christian name as his surname.

The Reformation and the translation of the Bible

The danger posed to Welsh in the wake of the abandonment of the language by the upper classes was averted by the Protestant Reformation. Protestantism elevated the vernacular as the language of worship. In the kingdom of England (which included the Welsh-speakers of Wales and the Cornish speakers of Cornwall) that meant that the language of worship would be English. There were, however, people in Wales who considered it invidious that the mass of the people – who had no knowledge of English – should be denied an understanding of the new religion. One of them was Sir John Price of Brecon, who in 1547 published the first printed book in Welsh. The book had no title and is generally known as *Yn y lhyvyr hwnn* (In this book), after its opening words. It contained the Lord's Prayer, the Creed and the Ten Commandments, together with instructions on how to read Welsh. Another advocate of religious literature in Welsh was William Salesbury, whose *Kynniver Llith a Ban,* a translation of the Epistles and Gospels of the first Book of Common Prayer, appeared in 1551. With Europe torn by religious dissension, the government came to realize that religious conformity was more important than linguistic uniformity. It was this consideration which led parliament in 1563 to pass an Act commanding the bishops of Wales and Hereford to ensure that Welsh translations of the Bible and the Prayer Book should be available by 1567 and that 'divine service shall be said throughout all the dioceses where the Welsh tongue is commonly used in the said Welsh tongue'. It was not the intention of the government to confirm the mass of the Welsh people in their monoglot state. The Welsh translations were to be placed in every parish church, but they were to be accompanied by English versions, so that those reading them might 'by comparing both tongues together the sooner attain to a knowledge of the English tongue'. The challenge was accepted by Richard Davies, bishop of St David's, and it was in his palace at Abergwili that the work of translating the New Testament and the Prayer Book was accomplished, largely by William Salesbury. The translation was published in 1567.

The task of producing a translation of the entire Bible was undertaken by William Morgan, vicar of Llanrhaeadr-ym-Mochnant

Title page of *Yn y lhyvyr hwnn*, the earliest printed book in Welsh.

on the borders of Denbighshire and Montgomeryshire. Its publication in 1588 was a crucial event in the history of the Welsh language. Since Morgan used the exalted diction of the poets of the strict metres, his style and vocabulary were highly literary and somewhat archaic. Even when published, the language of the Welsh Bible was markedly different from spoken Welsh, and over the centuries the difference widened as the spoken language evolved. Yet despite the archaisms (which became more marked in the revised edition of 1620) the Bible provided an exalted model of correct and majestic Welsh. As congregations heard its splendid rhythms Sunday after Sunday, the Welsh people became accustomed to a lofty image of their language. Welsh was the only one of the non-state languages of Europe to become the medium of a published Bible less than a century after the Protestant Reformation, a factor which goes far to explain the difference between the subsequent history of Welsh and that of others of those languages, Irish and Scots Gaelic in particular.

The Welsh humanists

The revised Bible of 1620 was the work of John Davies of Mallwyd in Meirionnydd, the most distinguished Welsh scholar of his day. He also published a Welsh grammar in Latin and a Latin–Welsh dictionary. Davies was a member of the remarkable band of Welsh lexicographers and grammarians who were imbued with the humanist ideas of the Renaissance. The earliest of them was William Salesbury who, in addition to his translation of most of the New Testament, published a collection of Welsh proverbs, a Welsh–English dictionary and a guide to Welsh pronunciation. Salesbury, an ardent Protestant, had a Catholic counterpart in Gruffydd Robert, an exile in Italy, who published a Welsh grammar in parts in Milan between 1567 and the 1580s. The Welsh humanists were concerned to demonstrate the richness of the Welsh language in idiom and vocabulary and to prove that it had been the language of learning and religion from its earliest days.

Yet despite their pride and confidence, the Welsh humanists were deeply aware that their language was under siege. While Davies and Morgan were labouring, other senior Welsh clerics, according to the poet Morris Kyffin, were saying that 'it was not expedient to allow the printing of any kind of Welsh book [for] the people should learn English and forget their Welsh'. 'Could the devil himself', asked Kyffin, 'put the matter better?' Gruffydd Robert lamented that Welshmen, after crossing into England,

Testament

Newydd ein Arglwydd

IESV CHRIST.

Gwedy ei dynnu, yd y gadei yr ancyfia=
ith, air yn ei grlydd oz Groec a'r Llatin, gan
newidio ffurf lipthyzen y gairiae-dodi. Eb law hyny
y mae pop gair a dybiwyt y bot yn andeallus,
ai o ran llediaith y'wlat, ai o ancynefin-
der y debnydd, wedy ei noti ai eg-
luzhau ar 'ledemyl y tu da-
len gydzychiol.

bot golaunt ir byc, a' charu o ddynion y tywyllwch

Matheu x iii,f.
Gwerthwch a veddwch o'ru dd
(LPyth a'r Dyn lle mae'r mydd
Ac mewn ban angen ay hydd)
I gael y Perl goel hap wedd.

The title page of the New Testament of 1567.

were determined to forget their Welsh, and in about 1600 the poet Edward ap Raff despairingly cried: 'The world has gone all English'. The decay of the bardic order, brought about not only by the Anglicization of the greater gentry, but also by the disastrous effect of inflation on the lesser gentry and the new tastes created by the availability of the printed book, caused anguish to those who continued to compose in the strict metres. 'This world is not with the poets,' mourned Edward Dafydd in 1655.

Welsh-language culture in the seventeenth century

By the seventeenth century Welsh had lost its status as a language of high culture. In that century, wrote the authors of the 1927 report *Welsh in Education and Life* (see pp. 63–4), 'the language was in a state of suspended animation'. Literature of distinction continued to be written, the work of Morgan Llwyd (1619–59) being pre-eminent. There were still those who had an interest in the literature of previous ages. Scribes such as John Jones, Gellilyfdy (died about 1658) tirelessly copied the works of early poets, and a few squires – Robert Vaughan of Hengwrt near Dolgellau (1592–1667) in particular – took pride in their collections of manuscripts. Yet such men as Vaughan were becoming increasingly rare. It was widely assumed that the extinction of Welsh was imminent, the author of the satirical volume *Wallography* (1682) hoping that 'if the stars prove lucky there may be some glimmering hope that the British language may yet be English'd out of Wales'. Yet the vast majority remained monoglot Welsh and they demanded some sort of literature. New poets of humble stock answered the call and the old strict metres were elbowed aside by free-metre poetry. 'Although the new generation of Welsh poets', wrote Professor Geraint Jenkins, 'were pale shadows of their illustrious professional forebears, their poetry fulfilled a much wider social function. Welsh poetry became an open rather than a closed shop.' Folk literature, previously too humble to be written down, began to be published. Thomas Jones, the almanacker, established himself in Shrewsbury in 1685, and his success was proof that literacy was no longer confined to the wealthy and leisured classes. The first book to be printed on a permanent printing press on Welsh soil – the press established at Atpar near Newcastle Emlyn by Isaac Carter in 1718 – was a ballad: *Cân o Senn i'w hen Feistr Tobacco* (A Song of Rebuke to his Old Master Tobacco). Carter soon transferred his press to Carmarthen, which became the first town in Wales to be the centre of vigorous publishing activity in the Welsh language, a role later undertaken by other towns, in particular Merthyr, Aberdare, Denbigh and Caernarfon.

Side by side with the growing stream of print was the revival of the eisteddfod. The use of the word _eisteddfod_ (from _eistedd_, to sit), dates from 1523, but the poetic and musical contest held by Rhys ap Gruffudd in Cardigan in 1176 is generally held to be the first recorded eisteddfod. Others were held in Carmarthen in about 1451 and in Caerwys in Flintshire in 1523 and 1567. Thomas Jones's almanacs advertised eisteddfodau from 1700 onwards and by the 1730s they had become fairly numerous, particularly in the north. In them, poets tested their skills and the victor was chaired and his health toasted. The meetings were often drunken and raucous affairs, but they were transformed into more decorous assemblies in the late eighteenth century, thus initiating an activity which was to become central to Welsh cultural life (see pp. 39–40, 108–9).

Religious education and the Welsh language

The jollifications of the poets caused grave concern to the godly, particularly those of Puritan sympathies. Puritans unable to accept the doctrines of the Church of England left the Anglican communion. They formed Nonconformist sects – Congregationalist, Baptist, Presbyterian and Quaker – and, following the Toleration Act of 1689, they were able to build chapels and organize themselves with a fair degree of freedom. Before the Act of 1689, however, they were subject to persecution. The main element within dissent was the 'middling sort' of people, and that became even more true as persecution drove the wealthy and the ambitious back to the Established Church. Thus Nonconformity in Wales became increasingly reliant upon people wholly Welsh in speech, with the result that it became, despite its English origins, an integral part of the life of Welsh-speaking Wales. The growth of Nonconformity was to have a profound impact upon the growth of the Welsh language – so much so that by the late nineteenth century there was a widespread assumption that a Welsh-speaker was by definition a chapel-goer.

In 1700, when nine out of ten of the people of Wales were Anglican in their religious allegiance, it was by no means apparent that this would be so. Although antagonism between Church and Chapel was to become a major theme in Welsh history, there were people from both sides of the denominational divide who were anxious to evangelize the people. In 1674, Thomas Gouge, a London Dissenter, established the Welsh Trust. Aided by contributions from Anglicans and Nonconformists, he sought to establish schools in which children would learn English, thereby making them 'more serviceable to their country' and capable of reading English devotional works. Many of Gouge's views were shared by Stephen Hughes, the 'Apostle of Congregationalism' in Carmarthenshire. Hughes, however, was appalled by the notion that children should have to learn English before their souls could be saved. 'It would be excellent', he wrote, 'if everyone in Wales could understand English. But Lord, how will that come about if thou dost not make miracles?' He persuaded Gouge to spend part of the funds of the Trust on publishing and distributing Welsh books. The work of the Welsh Trust was continued by the Society for Promoting Christian Knowledge (the SPCK), founded in 1699. As a result, some 545 books in Welsh were published between 1660 and 1730, five times the number published between 1540 and 1660. They included eleven editions of the Bible, four editions of the Welsh translation of *Pilgrim's Progress*, and fourteen editions of *Canwyll y Cymru* (The Welshman's Candle), a collection of edifying verses by Rhys Prichard of Llandovery. The finest literary work of the period was Ellis Wynne's *Gweledigaetheu y Bardd Cwsc* (The Visions of the Sleeping Bard, 1703), a book rich in satire and powerful language. Thus by the early eighteenth century publications in Welsh were proliferating; their content was largely devotional and they made a vital contribution to the religious and educational awakening of the eighteenth century. Like the Welsh Trust, the SPCK established schools; it assumed that the children would be taught in English, but in some districts, particularly in the north, Welsh was used – a marked contrast with Scotland, where the SPCK was strongly opposed to any use of Gaelic.

The eighteenth-century renaissance

The readiness to use Welsh to advance religious knowledge stemmed from expediency rather than from a belief in its inherent value. Yet the language did have its champions. The great lexicographer, John Davies, had argued that Welsh was a sister language of Hebrew and had thus been in existence before the Tower of Babel. According to Paul-Yves Pezron, a Breton monk, the Welsh were directly descended from Gomer, son of Japhet, son of Noah. There were still believers in the work of Geoffrey of Monmouth, who had claimed in 1137 that, as the Welsh were descendants of

The scholar and poet Lewis Morris (1701–65).

the Trojans, their lineage was among the most distinguished in Europe. In the early eighteenth century, druidism came into vogue and the Welsh poets were seen as the heirs of the learned druids. Belief in the ancient and lofty origins of the Welsh and their language served to swell a national pride that found expression in *Drych y Prif Oesoedd* (The Mirror of Past Ages, 1716), the work of Theophilus Evans, the vicar of Llangamarch, Breconshire. Presenting the history of the Welsh as a glorious epic, Evans greatly enhanced their pride and at least twenty editions of his book had been published by 1900. He treated evidence quite uncritically and was totally unconcerned to distinguish between myth and historicity.

When *Drych y Prif Oesoedd* appeared, the origins of the Welsh and their language had already become the subject of scholarly investigation. In 1697, Edward Lhuyd, the Keeper of the Ashmolean Museum at Oxford, set out on a four-year journey through the Celtic countries. He collected a vast amount of material and, through his analysis of it, became the founder of comparative Celtic philology. Lhuyd's scholarship proved too rigorous to find widespread acceptance, and myth and bizarre linguistic notions continued to play a major role in the Welsh consciousness. Nevertheless, his spirit of critical enquiry did find emulators. William Gambold, a protégé of Lhuyd, published in 1727 *A Grammar of the Welsh Language*, the first English book to be printed in Wales.

Lewis Morris of Anglesey (1701–65) also considered himself a follower of Lhuyd. Morris and his brothers were fired by an enthusiasm for the language and history of Wales; their letters, a thousand of which have been preserved, offer a panorama of Welsh cultural life in the mid-eighteenth century. Lewis Morris, the Deputy Steward of Crown Manors in Cardiganshire, longed to prove to the Anglicized Welsh gentry 'a fact that they have never heard of, that there was once culture and learning in Wales'. He encouraged his brother Richard, a clerk in the Navy Office, to establish in 1751 the Honourable Society of Cymmrodorion. Based in London, the Cymmrodorion had corresponding members in Wales and its founders hoped that the society would transform Welsh cultural life. Their hopes were not fulfilled but the activities of the Morrises and their circle undoubtedly stimulated interest in the Welsh language and its literature. Perhaps the greatest achievement of the circle was the publication by the cleric, Evan Evans, of *Some Specimens of the Poetry of the Antient Welsh Bards* in 1764, a work which provided for the first time a serious study of early Welsh poetry.

The spread of literacy

The activities of the Morris circle coincided with the much more momentous campaign of Griffith Jones, rector of Llanddowror, Carmarthenshire (1683–1761). In 1731 Jones began establishing schools with the aim of teaching both children and adults to read the Bible and to learn the catechism of the Anglican Church. The schools were held mainly in the winter when the demands of agricultural work were less. When the pupils had grasped the essentials of reading and had learnt the catechism, the teacher moved to another parish. They were therefore circulating schools and were cheap, flexible and efficient; above all they were, outside the English-speaking enclaves, conducted in Welsh. The SPCK supplied teaching materials, including over 70,000 Bibles, and the pious among the affluent provided the teachers' salaries, for virtually no support was given by the higher clergy of the Established Church. Between 1731 and his death in 1761, Griffith Jones established a total of 3,325 schools in nearly 1,600 different locations; they were attended by perhaps as many as 250,000 pupils. Given that at that time the total population of Wales was about 480,000, this very remarkable achievement was one of the most successful initiatives of its kind in Europe. Literacy gave Welsh a new prestige and enormously stimulated publications in the language; over 2,500 books in Welsh were published in the eighteenth century. In the period between the translation of the Bible and the Industrial Revolution, the circulating schools were undoubtedly the most crucial happening in the history of the Welsh language.

The Methodist Revival

The literacy campaign intertwined with the Methodist Revival. Methodism began as an evangelical movement within the Church of England, but the Methodism of Wales took a different path from that of England, as its leaders adopted Calvinist theology in contradistinction to the Arminianism of John Wesley. The Welsh Calvinistic Methodists remained within the Church of England from their beginnings in the 1730s until 1811, when they became a separate denomination. By 1811, membership of the denominations which had sprung from the Old Dissent had greatly increased because of the impetus of revivalism; with the creation of the new Calvinistic Methodist denomination, adherents of the Church of England became a minority in Wales, a fact which was to have a profound effect upon the concept of the Welsh nation. The Methodists were not particularly concerned to foster the Welsh language, but as they sought their converts among monoglot Welsh-speakers, they were obliged to cultivate the language as a vehicle of evangelical zeal. Indeed, they used the language in a more direct and less self-conscious way than did those who were deliberately seeking to contribute to the Welsh literary tradition. The sermons of the early Methodist leaders, particularly those of

Daniel Rowland, created a tradition of powerful preaching in Welsh. The travels of itinerant preachers to address those who spoke a different dialect led to the emergence of a standard spoken Welsh which could be understood throughout the country. The use of the hymn as a central feature of worship caused the superb compositions of William Williams of Pantycelyn, Carmarthenshire, and those of later hymn-writers such as Ann Griffiths to become the new folk-songs of the nation. The Calvinistic Methodists were the pioneers of Sunday schools; like the circulating schools, they were attended by adults as well as children, and they helped to maintain the levels of literacy in Welsh achieved by Griffith Jones. The new denomination developed a more structured and centralized form of government than that of the older denominations such as the Baptists and the Congregationalists; it operated at all levels through the medium of Welsh, thus giving ministers and laymen opportunites to make public use of their mother tongue.

The Established Church and the Welsh language

One of the major reasons for the advance of Methodism and the growth in the membership of the old dissenting denominations was the perception that they were more prepared to serve the needs of Welsh-speakers than was the Church of England. From the time of William Salesbury and Richard Davies, the Anglican Church had made an honourable contribution to Welsh-language culture, but by the late eighteenth century the upper reaches of the Church of England in Wales had become thoroughly Anglicized. No native Welshman was appointed bishop in Wales from the accession of the Hanoverian dynasty in 1714 until 1870, and Welsh-speaking clerics, viewed by their superiors as rustics, rarely received a position beyond that of parish clergyman. The scholar Evan Evans, who spent his life as a curate, angrily denounced the *Esgob Eingl* (the English bishops) who, by appointing 'unfit shepherds', were driving their flocks into the arms of the Methodists. One of the 'unfit shepherds' was Thomas Bowles, a septuagenarian Englishman who in 1766 was appointed rector of two parishes in Anglesey in which only five of the 500 parishioners had a knowledge of English. Members of the Cymmrodorion and others sought to oust him from his living but, in the court proceedings, Bowles's attorney argued that as 'Wales is a conquered country . . . it is the duty of the bishops to promote the English in order to introduce the language.' Because he had been legally inducted,

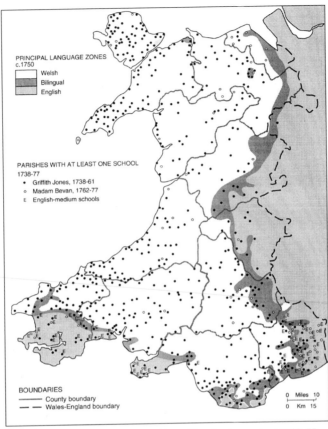

PRINCIPAL LANGUAGE ZONES
c.1750

◼ Welsh

◼ Bilingual

◻ English

PARISHES WITH AT LEAST ONE SCHOOL
1738-77

• Griffith Jones, 1738-61

○ Madam Bevan, 1762-77

E English-medium schools

BOUNDARIES

—— County boundary

— — Wales-England boundary

0   Miles   10

0   Km   15

Principal language zones *c.*1750: parishes with at least one school 1738–77.

Bowles was permitted to keep his living, but the judge declared that ignorance of Welsh should debar a clergyman from being appointed to a parish where the majority of the parishioners spoke only Welsh.

The distribution of Welsh-speakers in 1750

Despite the appointments of monoglot Englishmen such as Thomas

Bowles, the parish clergy in the greater part of Wales were Welsh-speaking and the services were in the Welsh language. Indeed, information relating to the language of services is the best available evidence concerning the distribution of the Welsh language in the eighteenth century. The information may not be wholly reliable, for clerics such as Thomas Bowles or pressures from assertive immigrants or Anglicized landowners may have caused services to be held in English in parishes where Welsh would have been more appropriate. Nevertheless, details of the language of services in parish churches provide a convincing picture of the language zones of Wales. In about 1750 Welsh was the sole language of services in over 80 per cent of the country; some western towns were centres of Anglicization, and a bilingual zone along the eastern border and the southern coastlands divided the solidly Welsh areas from districts which were almost totally Anglicized. Of these districts, the largest were south Pembrokeshire, which had been Anglicized in the Middle Ages (see p. 20), and Radnorshire, where the Welsh language collapsed in the eighteenth century.

IV The Welsh language in the era of industrialization

Demographic and economic change
Wales in 1750 was a country almost wholly rural in its economy, with hardly a town exceeding 3,000 in population. This pattern was to become vastly more complicated as a result of the surge of economic activity which occurred from about 1770 onwards. Wales probably had about 489,000 inhabitants in 1770, most of whom were employed in the cultivation of the land or in work directly dependent upon agriculture. By 1801, when the first official census was held, the population had risen to 587,000 and by 1851 Wales had 1,163,000 inhabitants, only a third of whom were involved in agriculture. A wide variety of industries developed in north-east Wales, including copper and lead smelting, iron-working, brick making and the production of chemicals. The north-west was involved in copper mining and quarrying, while in mid Wales woollen production was entering the factory phase. Even more momentous developments were afoot in south-east Wales. The exploitation of the south Wales coalfield, initiated in the 1770s, gathered pace in the early nineteenth century. The ironworks of Dowlais and Cyfarthfa near Merthyr Tydfil became

35

the largest in the world. In the 1840s, the coalfield was producing 700,000 tons of iron a year and Sir John Guest of Dowlais probably had more employees than any other industrialist on earth. By 1851, there were 46,000 people living in Merthyr, making it by far the largest town in Wales. Mass communities were developing elsewhere in the narrow valleys of northern Glamorgan and Monmouthshire, in areas which a hundred years previously had been virtually uninhabited.

Such revolutionary changes could not but have a profound effect upon the Welsh language. The growth of industry allowed Wales to sustain far more people than had been possible under the old agricultural economy. Some of them came from beyond the borders of Wales. In 1851, the Welsh population included 115,000 people born in England and 20,000 born in Ireland. The vast majority of the inhabitants of the industrial districts had, however, either been born there or had moved there from the rural areas of Wales. Most of those areas were Welsh-speaking and, in colonizing their own country, the Welsh brought their language from the countryside to the towns. This was true of the old towns as well as of the new industrial districts; Welsh was widely spoken in Newport in the 1830s, and in that decade perhaps half the population of Cardiff had a knowledge of the language. Alone among the Celtic languages, Welsh has had a considerable degree of success in becoming an urban tongue. This is reflected in the rise in the number of Welsh-speakers. Although official statistics relating to the numbers in Wales able to speak Welsh and English are not available until 1891, it is likely that Wales had about 470,000 Welsh-speakers in 1801 and about 800,000 in 1851. By 1851, large numbers of Welsh-speakers lived in mass urban communities in which the language could be used in a new range of activities. Welsh-speakers were becoming not only more numerous but also more prosperous. This helps to explain the far greater scale of activities carried out through the medium of Welsh by the first half of the nineteenth century. Cultural societies proliferated, eisteddfodau multiplied and publishing expanded vastly. Between 1800 and 1850, about 3,000 books were published in Welsh and dozens of periodicals were established.

Although Welsh-speakers increased in absolute terms between 1801 and 1851, in proportionate terms there was a decline, from about 80 to about 67 per cent. Welsh-speaking communities proved adept at assimilating incomers and in the late nineteenth century many Welsh-speakers were descendants of earlier incomers. But where incomers were very numerous, assimilation proved difficult. It is estimated that 12 per cent of the population of Merthyr in the 1840s came from outside Wales, a percentage low enough to permit large-scale assimilation; it was 35 per cent in Blaenafon and 44 per cent in Pontypool, districts which were being rapidly Anglicized by the mid-nineteenth century. In north-east Wales, some industrial centres remained stubbornly Welsh, probably because of selective migration, but in general the bilingual zone was becoming wider; Daniel Owen, the most talented of Welsh-language novelists, was born in Mold, Flintshire in 1836 and his work is clearly based on experience of a bilingual community. On the other hand, in the quarrying areas of the north-west, where the industrial districts attracted only short-distance migrants, mono-lingualism in Welsh persisted well into the twentieth century.

Linguistic and cultural innovation

While the Industrial Revolution was transforming the Welsh economy, the Welsh language and its culture were being transformed by the work of scholars and enthusiasts. John Walters's English–Welsh dictionary, published between 1770 and 1794, contained many new words invented to meet contemporary demands. William Owen Pughe was so enthusiastic a coiner of words that his Welsh dictionary, published in 1803, contained far more entries than did Dr Johnson's English dictionary. Some of the coinages proved unacceptable, but so numerous were those that were adopted in speech and print that the historian Prys Morgan claims that no intelligent discussion could be held in Welsh today but for the energy and the ingenuity of the neologists of the late eighteenth and early nineteenth centuries.

COINAGES OF THE LATE EIGHTEENTH AND EARLY NINETEENTH CENTURIES	
diddorol (interesting)	darganfyddiad (discovery)
geiriadur (dictionary)	cyfrifoldeb (responsibility)
cyngerdd (concert)	pwyllgor (committee)

Iolo Morganwg (1747–1826).

In addition to his dictionary, Pughe compiled two grammars of the Welsh language in which his inventiveness found full range. He believed that the task of the grammarian was to describe a language not as it is but as it should ideally be. He therefore devised a new orthography for Welsh, and sought to eliminate irregular verbs and plurals and to create a consistent grammar. His work had an unfortunate influence upon nineteenth-century Welsh literature, for it encouraged an affected style of writing and led to the adoption of idioms alien to the spoken language. Pughe was also involved in the publication of *The Myvyrian Archaiology* (1801–7), three volumes which made available a wide sweep of medieval Welsh poetry and prose.

The chief editor of the *Archaiology* was Edward Williams of Flemingston in the Vale of Glamorgan. Better known as Iolo Morganwg (Ned of Glamorgan), he is the most exotic figure in the whole history of the Welsh language and its literature. He allowed his enthusiasm for the past and for the history of his native county of Glamorgan to run out of control. Where material did not exist, he invented it; much of the second and third volumes of the *Archaiology* consists of Iolo's forgeries. The fabrication of literature was a widespread phenomenon in the eighteenth century, and so skilled was Iolo that the full extent of his forgeries was not discovered until the twentieth century.

Forging literature was only a part of Iolo's invention of tradition. He claimed that the Welsh bardic order was descended from the druids, that the Gorsedd (congress) of the Bards of the Isle of Britain had existed from time immemorial and that knowledge of the druidic lore had survived only in Glamorgan. He made public the ceremonies of the druids at a gathering of London Welshmen on Primrose Hill in 1792 and persuaded the Welsh literati to join the order of bards. Throughout the nineteenth century there were firm believers in the antiquity of the Gorsedd, and the supposed venerability of the tradition gave added prestige to the Welsh language with which it was associated.

The Eisteddfod

In the late eighteenth century, the Gwyneddigion Society, an association of London Welshmen more populist and radical than the Cymmrodorion, became involved in organizing eisteddfodau. They were more formal occasions than the rather ramshackle meetings held earlier in the century; competitions were announced in advance, programmes were printed, adjudications were published and medals were awarded to successful competitors. The meeting at Corwen in 1789 is considered to be the first modern eisteddfod. Others were held in the 1790s but, with the worsening of the conflict with France, they petered out. They were revived after 1815, and in 1819, at Carmarthen, Iolo Morganwg succeeded in linking the eisteddfod with the Gorsedd; this linkage still survives. In the 1820s and 1830s, the eisteddfod was organized on a provincial basis, largely through the efforts of a group of

The National Eisteddfod at Chester, 1866.

Anglican clergymen. Chief among them was Thomas Price (Carnhuanawc), who was the leading figure in the eisteddfodau held at Abergavenny from 1834 to 1853. The Abergavenny eisteddfod received the patronage of Lady Llanover, who provided hospitality at Llanover Court for Celtophiles from all over the world. The meetings at Abergavenny and elsewhere created a widespread literary enthusiasm and the prizes they offered stimulated the production of scholarly works; chief among them was *The Literature of the Kymry*, submitted to the Abergavenny eisteddfod of 1848 by Thomas Stephens, a chemist at Merthyr. Merthyr's vigorous literary life attracted Lady Charlotte Guest, the wife of Sir John Guest, proprietor of the Dowlais Iron Company; her English translations of the *Mabinogi* appeared in three volumes between 1838 and 1849. The example of the provincial eisteddfodau led to the establishment of local meetings, and by the late nineteenth century there was hardly a village or hamlet in Welsh-speaking Wales that did not have its eisteddfod. The provincial eisteddfodau, with their reliance on upper-class patronage, tended to give precedence to English, but the smaller ones were conducted entirely in Welsh.

40

(RHIFYN III.)

CYLCHGRAWN CYMRAEG:

N E U,

DRYSORFA GWYBODAETH.

Am AWST 1793.

Y Cylchgrawn uniawn a'i enwi—drws yw
I dryſſor goleuni;
Llyfr hoff, hardd, er hyfforddi
Trigolion bro trwy gael bri.

D. SANDERS.

GYMRO HAWDDGAR,

WELE y trydydd Rhifyn yn ei gylch yn dy annerch: y mae'n dwyn goleuni i'th dŷ; na ddigia wrtho, canys nid yw yn meddwl dy dramgwyddo, eithr dy hyfforddi'n raddol mewn pob gwybodaeth ddefnyddiol: os gweli ynddo rai pethau anhawdd eu deall, darllain hwynt drachefn a thrachefn, a gofyn i'th gymmydog deallus beth yw yſtyr neu arwyddoccad y peth neu'r peth.

Nid yw'r Cymry yn yr oes ddiweddaf wedi gweled fawr lyfrau yn y iaith Gymraeg ond llyfrau crefyddol, am hynny y mae'r geiriau a'r llyfrau ſy'n trin am naturiaethau a chyfreithiau yn fwy dieithr iddynt. Amcan a diben y *Dryſorfa Gwybodaeth* yw goleuo'r wlad mewn pethau naturiol yn gyſtal ac yſbrydol. Y mae'r Cyhoeddwyr yn rhwymedig i'r dyſgedigion haelionus, o bob enw, ſydd yn addaw eu cynnorthwyo â defnyddiau defnyddiol ar bob teſtun. Nid oes ond dau beth yn attal y *Cylchgrawn* rhag cymmeryd lle yn gyffredinol trwy Gymru; hynny yw, yr anhawſdra o'u doſbarthu a chaiglu'r arian am danynt. At ddiwygio hyn, y mae'r Cyhoeddwyr yn gobeithio y bydd i un neu ddau ag ſy'n caru eu gwlad un-iaith a lles cyffredin, i gymmeryd rhan o'r gwaith a'r baich arnynt ymhob cwrr o Gymru; a dymunol fyddai cael un o bob plaid neu ſeɛ̃ o grefyddwyr, fel y byddo rhagfarn i gael ei chadw i lawr. Y mae'r Cyhoeddwyr wedi cael eu cyhuddo ar gam eiſioes, am nad oes rhagor ynghyd â'r gorchwyl, canys fel y dywedodd Mr. *J. Griffith,* " Y mae gormod o ddynion annyſgedig, a dyſgedig hefyd, na's gallant roi gair da i ddim ond eu heiddo'u hunain."—Meddyliodd rhai, am ein bod wedi cyffwrdd ag yſpryd erledigaethus *Calfin.* mai condemnio eu holl athrawiaeth oedd ein hamcan, ond mae'n eglur i'r darllenydd yſtyriol, nad oes dim rhagor yn cael ei amcanu nâ goſod allan yr atgaſrwydd o yſbryd erledigaethus, a'r ynſydrwydd o fod dynion yn galw eu hunain ar enw neb heblaw Criſt.

Pe baem yn ſylwi ar yr amrywiol leiſiau ſydd yn y byd, nid elem fawr ymlaen yn ffordd y bywyd; y mae un yn gwaeddi yn erbyn *Arminius,* a'r llall yn erbyn *Arius,* a'r trydydd yn gwaeddi'n groch fod y diafol yn well nâ Dr. *Prieſtley,* a'r pedwarydd yn tyngu nad oes braidd ddim gwahaniaeth rhwng *Soſiniaeth* a *Sabeliaeth;* y pummed a haera fod *Trinitariaeth* yn fwy atgas nâ dim, am fod yr athrawiaeth hon yn

Q

gwneud

Y Cylchgrawn Cymraeg. Five numbers of this quarterly appeared in 1793–4.

41

The growth of the Welsh-language press

The early years of the eisteddfod movement coincided with the rise of the Welsh provincial press. In 1735, Lewis Morris had sought to establish a Welsh periodical, but he succeeded in bringing out only one issue. Several magazines were launched by the Radicals of the 1790s, but they were discontinued because of the hostility of the authorities, the burden of stamp duty and the lack of an effective distribution system. The periodicals which had the best chance of survival were those which could rely on a denominational network; *Yr Eurgrawn Wesleyaidd*, the organ of the Welsh Wesleyan Methodists, was published from 1809 to 1983. The first weekly newspaper published in Welsh was *Seren Gomer*, launched at Swansea by Joseph Harris in 1814; it died within the year, but was revived as a fortnightly in 1818 (it became a monthly in 1820). A number of other monthlies were launched in the 1820s; in the main, they were intended to serve the denominations, but they also contained articles on politics and literature. *Y Diwygiwr* (The Reformer), begun in 1835, was more openly political; far more political were *Y Gweithiwr/The Worker*, a bilingual trade-union paper published in Merthyr in 1834, and *Utgorn Cymru* (The Trumpet of Wales), a Chartist journal published, also in Merthyr, from 1840 to 1842. The first true newspaper in Welsh was *Yr Amserau* (The Times), founded in Liverpool in 1843. In 1859 it was merged with *Baner Cymru* (The Banner of Wales), published by Thomas Gee at Denbigh, and by the late nineteenth century *Baner ac Amserau Cymru*, which then appeared twice a week, claimed a readership of over 50,000. In 1845 Thomas Gee launched *Y Traethodydd* (The Essayist), a quarterly modelled on the great English quarterlies of the period. The Welsh periodical press was highly influential in expressing and moulding public opinion. Its existence also proved that the language was capable of being a medium of mass communication.

Attitudes to Welsh in the first half of the nineteenth century

The Welsh press was written by and for members of the lower middle and working classes, for by the nineteenth century there were no upper-class Welsh-speaking families. In the Welsh countryside, the Anglicization of the gentry had long linked the speaking of English with superior status. Although Wales was to produce native industrialists, most of the pioneers of industrialization were incomers. As the poet Walter Davies put it in 1815: 'The Welsh have the labour, the strangers have the profit.' In discussing the Welsh workman in 1847, the author of a government report stated that 'his language keeps him under the hatches . . . he is left to live in an under-world of his own and the march of society . . . goes completely over his head.' Schools conducted through the medium of English were considered to be the means whereby this undesirable state of affairs could be brought to an end. English education, it was considered, would also curb the Welsh tendency to riot, of which there was much evidence in the 1830s and 1840s. 'A band of efficient schoolmasters,' wrote one commentator, 'is kept up at a much less expense than a body of police or soldiery.' A complete network of elementary schools was not created in Wales until the 1870s. The main provider of elementary education in the first half of the nineteenth century was the National Society, which was concerned to teach the principles of the Established Church. Its schools generally taught through the medium of English, much to the confusion of monoglot Welsh children. Yet, in the first half of the nineteenth century at least, the impact of English-medium schools can easily be exaggerated. In the counties of Carmarthenshire, Pembrokeshire and Glamorgan in 1846, only 30,000 pupils attended day schools, compared with the 80,000 who attended the largely Welsh-medium Sunday schools.

The use of English in day schools probably represented the general wish of parents; after all, Welsh could be learned at home and in the chapel. In 1846, a small farmer in Carmarthenshire declared that 'he would sooner pay twice as much to an English master who knew no Welsh'. English was perceived as being useful and profitable, a viewpoint encouraged by the Utilitarianism which was winning increasing numbers of adherents among the Welsh middle class. The belief arose that Welsh should be the language of sacred things and English of secular things, a belief which did much to narrow the sphere in which the Welsh language operated.

The Blue Books controversy

In 1846 the role of the Welsh language in education was extensively investigated by the commission set up to inquire into the state of education in Wales and 'especially into the means afforded to the labouring classes for obtaining a knowledge of the English language'. The inquiry was instituted following a speech by William Williams, MP for Coventry and a native of Llanpumsaint, Carmarthenshire, in the House of Commons on 16 March 1846. The commission consisted of three young barristers, English and

> They (the young people) often meet at evening schools in private houses for the preparation of the pwnc and this frequently tends to immoralities between the young persons of both sexes, who frequently spend the night afterwards in the hay-lofts together. So prevalent is the want of chastity among the females, that, although I promised to return the marriage fee to all couples whose first child should be born after nine months from the marriage, only one in six years entitled themselves to claim it. Most of them were in the family-way. It is said to be a customary matter for them to have intercourse together on condition that they should marry if the woman becomes pregnant; but the marriage by no means always takes place. Morals are generally at a low ebb, but want of chastity is the giant sin of Wales. I believe that the best remedy for the want of education is that of the establishment of good schools such as I have described.
>
> Evidence of Revd L. H. Davies, Troed-yr-aur, Cardiganshire, published in the Education Report of 1847.

Anglican; they collected a vast quantity of material, and their report, 1,252 pages long, was ready by 1 April 1847.

It drew a dark picture of Welsh society, emphasizing the vast gulf which separated the almost totally English-speaking wealthier classes from the largely monoglot-Welsh poorer classes. Although there were some schools of distinction, most were hopelessly inadequate; in any case, the numbers attending schools represented no more than a third of the children between five and ten years of age. The commissioners were convinced that the Welsh language was a vast drawback and they quoted a large number of letters, mostly from Anglican clergymen, which insisted that the moral and material condition of the Welsh could not be improved without the general introduction of the English language. Some of the letters went further, claiming that Welsh women were nearly all unchaste and suggesting that the meetings of the Nonconformists were occasions for illicit sex. The 'Treachery of the Blue Books' gave rise to a great furore which has been seen as the wellspring of many of the most important developments in Wales in the second half of the nineteenth century. It greatly exacerbated the relationship between Church and Chapel; it forced the Methodists into alliance with the denominations of Old Dissent; it inspired the Welsh to seek to prove that in purity and respectability they were unrivalled. Where the Welsh language was concerned, it had contrary effects; for some Welsh leaders, this evidence of English contempt was a goad to action and, by mid-century, men like Michael D. Jones were giving voice to a new linguistic nationalism; to others of those leaders – perhaps the majority – the removal of English contempt could only be ensured by making the Welsh as similar to the English as possible.

Attitudes to Welsh in the second half of the nineteenth century

The history of the Welsh language in the second half of the nineteenth century is extremely complicated, with wholly contradictory forces at work. Although the period saw the birth of modern Welsh nationalism, some of the clearest voices from within Welsh-speaking Wales were those accepting, indeed welcoming, the demise of Welsh distinctiveness. The legacy of the 'Treachery' of 1847 was not the only factor involved. These years saw the virtual completion of the Welsh railway network; with the country so manifestly being opened up to English influence, it seemed that the maintenance of linguistic distinctiveness was no longer a viable proposition. They were also years in which Britain could be convincingly portrayed as the greatest and most envied country on earth; to be an integral part of that glory, to share in it as equal partners with the English and the Scots, seemed a wholly laudable ambition. Although Darwin's theory of evolution (1859) caused distress to the devout, his notion of the survival of the fittest was soon adapted to the social field and there were many who believed that it was scientifically possible to prove that wholly inevitable forces would bring about the extinction of the Welsh language. The emphasis on competition, implicit in Darwinism, coincided with the tenets of capitalism. To resist the effects of competition, between species or languages, was to resist the ordinances of God. Utilitarianism, the advocacy of what is useful and what furthers progress, was the dominant creed of middle-class Nonconformists. Welsh, it was believed, stood in the way of Progress and was therefore doomed. The qualities enshrined in Welshness would not, it was argued, be threatened by the demise of the language for, as Matthew Arnold claimed in 1867, the genius of the Celts

45

lay in their imagination and their awareness of the spiritual and the mystical; these were qualities central to Britain's greatness and were independent of language.

Indicative of such prevailing intellectual ideas was the effort to Anglicize Nonconformity. It was believed that newcomers to Wales could be assimilated religiously if not linguistically, and denominational leaders accordingly set about establishing English-language chapels in largely Welsh-speaking areas. They urged prominent members of Welsh-language chapels to attend them in order to create a core congregation which might prove attractive to English incomers. Among the Calvinistic Methodists, Lewis Edwards, the editor of *Y Traethodydd*, was a particularly active advocate of the 'English causes', and he believed that the campaign was comparable with Paul's mission to the Gentiles.

Yet, although many of the developments of the mid-nineteenth century seemed to augur ill for the well-being of the Welsh language, there were other more positive factors. In many ways the position of Welsh was more favourable than that of some of the other non-state languages of Europe. It had a standard literary form which the majority of the population could read; in religion, particularly where the Nonconformist chapels were concerned, it had a recognized and dignified role; although some communities in Wales were suffering severe poverty, the generality of Welsh-speakers were not abject paupers, and their language could therefore be maintained by material means. Although the creation of the railway network seemed to pose a threat to the continuance of Welsh, that same network could function as an ally of the language; it greatly facilitated the distribution of Welsh publications and it allowed people to travel on a wholly unprecedented scale to gatherings such as eisteddfodau. Furthermore, the railway undermined the localism of Welsh communities, giving rise to a concept of a wider Welsh allegiance. The growth of that allegiance led to a demand for specifically Welsh institutions. The University of Wales was founded in 1895, a federal institution consisting at that date of three University Colleges. Charters were secured in 1907 for the National Museum and the National Library. In the history of the Welsh language, the establishment of the National Library was particularly significant, for it provided a permanent home for the manuscripts which were proof of the longevity and richness of the Welsh literary tradition, and it ensured that virtually all the material necessary for a study of the language was available under a single roof.

Pupils and teachers outside the intermediate school in the Welsh community of Chubut, Patagonia, 1908.

Welsh-language culture

While Welsh in the later nineteenth century was being subjected to contradictory forces and was the subject of contradictory attitudes, the culture expressed through the language showed marked vitality. Although Welsh had lost ground in the rural borderlands, particularly in Radnorshire and in the eastern parts of the counties of Montgomery, Brecon and Monmouth, it continued to be the main – indeed, frequently the sole – language of the inhabitants of most of the rest of Wales; George Borrow, on his walking-tour in 1854, noted many instances of English greetings being answered with the words: 'Dim Saesneg' (No English).

As the majority of Welsh-speakers knew no other language, there was a demand for reading material in Welsh on almost every subject. In 1854, Thomas Gee began publishing his *Gwyddoniadur* (Encyclopaedia), a venture in ten volumes, completed in 1871 at a cost of £20,000. Books of poetry were extensively bought, with volumes by the highly popular Ceiriog (John Ceiriog Hughes) selling over 20,000 copies. The Welsh periodical press entered its golden age. In 1866, it was estimated that the five quarterlies, twenty-five monthlies and eight weeklies published in Welsh had a combined circulation of 120,000.

Welsh-language culture was not confined to Wales. In 1865, 163 Welsh people sailed to Patagonia, a venture largely initiated by Michael D. Jones; they were later joined by other colonists, establishing in the Chubut valley a self-governing community which ran its affairs entirely through the Welsh language. The community eventually came under pressure from new migrants and from the Argentine government, but there are still Welsh-speakers in Patagonia. In numerical terms, migration to North America was far more significant. By 1872, there were 384 Welsh-language chapels in the United States and, in industrial Pennsylvania and rural Wisconsin in particular, there were extensive communities which were largely Welsh in speech. More substantial were the Welsh-speaking communities in England. By the late nineteenth century, there were almost a quarter of a million people born in Wales living in England. The largest community was that of Merseyside; Liverpool had over fifty Welsh chapels and it has been claimed that the city produced the only example in the nineteenth century of a Welsh-speaking urban élite.

Within Wales and in immigrant communities outside Wales, Welsh-language culture in the later nineteenth century was above all the culture of Nonconformity. The chapels were a vast arena of Welsh-language activity, with millions of Welsh sermons being preached annually and Welsh books of hymns and of biblical commentary being brought out on a massive scale. The close link between the Welsh language and Nonconformity had its negative aspects. As Professor Ieuan Gwynedd Jones put it, the language 'entered into alliance with the chapel on the terms of the chapel and English became the language for what [Welsh] scorned or feared to express'. Welsh-language culture came to be permeated

---

'I see the Methodists', says Dr Jones, 'turning Wales into a country without history, without a memory, without a past.'

'A chosen people, a holy nation,' replies John Elias, 'that is our Wales, a nation with the Lord as its God. The goal of the Methodists is to create that nation.'

J. Saunders Lewis, *Merch Gwern Hywel*, Llandybïe, 1964 (translation).

by the Nonconformist ethos to such an extent that it was rejected by many, particularly by those of hedonistic, libertarian or modernistic sympathies. Furthermore, the awareness among the Nonconformists of their numerical preponderance led them to portray the Church of England in Wales as an alien force and to demand the abolition of its status as the Established Church. Over the centuries, the Anglicans had been the chief sustainers of Welsh traditional culture; indeed, many aspects of that culture had been spurned by the people of the Chapel, particularly by the Calvinistic Methodists. In order to defend the establishment, the Anglicans were obliged to rely upon their links with England, and the denominational divide served to vitiate attempts to create a united Welsh patriotism. Although individual Anglicans continued to be active in Welsh-language movements, the vehemence of the disestablishment campaign cooled the ardour of many. The campaign culminated in 1920 with an allegedly national victory, but it was probably conducted at the expense of other activities which could have been based upon consciousness of a shared heritage.

Welsh and education in the late nineteenth century

Denominational bitterness was particularly marked in the field of elementary education. Indeed, the dispute over the nature of religious education in elementary schools delayed the establishment of a complete network of such schools until the 1870s. Nevertheless, the 1850s saw a marked rise in the number of elementary schools and the state became increasingly involved in financing them. In 1861, through the 'Revised Code', government payments to schools were replaced by a capitation grant of twelve shillings per child per year; two-thirds of the money could be withheld if pupils failed to satisfy inspectors in annual examinations that they were making progress in arithmetic and in the reading and writing of English. The new code did not prohibit the use of Welsh, but as the livelihood of teachers depended to a large extent upon whether or not their pupils had at least a mechanical knowledge of English, they had a pecuniary interest in boycotting the Welsh language. There was therefore no motive for equipping them to teach the language and it disappeared completely from the timetable of training colleges. Some teachers actively persecuted children who spoke Welsh in school, but the 'Welsh Not' – the tallystick worn by erring pupils – was probably not as widely used as twentieth-century mythology would suggest.

Public involvement in elementary education increased greatly after the passage of the Education Act of 1870. Local school boards were created with the duty of establishing schools in those areas not adequately provided for by the voluntary societies, a much-needed reform which had been long delayed because of disputes over the kind of religious education to be offered in state schools. By 1880, when attendance became compulsory, elementary education was available everywhere in Wales. The payment-by-results system was retained and thus the completed network of schools provided education which was almost entirely in English. The Education Act of 1870 is widely considered to be one of the most grievous blows ever suffered by the Welsh language. Its impact has been exaggerated. It did not suddenly impose a system of English-medium education; as has been seen, the practice of teaching Welsh-speaking children in English goes back to the seventeenth century. In those areas where the language was already weak, compulsory education through the medium of English probably proved to be the final blow, but there were so many factors at work that it would be naive to consider the language used in schooling to be the sole determinant of linguistic change. Nevertheless, the link between personal advancement and English was powerfully reinforced by the spread of English-medium education, not only at the elementary but at the intermediate and higher levels also.

Welsh did, however, make a crucial breakthrough in the field of education in the late nineteenth century. Many educationists were disturbed by the practice of teaching monoglot Welsh children solely through the medium of English; while many of them accepted that the primary purpose of the elementary schools was to give the pupils a knowledge of English, they argued that this could best be done through the medium of the mother tongue. Chief among them was Dan Isaac Davies, an inspector of schools in Glamorgan. At the National Eisteddfod at Aberdare in 1885, he established the Society for the Utilization of Welsh in Education, a title to which the words 'for the better teaching of English' were sometimes added. English was emphasized partly to allay the suspicions of the authorities, for Davies and his fellows undoubtedly had a sincere concern for the well-being of Welsh. The usual title of the society was the simpler and more direct Welsh Language Society or Cymdeithas yr Iaith Gymraeg (of the first creation). In 1885, Davies published a collection of his articles, *Tair Miliwn o Gymry Dwy-ieithawg* (Three million bilingual Welsh

Sir Owen M. Edwards (1858–1920), writer and educationist.

people), in which he foresaw that, given an enlightened educational policy, Wales would have three million bilingual citizens by 1985. He was largely responsible for the memorandum on the use of Welsh submitted to the Royal Commission on Elementary Education, and in 1886, shortly before his untimely death, he gave evidence before the commission.

On the basis of the Royal Commission's report, capitation grants were made to schools which taught Welsh, the use of bilingual books was authorized and the teaching of the geography and history of Wales was encouraged. The concession, made in 1890, was niggardly enough. No school was obliged to use Welsh; where it was used, it was grafted upon a basically English curriculum, and it was very rare for schools to make the step from lessons on the mother tongue to lessons in the mother tongue. It was, nevertheless, a development of fundamental importance that Welsh had won a toehold in the education system; indeed, all the advances made by Welsh in schools in the twentieth century had their origins in the victory of 1890. Those advances became more marked in the early twentieth century under the influence of Owen M. Edwards, the Welsh Board of Education's Chief Inspector of Schools from 1907 to 1920. Edwards was also a tireless producer of children's books and his monthly, *Cymru'r Plant*, had a circulation of over 12,000. Developments at the secondary level were less marked. The Welsh Intermediate Education Act of 1889 led to the establishment of ninety-five secondary schools by 1900, fewer than half of which offered Welsh lessons. The Central Welsh Board, created as an examining body in 1895, prepared examination papers in Welsh at the senior and higher level. Gradually, under the influence of O. M. Edwards, the language and its literature became a recognized subject at the secondary level, although the atmosphere of the secondary schools, even in the most intensely Welsh-speaking areas, remained almost wholly English.

The academic study of Welsh

The publication of Kaspar Zeuss's *Grammatica Celtica* in 1871 at last placed Celtic philology on a sound basis. German scholarship inspired the work of John Rhŷs, the first Professor of Celtic at Oxford (1877), whose *Lectures on Welsh Philology* proved that the seed sown by Edward Lhuyd was at last bearing fruit. The chair of Celtic at Oxford was established on the urging of Matthew Arnold who, although anxious to see the demise of the Celtic languages, was an ardent advocate of their academic study. With Celtic studies earning respectability, they were deemed to be worthy of a place in the new university colleges established in Wales. The college at Aberystwyth, opened in 1872, created a chair of Welsh in 1875; a chair of Celtic was one of the foundation chairs of the college opened in Cardiff in 1883; Bangor, opened in 1884, created a lectureship in Welsh in 1889 and Swansea, opened in 1920, had a chair of Welsh from its inception. The establishment of university departments of Welsh was a crucial development in the history of the language. Although, until the

52

1920s at least, lectures in departments of Welsh were given in English and the work of the departments was hindered by a lack of adequate linguistic studies and of published texts, the situation was gradually rectified by the labours of university teachers, whose academic work transformed Welsh scholarship. Chief among them was John Morris-Jones, who taught Welsh at Bangor from 1889 until 1929. Through his efforts, the orthography of Welsh was firmly established, its grammar rigorously described and the system of strict-metre poetry lucidly analysed. The succession of graduates in the language added greatly to its prestige; in the twentieth century, students of and graduates in Welsh have provided the shock troops of Welsh-language movements and have constituted a very high proportion of the practitioners of Welsh literature.

Welsh in law and administration

The partial success in anchoring the Welsh language in the education system was not paralleled in the fields of law, administration and commerce. Unlike the Czechs, who made official status for their language the cornerstone of their policy, the Welsh of the late nineteenth century were pusillanimous when it came to their linguistic rights. Small rural businesses did exist which conducted their affairs in Welsh, and official notices in the language were not unknown. There were occasional agitations against monoglot English judges, but the matter was only fitfully pursued. In courts and official meetings, translations were frequently used – 34 per cent of the witnesses who appeared before the Royal Commission on Land in Wales in the 1890s gave their evidence through a translator – but there were few who advocated the notion that official bodies should conduct their business in Welsh. One who did do so was Michael D. Jones, the architect of the Patagonia venture and the father of modern Welsh nationalism. Another was Emrys ap Iwan, (Robert Ambrose Jones, 1857–1906), who was aroused to anger by the efforts of his denomination, the Calvinistic Methodists, to establish English causes. Emrys ap Iwan was a tireless journalist and pamphleteer; his ardent advocacy of the Welsh language and his vision of a group of 'covenanters' prepared to defend it made him the hero of subsequent generations of linguistic nationalists. The issue of the use of Welsh for official business came to the fore following the creation of the County Councils in 1889. Michael D. Jones raised it at the first meeting of the Meirionnydd County Council, a body consisting of six English monoglots, three Welsh monoglots and fifty-seven members who were far more fluent in Welsh than in English. The matter was put before the Attorney-General, who ruled that 'the proceedings of county councils must be carried out and recorded in the English language'. Michael D. Jones distanced himself from the council, the members of which struggled on as best they could in English.

The census of 1891

In the 1890s official statistics relating to the distribution of Welsh and English in Wales became available for the first time. The census of 1891 was the first to concern itself with the linguistic situation in Wales; forms were distributed asking the country's inhabitants to note 'English' if they spoke English only, 'Welsh' if they spoke Welsh only and 'Both' if they spoke both languages. In January 1992, the enumerators' returns, giving information household by household, became available for public inspection, thus allowing the distribution of the two languages to be studied in far greater detail. Henceforth, decade by decade, further sets of returns will become available, making possible a minute scrutiny of linguistic change in twentieth-century Wales.

The census of 1891 showed that 54.4 per cent of the population of Wales over the age of two spoke Welsh, the percentage varying from 95 per cent in Cardiganshire to 6 per cent in Radnorshire. The total number of Welsh-speakers in Wales was 910,289. There were tens of thousands of Welsh-speakers elsewhere in the United Kingdom, but they were not recorded; if the numbers of Welsh-speakers in other parts of the United Kingdom, the colonies and dominions, the United States and Patagonia are added to those in Wales, the total number in 1891 undoubtedly exceeded a million. Of the 910,289 in Wales, 56 per cent (508,036) were returned as speaking Welsh only. The number of monoglots declined to 208,905 in 1901 and to 190,292 in 1911, suggesting that they were either overestimated in 1891 or underestimated in subsequent censuses. It is likely that many of those returned as bilingual in the censuses of the early twentieth century had only a very minimal knowledge of English; on the other hand, the drastic drop in Welsh monolingualism between 1891 and 1901 – from 32.1 per cent to 7.3 per cent in Merthyr, for example – indicates that the way the question was posed in 1891 led large numbers who spoke Welsh habitually, but who had some knowledge of English, to return 'Welsh' rather than 'Both'. Sometimes the enumerator felt obliged to alter the returns; in those for Clydach Dingle near

Bryn-mawr in Breconshire, for example, 'Welsh' was frequently crossed out and 'Both' substituted.

If the figures for 1891 are taken as they stand, they show that 54.4 per cent of the inhabitants of Wales claimed a knowledge of Welsh and 69.7 per cent claimed a knowledge of English. The situation had changed markedly since 1801, when the population was probably 70 per cent monoglot Welsh, 20 per cent monoglot English and 10 per cent bilingual. Between 1801 and 1891, the population of Wales trebled; the number of Welsh monoglots rose by 25 per cent and the number of English monoglots rose seven-fold; the number with a knowledge of Welsh doubled and the number with a knowledge of English rose seventyfold. Yet in 1891, although English was widely known, Welsh was probably more widely spoken. Furthermore, there were areas where English had hardly penetrated at all. All the inhabitants of the parish of Blaenpennal were Welsh-speaking and 96 per cent of them had no knowledge of English. Blaenpennal lies in the heart of Cardiganshire, but the situation was not widely different in Llan-gadwaladr in Denbighshire, a parish only three miles from the English border; there 99.5 per cent of the inhabitants were Welsh-speaking and 88 per cent had no knowledge of English.

Blaenpennal and Llangadwaladr were rural districts where depopulation was already taking its toll. The 1880s were particularly difficult years in the countryside, accelerating the haemorrhage of rural communities which was to have a profound effect upon the fortunes of the Welsh language. Between 1881 and 1901, 160,000 people migrated from the Welsh countryside. In the same period, 130,000 people migrated to the industrial areas of south-east Wales. Up to the late nineteenth century, the bulk of those flood-ing into the valleys of the coalfield came from the rural counties of Wales, which were largely Welsh in speech. The migration added to the numbers of Welsh-speakers in the coalfield, and the census of 1891 shows that almost half those claiming to speak Welsh lived in the industrial belt between Llanelli and Pontypool. In the Rhondda, of the first seven households in Dumfries Street, Treorci, one was monoglot English, two were bilingual and four were monoglot Welsh. Many English-speaking migrants had been assimilated, and it was claimed that the collieries of the Rhondda were the best linguistic schools in Wales. The returns for 1891 suggest that, in the upper Rhondda at least, there was very little linguistic loss between generations, the children of Welsh-speaking parents almost invariably having a knowledge of the language.

Road, Street etc. & Number of House	Name and Surname of Person	Relation to Head of Family	Age last Birthday	Profession or Occupation	Where Born	Language Spoken
39 Cwmnantgam	William Bowen	Head	41	Blacksmith	Llanelly	Both
	Elizabeth Bowen	Wife	40		Llanelly	Both
	Elizabeth Bowen	Daughter	16		Llanelly	English
	Keturah Bowen	Daughter	14		Llanelly	English
	John Bowen	Son	12		Llanelly	English
	Anne Bowen	Daughter	9		Llanelly	English
	Charlot Bowen	Daughter	6		Llanelly	English
	Harriet Bowen	Daughter	3		Llanelly	English
	John Parry	Father-in-law	66	Coal Miner	Llanelly	Welsh

Extract from the 1891 Census for the parish of Llanelly, Breconshire.

Further east, the pattern was rather different. In Bryn-mawr there was a high incidence of marriages between monoglot English-speakers and bilinguals, with the children almost always being monoglot English. English monolingualism in offspring was also common where both parents were bilingual, and there are examples of families in which the elder children had a knowledge of Welsh and the younger ones did not. Even more striking are three-generation households with monoglot Welsh grandparents, bilingual parents and monoglot English children. There is some evidence that English-speaking families were larger, a phenomenon which, if widespread, could have been of considerable significance. Yet even on the eastern fringes of the coalfield there is evidence that English incomers mastered Welsh; Sir Joseph Bailey's mansion in the parish of Llangatwg had a number of servants from England, a feature of many gentry households and a potent cause of Anglic-ization, yet his gamekeeper, a native of Bermondsey, is recorded as speaking Welsh.

The censuses of 1901 and 1911

The two subsequent censuses, those of 1901 and 1911, are as yet only available as published reports. The reports differ from that of 1891; they give details of children over the age of three rather than two, they break down their figures by age-group and their tables are arranged by county rather than by registration district. They record an increase in the number of Welsh-speakers – 929,824 in 1901 and 977,366 in 1911 – but a decrease in the pro-portion of the Welsh population claiming to speak the language – 49.9 per cent in 1901 and 43.5 per cent in 1911. At the same time, the proportion claiming to speak English rose to 84.9 per cent in 1901 and to 91.5 per cent in 1911. Thus, by the early twentieth century, the majority of the inhabitants of Wales no longer had a knowledge of the Welsh language. It was a change of momentous importance. Until the twentieth century, it was possible to define the Welsh as a people who were predominantly Welsh-speaking. That definition was no longer viable, and a new definition was needed. Welsh-speakers continued to use *Cymro* to mean Cambrophone, and *Sais* to mean Anglophone, but when the words were translated as Welshman and Englishman they carried the implication that those lacking a knowledge of Welsh were not part of the Welsh nation, a suggestion fraught with controversy and bitterness

Industrialization and the Welsh language

The decline in the proportion speaking Welsh between 1891 and 1911 was largely the consequence of the marked rise in the population of Wales, from 1,771,451 to 2,420,921. The rise was partly the consequence of the excess of births over deaths, particularly in the coalfield, an area of high fecundity. It was also the result of very considerable immigration into Wales, for Wales in the first decade of the twentieth century was second only to the United States in its ability to attract immigrants. In that decade, over a 100,000 people moved into industrial Wales from England, causing a government report in 1917 to comment: 'Until some fifteen or twenty years ago, the native inhabitants had in many respects shown a marked capacity for stamping their own impress on all newcomers . . . [but] of more recent years the process of assimilation has been unable to keep pace with the continuing influx of immigrants.'

The ability of the industrial areas to attract migrants from England and the Anglicization caused by the rapid inflow of the years immediately before the First World War gave rise to the belief that the industrialization of Wales was fundamentally harmful to the Welsh language. The belief has been strongly contested by the economist, Brinley Thomas, who has argued that 'from the point of view of the Welsh language, industrialization in the nineteenth century was the hero not the villain of the piece'. Without industrialization, Wales would have been able to sustain a population of hardly more than half a million, and its resources would have been inadequate to support ambitious cultural activities and institutions. Indeed, the Welsh language might well have met the same fate as Irish, which virtually collapsed under the weight of poverty, famine and emigration. 'The unrighteous Mammon', wrote Thomas, 'in opening up the coalfields at such a pace unwittingly gave the Welsh language a new lease of life and Welsh Nonconformity a glorious high noon.' Yet Thomas admitted that the helter-skelter growth of the early twentieth century was harmful to Welsh, although he maintained that the rapid expansion of the Welsh economy in the early years of the century did less harm than did the rapid contraction which that economy was subsequently to experience.

The period of the coalfield's most rapid expansion was also that in which socialism, trade unionism and labour politics became dominant forces. The South Wales Miners' Federation was founded in 1899; Keir Hardie was elected for Merthyr Tydfil as the sole socialist member of the House of Commons in 1900 and by 1914 anti-capitalist and syndicalist ideas had made the south Wales valleys a veritable industrial cockpit. Ever since the emergence of the New Unionism in the 1880s, many Welsh workers had been drawn into British unions which had little interest in specifically Welsh issues. While the sympathies of the coalminers were always more localized, the desire for community solidarity created hostility towards any factor which could be considered socially divisive. The Welsh language could appear to be one such factor. Describing the different groups which settled in the Rhondda valley, the author Gwyn Thomas noted: 'The Welsh language stood in the way of our fuller union and we made ruthless haste to destroy it. We nearly did.' The alliance between Liberalism, Nonconformity and Welshness was so strong that it seemed consistent, on rejecting one, to reject all three. As Ieuan Gwynedd Jones put it, 'To abandon Welsh became not only a valuational but also a symbolic gesture of rejection and of affirmation – the rejection of the political philosophy and the sham combination of Lib-Labism and the affirmation of new solidarities and new idealism based upon a secular and anti-religious philosophy.'

V War, depression and the Welsh language

The First World War
By the second decade of the twentieth century the Welsh-language community no longer embraced the majority in Wales. It was subject to formidable and often contradictory forces, both negative and positive, and then, from 1914 to 1918, it experienced the pressures of total war. The most obvious impact of the First World War upon the Welsh language was the carnage it caused among young, Welsh-speaking Welshmen. There was a lost generation of Welsh-speakers, perhaps 20,000 in all. The best remembered of the casualties was Hedd Wyn (Ellis Humphrey Evans), the shepherd-poet of Trawsfynydd, who was killed twenty-seven days before he should have been chaired at the National Eisteddfod held at Birkenhead in 1917.

The ravages of the decade from 1911 to 1921 are apparent in the census of 1921, the first to provide statistics at parish level. It showed that the proportion of the inhabitants of Wales speaking Welsh had fallen from 43.5 per cent to 37.1 per cent and that the total number had declined from 977,366 to 922,092.

Hedd Wyn (Ellis Humphrey Evans, 1887–1917), the Welsh poet killed during the First World War.

The inter-war years

By 1921, the social and economic impact of the First World War was becoming clear. Pressures upon the owners of great estates, pressures which had been multiplying since the mid-nineteenth century, had become intense from 1914 onwards and, when the war ended, most landed proprietors placed much of their land on the market. The gentry houses, which had been centres of Anglicization since the sixteenth century, became virtually extinct. Yet rural communities hardly benefited. The post-war depression in agriculture continued almost until the Second World War, and the 1920s and 1930s were a period of severe hardship among those cultivating the land. Rural depopulation continued apace, leaving an ageing population in the countryside. In every year of the late 1920s and the 1930s, deaths exceeded births in the counties of Anglesey, Caernarfon, Meirionnydd and Cardigan. They were the only counties in Wales in which that happened; as they were also the counties where Welsh-speakers were most prevalent, the consequences for the language were severe.

The impact of the post-war depression on heavy industry was far more dramatic. By 1925, the coal industry of south Wales was in dire straits and it experienced virtually no recovery until the Second World War. Migration into the coalfield ceased, giving rise to the hope that, with a more stable population, the linguistic assimilation of earlier newcomers would be accomplished. But the population did not remain stable. In August 1932, unemployment among insured males in Wales reached 42.8 per cent, and to abandon Wales seemed to be the only option for those who sought a future. Between 1925 and 1939, 390,000 people moved out of Wales, mainly to the Midlands and the south-east of England. The districts worst hit by the depression were the valleys of the eastern half of the coalfield, where the Welsh language was already in decline. If migration to England was the only option for the younger generation, there seemed little point in ensuring that they had a command of Welsh – a consideration similar to that which had caused huge numbers of Irish-speakers to fail to pass Irish on to their children. By the 1930s, there were communities in the coalfield in which Welsh-speakers constituted three-quarters of those over sixty-five, but less than a quarter of those under eleven. The penury of chapel-goers prevented them from maintaining the range of chapel-based activities which had been central to the Welsh-language culture of the coalfield. Furthermore, it was widely believed that scientific socialism was the only answer to the depression and to the injustices of society; those holding such beliefs frequently regarded religion as 'the opium of the people', and were contemptuous of chapel activity and of its close associate, the Welsh language.

There were other developments which represented a threat to Welsh. London daily newspapers had been reaching Wales from the late nineteenth century onwards. The demand for fresh news soared during the First World War, and it was a demand which the Welsh weeklies and monthlies were unable to meet. In the

At the Urdd's camp at Llangrannog.

1920s, when the popular dailies indulged in a lively circulation war, the taking of a daily London newspaper became an ingrained habit over much of Wales and sales of Welsh periodicals declined sharply. In the 1920s also, the cinema won huge popularity and talkies were widely available after 1927. The films were largely imports from America, but wherever they came from, they were not Welsh. The BBC began broadcasting from Cardiff in 1923 and from Swansea in 1924. Cardiff became the headquarters of the West Region, created to serve the West of England as well as Wales. Its programmes included an occasional song in Welsh and sometimes a brief Welsh talk, but the service was overwhelmingly English. The 1920s saw the completion of a network of bus routes, and the growing popularity of the private car and the motor cycle, with the result that the population became increasingly mobile. The charabanc won wide favour, allowing areas distant from railways to be opened up to mass tourism. Remote villages, where no language but Welsh had been heard for fifteen centuries, now resounded in summer with English voices.

Yet not all the developments of the inter-war years were hostile to Welsh. Indeed, considering the impoverishment of Wales in the 1920s and 1930s, the promoters of the language proved remarkably active and inventive. A development of the greatest importance occurred in 1922 with the launching by Ifan ab Owen Edwards (the son of O. M. Edwards) of Urdd Gobaith Cymru (The Welsh League of Youth). The Urdd sought to attract the young to the Welsh language through games, athletics and camps, as well as through more traditional cultural activities. By 1934 it had 50,000 members and its rapid growth is the clearest evidence in the inter-war years of the strong appeal of Welshness.

Three years after the launching of Urdd Gobaith Cymru came the establishment of Plaid Genedlaethol Cymru (The National Party of Wales). Saunders Lewis, its leading figure, insisted that the new party should concentrate its efforts upon the defence of the Welsh language. Initially it functioned entirely through the medium of Welsh and its activities were almost wholly centred upon Welsh-speaking areas. Although the party attracted minimal support, its concept of the sovereignty of Welsh brought a new element into discussions about the Welsh language.

Welsh writing in the 1920s and 1930s
Welsh literature, which had been undergoing a renaissance since the beginning of the century, reached new heights in the 1920s and 1930s. A more naturalistic style of poetry replaced the turgid productions of the nineteenth century, and was splendidly exemplified in the work of T. Gwynn Jones, T. H. Parry-Williams and R. Williams Parry. In the field of prose, there were the short stories of Kate Roberts, the essays of R. T. Jenkins and the early writings of Saunders Lewis. Much of their work was published in *Y Llenor*, the quarterly edited by W. J. Gruffydd, the professor of Welsh at Cardiff. Gruffydd represented a new phenomenon – a professional man and a figure of power in academic circles who was dedicated to the Welsh language and always ready to defend it with total confidence and brilliant satire.

The Welsh language and developments in education
Among W. J. Gruffydd's contributions to the Welsh language was his role in drawing up the report *Welsh in Education and Life*, published in 1927. The report was prepared by a committee appointed by the President of the Board of Education, who requested its members to 'inquire into the position occupied by Welsh in

the educational system of Wales, and to advise how its study may be promoted'.

The tone of the 1927 report was vastly different from that of the infamous Blue Books of eighty years previously. Indeed, a later government report was to comment that *Welsh in Education and Life* was imbued with 'an almost religious zeal'. Its authors noted that, although Welsh had made remarkable advances in schools since the 1880s, the policies of local authorities were imprecise, the training of teachers inadequate and the resources available to them insufficient. In their recommendations, they set out policies for the different linguistic areas of Wales and urged the allocation of considerable resources to the training of teachers and the preparation of teaching materials. They were particularly concerned about the education of the children of Welsh-speaking families in the larger towns. 'Welsh Wales', they wrote, 'will be unable to develop a middle class because the members of that class will necessarily become Anglicized as they rise in the social scale, unless some immediate provision is made for their children in those areas in which economic conditions have forced the parents to settle.' Interestingly, in view of subsequent developments, they did not recommend that schools in places like Cardiff should be designated Welsh schools, on the grounds that the distance the children would have to travel would be too great and that such designation 'might cause the relinquishing of all Welsh teaching in the other schools'.

Developments in broadcasting

The authors of *Welsh in Education and Life* were particularly concerned about the impact of broadcasting. 'We regard the present policy of the British Broadcasting Corporation', they wrote, 'as one of the most serious menaces to the life of the Welsh language.' Agitation to secure a broadcasting station for Wales by breaking the link with the West of England intensified in the 1930s, when there were some who considered direct action against the BBC. The Corporation eventually acquiesced in the demand and the Welsh Region of the BBC came into existence on 4 July 1937. Much of its output consisted of the London regional programme, but Cardiff 'opt-outs' – in Welsh on all manner of subjects and in English on matters relating to Wales – were greatly facilitated once the listeners in the West of England had their own service. To make the best of resources, the producers and presenters appointed at Cardiff were expected to be able to deal with programmes in both English and Welsh. Those whose first language was Welsh also spoke English, but those whose first language was English generally did not speak Welsh; the new recruits to the station were therefore largely drawn from the Welsh-speaking community, giving rise to the notion that Welsh-speakers had a stranglehold on the BBC in Wales. The recruits were, however, anxious to be even-handed; work in English by Welsh writers – the Anglo-Welsh literature which flourished so greatly in the 1930s – found a generous patron in the BBC. In the history of the Welsh language, the creation of the Welsh Region of the BBC was a highly important development. Initially, Welsh-language programmes tended to be rather stilted versions of English programmes, but the service eventually found its own voice, despite the set-back occasioned by its suspension during the Second World War. The BBC became a significant patron of Welsh literature, commissioning plays and supplementing the income of indigent Welsh writers. Standard spoken Welsh, pioneered by itinerant evangelists in the eighteenth century, was heard by fewer people as chapel-going declined; the BBC stepped into the breach and evolved a suppler, more popular speech, which did much to unite a language in which dialect differences were still considerable. In a country which had so few national bodies, the Welsh Region became a cherished institution. Created for sound radio, it offered a ready model when television ultimately arrived although, like the Welsh radio service, the Welsh television service was not won without a struggle (see below pp. 96–100).

The Welsh Courts Act, 1942

Recognition in schools, in academic studies and in sound radio notwithstanding, in the courts of law the spirit of the language clause of the Act of Union still held sway. This became apparent at the assizes in Caernarfon in 1936, when Saunders Lewis and two of his fellow nationalists were on trial for setting fire to a bombing school on the Llŷn peninsula. Plans for bombing schools in England had been frustrated by the opposition of naturalists and historians, but the government refused to accept a deputation opposing the one in Llŷn. Incensed by the government's attitude and fearful that the Welsh language would be threatened in 'this essential home of Welsh culture, idiom and literature', Saunders Lewis and his associates committed arson and then gave themselves up to the police. At Caernarfon, the judge contemptuously refused their demand to address the court in Welsh. The Caernarfon

Lewis Valentine, Saunders Lewis and D. J. Williams, the three nationalists who set fire to the bombing school in Llŷn.

jury failed to agree on a verdict; the case was transferred to the Old Bailey, where the three defendants received prison sentences of nine months. The subordinate status of the Welsh language, starkly revealed by the behaviour of the judge at Caernarfon, inspired the launching at the National Eisteddfod of 1938 of a petition seeking the repeal of the language clause of the Act of Union and demanding that Welsh be granted an equal status with English. More than a quarter of a million people signed the petition, which was supported by thirty of the thirty-six Welsh MPs. The petition led to the Welsh Courts Act of 1942, which laid down that 'the Welsh language may be used in any court in Wales by any party or witness who considers that he would otherwise be at a disadvantage by reason of his natural language of communication being Welsh'. It also declared that the court, rather than the person using Welsh, should be responsible for paying the interpreter. The Act fell far short of what the petition had demanded; indeed, in the matter of payment, it merely brought Welsh into line with languages such as Greek or Arabic, which were occasionally used in courts in the south Wales ports.

The Second World War

The impact of the severe depression of the 1930s upon the Welsh language cannot be measured with exactitude because, with the Second World War raging, no census was held in 1941. When hostilities broke out, there were many in Wales who believed that another experience of total war would lead to the obliteration of the distinctiveness of Wales. The founding in December 1939 of Pwyllgor Amddiffyn Diwylliant Cymru (The Committee for the Defence of the Culture of Wales) reflected that concern. (The committee later became known as Undeb Cymru Fydd – The New Wales Union.) In fact, the war proved less of a threat than had been feared. Casualties were a third of those of the First World War. The belief that the major cities of England would be destroyed by bombing caused over 200,000 people to move to Wales in the first two years of the war; most of the adults stayed only briefly, and the young evacuees billeted on Welsh-speaking households were rapidly assimilated. By 1945, the War Office had taken over at least 10 per cent of the land of Wales, but most of it was returned to civilian use after the war ended. In one district, however, the activities of the War Office had a marked impact on the Welsh language. Mynydd Epynt in Breconshire – an area of 16,000 hectares – became a permanent military training ground. It had been the home of a Welsh-speaking community of about 400 people; they were dispersed, and the boundary of Welsh-speaking Wales was pushed fifteen kilometres westwards.

The censuses of 1931 and 1951

In 1931, 36.8 per cent of the inhabitants of Wales – 909,261 people in all – claimed to be able to speak Welsh; by 1951, the figures had declined to 28.9 per cent and 714,686. While most of the western rural counties recorded a decline of about 8 per cent, the decline in Glamorgan was 33 per cent, an indication of the ravages of the depression. In 1951, apart from an area north of Llanelli and Swansea in the western part of the south Wales coalfield and a group of parishes in the quarrying districts of the north-west, all areas with a high percentage of Welsh-speakers were rural. As some of them were thinly populated upland regions, a percentage survey overemphasizes the importance to the language of rural communities; conversely, it underestimates the importance of urban communities. Less than 10 per cent of the population of Cardiff spoke Welsh, yet the city had 10,000 Welsh-speakers in 1951, almost a third of the number in the county of Meirionnydd. One striking feature which emerged from the census of 1951 was that, although the majority of the inhabitants in the rural areas which made up the greater part of the surface area of Wales still had a command of Welsh, the language was no longer the prevailing medium over unbroken swathes of territory, as it had been a generation earlier. Instead of a solid, Welsh-speaking bloc, there was a series of nuclei, surrounded by areas of considerable Anglicization – a feature which was to become more marked in the future. Another of the census's revelations was the virtual disappearance of monolingualism in Welsh. Although adults who had no knowledge of English were to be found until the 1960s, entire communities living their lives exclusively through the medium of Welsh no longer existed.

3 The Welsh Language Today

I The numbers and distribution of Welsh-speakers

The evidence of the census

The census of 1991 revealed that 508,098 of the inhabitants of Wales, 18.6 per cent of the population over the age of three, claimed to have a knowledge of Welsh. Because of changes in the enumeration system, these figures are not strictly comparable with those of previous censuses. Nevertheless, they offer some grounds for optimism about the future of Welsh. The percentage of 18.6 represents a minute decline from the percentage for 1981 (18.7 per cent); the number of Welsh-speakers recorded represents a very slight increase over that for 1981 (503,520).

The most remarkable feature of the 1991 census is the advance among the younger age groups. In 1981, 18 per cent of those between the ages of three and fifteen claimed to be able to speak Welsh, a figure which had risen to 22 per cent by 1991. For the first time since 1891, when the census first concerned itself with the language, knowledge of Welsh is more widespread among children than it is among the population as a whole. In 1991, 61 per cent of the inhabitants of the county of Gwynedd had a knowledge of Welsh, compared with 77.6 per cent of those between three and fifteen; in the Llŷn peninsula, the percentages were 75.4 and 94.1.

The differentials recorded in the Anglicized districts were even more striking. In the north-eastern district of Alyn and Deeside, 9.6 per cent of the total inhabitants had a knowledge of Welsh, compared with 27.2 per cent of those between three and fifteen; in Radnorshire, the percentages were 8.3 and 27.6. It is, perhaps, difficult to accept that over a quarter of the children of Radnorshire are fluent Welsh-speakers. Nevertheless, parents are aware that the schools have enabled their children to gain some knowledge of the language, a fact which they are eager to have recorded in the census. That eagerness is indicative of a change in attitude, for in earlier censuses many of those with some knowledge of the language were reluctant to record the fact on the census form.

To those concerned with the welfare of the Welsh language, the census returns of 1991 were particularly gratifying when set

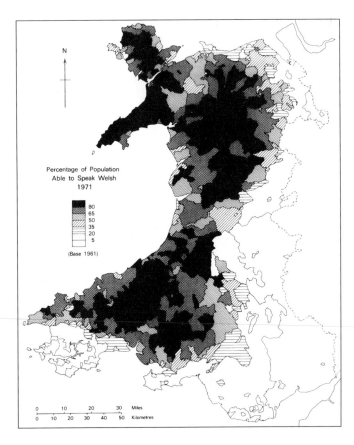

Percentage of Population
Able to Speak Welsh
1971

80
65
50
35
20
5

(Base 1961)

N

0   10   20   30   Miles
0   10   20   30   40   50   Kilometres

against the returns of the four previous censuses. The percentage of the inhabitants of Wales able to speak Welsh declined from 28.9 per cent in 1951, to 26 per cent in 1961, to 20.9 per cent in 1971, and to 18.7 per cent in 1981. The number able to speak the language was 714,686 in 1951, 656,002 in 1961, 542,425 in 1971, 503,520 in 1981. Numbers declined by 8 per cent in the 1950s, 17 per cent in the 1960s and 6 per cent in the 1970s. The dramatic drop in the 1960s was partly the result of a change in the questions asked in the census; the census of 1971, unlike previous ones, contained questions on the ability to read and write

Welsh in addition to one on the ability to speak the language. Many of those able to converse in Welsh were reluctant to admit that they were illiterate in the language and therefore stated that they were monoglot English-speakers. As the census records the linguistic abilities of all those over the age of three and therefore includes children under school age, it is hardly surprising that there were in all districts Welsh-speakers unable to read and write the language. Literacy levels varied, Dwyfor (the Llŷn peninsula) scoring highest with 89.76 per cent and Port Talbot lowest with 54.83 per cent. High percentages in Cardiff (72.14) and Taff-Ely (the southern part of the present borough of Rhondda Cynon Taf – 76.4) can be attributed to the attraction those areas had for middle-class Welsh-speakers (see below pp. 75–6) and to the growth of Welsh-medium education (see below pp. 79–86).

Until 1981, the census concerned itself not only with the ability to speak Welsh but also with the ability to speak English. It was probably in the 1960s that the last adult Welsh-speaker with no knowledge of English died, but monolingualism in Welsh among small children continued to be considerable. There were also bilingual persons who chose to declare themselves monoglot Welsh. Saunders Lewis argued in 1962 that the census was not a disinterested attempt to collect data on the linguistic situation in Wales. Rather, it was the authorities' way of finding the answer to the question: 'Can Wales be administered in English?' Those who wished to be administered through the medium of Welsh should, he declared, state that they were monoglot Welsh. Such a consideration helps to explain the 25 per cent increase (from 26,223 to 32,725) in recorded Welsh monolingualism between 1961 and 1971. In 1981 the figure fell back to 21,283, representing 0.8 per cent of the inhabitants of Wales over three years of age. The census form of 1991 did not contain a question about English, partly no doubt because those who compiled it believed that monolingualism was no longer an issue; furthermore, if questions concerning the ability or inability to speak English were raised in Wales, they could also be raised in the large conurbations in England which contained a significant number of immigrants from countries such as India, an issue to which the authorities did not wish to address themselves.

Areas with a high percentage of Welsh-speakers

On maps recording the data contained in the census reports in the late twentieth century, the most prominent feature is the

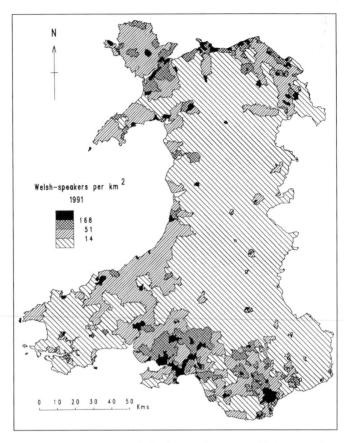

N

Welsh-speakers per km^2
1991

168
51
14

0 10 20 30 40 50
Kms

continuing contraction of districts having a very high proportion of Welsh-speakers. In 1961, 36.8 per cent of the surface area of Wales consisted of communities – 279 in all – in which over 80 per cent of the inhabitants had a knowledge of Welsh. In 1981, the figure had fallen to 9.7 per cent and a total of sixty-six communities. In 1991, Wales was organized into 912 wards; of these, there were thirty-two where 80 per cent or more of the population were Welsh-speakers.

By the late twentieth century, five core areas could be identified: central Anglesey; the old quarrying areas of Gwynedd and the

Llŷn peninsula; an extensive area centred upon Penllyn in eastern Meirionnydd but extending into Conwy, Denbighshire and Montgomeryshire; a group of scattered nuclei in the upland southwest; and an extensive area of the most westerly of the valleys of the south Wales coalfield. By 1991, the position of the language had deteriorated in all these areas, although the first three still contained clusters of wards where the ability to speak Welsh was wellnigh universal.

The core areas were surrounded by extensive tracts in which over half the inhabitants had a knowledge of Welsh. In 1961, 57 per cent of the territory of Wales had a Welsh-speaking majority, a proportion which had fallen to 47 per cent by 1981. In 1991, seven of the thirty-seven districts of Wales had Welsh-speaking majorities, and those districts constituted 33.9 per cent of the surface area of Wales. The Welsh-speakers of that 33.9 per cent represented 41.6 per cent of the total number of Welsh-speakers in Wales.

Areas with high numbers of Welsh-speakers

Thus, by the late twentieth century a new phenomenon had emerged: the majority of the speakers of Welsh were, by then, living in areas where the language was not that of the majority. That did not necessarily mean that Welsh-speakers in such areas made little use of the language; many of them consciously sought opportunities to do so, and thus, over the greater part of the surface area of Wales, Welsh has become the language not of the entire community, but of networks within the community.

The fact that the majority of Welsh-speakers live outside the areas in which Welsh is the language of the community as a whole is illustrated by a map showing the density of Welsh-speakers per square kilometre. Apart from the quarrying districts of Caernarfonshire and the westernmost region of the southern coalfield, where there are substantial clusters of Welsh-speakers living in a largely Welsh-speaking environment, the other substantial clusters are in the resorts of the north Wales coast, the districts round Wrexham, Llanelli, Swansea, Cardiff and parts of mid Glamorgan, all of them areas in which fewer than half the inhabitants speak Welsh. Thus while a map concerned with percentages gives the impression that the strength of the language lies in the western inland areas of Wales, maps concerned with density or absolute numbers suggest that its strength lies along the northern and southern coasts.

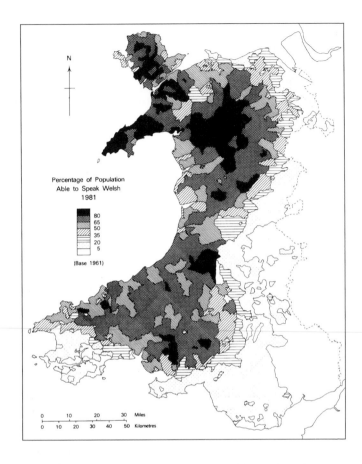

Percentage of Population
Able to Speak Welsh
1981

80
65
50
35
20
5

(Base 1961)

N

0   10   20   30   Miles
0 10 20 30 40 50 Kilometres

The areas in which there were considerable numbers, but not a majority, of Welsh-speakers fall into two categories. On the one hand there are those in which Welsh-speakers were a majority in the fairly recent past, but where slippage between generations means that knowledge of the language is heavily concentrated among the older age groups. This is particularly true of parts of the north-eastern coalfield and of much of west and north Glamorgan. In 1971, 41 per cent of the Welsh-speakers in the borough of Merthyr Tydfil could be found among the 15 per cent of its inhabitants who were over sixty-five. As the older generation died, knowledge of the language slumped dramatically. Indeed, the loss of 206,479 Welsh-speakers between 1951 and 1981 is largely explained by the generational slippage in such places as Merthyr. Such generational slippage seems to be less in evidence in the late twentieth century. In 1991, in households in which the parents were married and were both Welsh-speaking, 91.1 per cent of children between the ages of three and fifteen had a knowledge of the language.

The other category is markedly different. It consists of areas where the percentage of Welsh-speakers had long been low, but where employment opportunities encourage an inflow of substantial numbers of people from Welsh-speaking areas. Such areas include towns of planned expansion, like Newtown, and growing administrative centres such as Mold and Llandrindod. Above all, they include Cardiff and its immediate hinterland.

The position of Cardiff

The number of Welsh-speakers in the capital rose from 9,623 in 1951 to 17,236 in 1991, an increase of 79 per cent. In a wide belt round the city, the percentages speaking Welsh doubled and trebled, admittedly from low bases. By 1991, over 10 per cent of all the Welsh-speakers of Wales lived within twenty-five kilometres of Cardiff, compared with less than 5 per cent forty years earlier. The phenomenon has attracted the interest of urban geographers, prompting them to write of Cardiff's 'quiet revolution'. The percentage remains low – in hardly any locality around the city do Welsh-speakers constitute as much as one in five of the population – and doubts have accordingly been expressed whether such a scattered linguistic community is able to create the social networks necessary for language maintenance. Yet with several of the wards of the city having, by 1991, more than 350 Welsh-speakers per square kilometre, there are enough of them in close proximity to each other for such networks to be created. Furthermore, since 1991 there is evidence that the 'quiet revolution' has continued and even accelerated. Most of the Welsh-speaking migrants to Cardiff are employed in administration, education and the media; having middle-class occupations, they have settled in middle-class areas, and it is noticeable that the rise in the number of Welsh-speakers has occurred almost exclusively in the more affluent parts of the city. Ever since the Anglicization of the gentry, the speaking of Welsh has been associated with low social

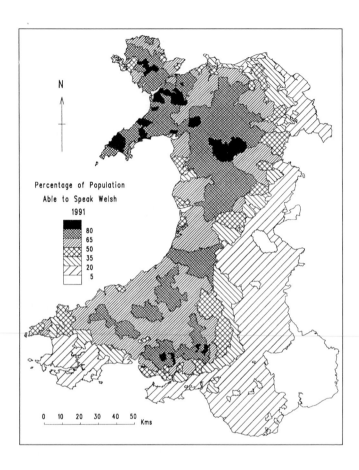

N

Percentage of Population
Able to Speak Welsh
1991

80
65
50
35
20
5

0 10 20 30 40 50
                    Kms

status; its association with high status, apparent in Cardiff but also elsewhere, is a new development.

Economic change and Welsh-speaking communities

While the growth of Welsh-medium education and a selective pattern of migration were strengthening the position of the Welsh language in some parts of Wales – Cardiff in particular – economic change was undermining the viability of traditional Welsh-speaking communities. Particularly significant was the contraction of employment in the industries which had been the mainstay of those communities. The quarries of Gwynedd, which had employed 20,000 men in the 1890s, employed only 500 in the 1990s. The coal-mines and tinplate works of east Carmarthenshire and west Glamorgan – districts which contained about a quarter of all the Welsh-speakers of Wales – contracted rapidly. Carmarthenshire had 14,644 coalminers in 1921 and only a few hundred in 1991. Even more significant numerically was the decline in employment in agriculture. Anglesey, Caernarfon, Meirionnydd, Cardigan and Carmarthen – the only ones among the ancient counties to have substantial Welsh-speaking majorities – had 40,000 families involved in agriculture in 1921 and hardly a third of that number in 1991. Farming has a rich Welsh vocabulary, and this is also true to a considerable extent of slate-quarrying and coal-mining. As employment in those industries contracted, tens of thousands of Welsh-speakers found jobs in new fields – in offices, the service industries and light manufacturing in particular – fields in which any traditional use of Welsh was minimal. Many, young people especially, failed to find any work in their home neighbourhoods; they moved out, thus distorting the age structure of the population. Between 1921 and 1971 the population of the strongly Welsh-speaking industrial parish of Llan-giwg in west Glamorgan fell by 25 per cent, and that of the quarrying parish of Llanddeiniolen in Caernarfonshire by 20 per cent. Even more striking was the population decline in the countryside, with the number of inhabitants declining by 43 per cent in the Rural District of Penllyn and by 38 per cent in the Rural District of Tregaron.

The impact of in-migration

The contraction of employment in agriculture meant that the housing stock in the countryside exceeded the needs of the local economy. Many of the houses were bought as holiday homes; by the 1970s, districts such as Llŷn had parishes in which over a quarter of the dwellings were holiday homes. As their purchasers came largely from the conurbations of England, this growth created a temporary English-speaking presence in even the remotest parts of Welsh-speaking Wales. Many owners settled permanently in their second homes on retirement. Others from over the border who settled permanently in Wales included those inspired by the self-sufficiency movement which flourished in the 1960s. As land appeared cheap in Wales, there was a marked influx, particularly

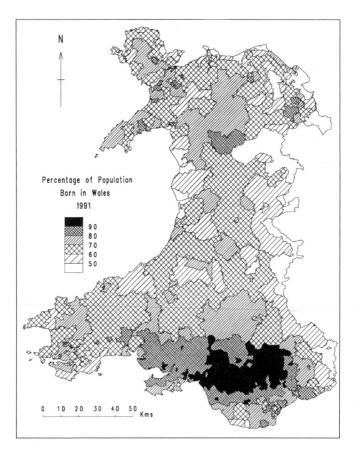

Percentage of Population
Born in Wales
1991

90
80
70
60
50

0   10   20   30   40   50   Kms

into the rural south-west, where in some of the parishes of south
Cardiganshire and north Carmarthenshire the proportion born
outside Wales rose to almost 50 per cent. At the same time tourist
resorts, which had long been centres of Anglicization, became
increasingly attractive to incomers. By the 1970s, the majority of
the inhabitants of Colwyn Bay, Abergele and Prestatyn had been
born in England, but by that time the same was true of more
remote districts, such as the parish of Llanfair Mathafarn Eithaf
on the east coast of Anglesey. The Snowdonia region, traditionally

considered a heartland of the Welsh language, proved so attractive to English mountain-lovers that those born in Wales became a bare majority in such parishes as Capel Curig. The existence of military bases, such as the one at Valley in Anglesey, meant that the majority of the population of those districts came from England. The expansion of centres of higher education led to the appointment of English academics, and attempts to industrialize rural Wales created jobs which attracted English managers and key workers. Some of the incomers were intrigued by the distinctiveness of Wales and set about learning Welsh. Indeed, in 1991, 10 per cent of the Welsh-speaking inhabitants of Wales had been born outside the country. Others, feeling that all they had done was to move from one place to another within their country of Britain, were annoyed at any suggestion that they should be assimilated into a culture which they considered inferior. Some of the incomers were considerably perturbed at finding that they had, by moving, deprived themselves of some of their favourite television programmes. Many were parents of school-age children who reacted angrily to the discovery that lessons in the local primary school were conducted largely through the medium of Welsh. On the other hand, the Welsh population, feeling under siege and fearing that the influx would squeeze them out of existence, also began to voice concern. Thus the traditionally Welsh-speaking areas of Wales became areas of potential conflict.

II Education

In any community in which the original native language coexists with the dominant language of the state, the issue of language in education is almost certain to be a contentious matter. It was a major cause of dissension in the old Austro-Hungarian Empire and has aroused passions among peoples such as the Quebecois and the Basques. It also arouses passions in Wales. Broadcasting has perhaps been the most disputatious issue where the Welsh language is concerned (see pp. 64–5, 96–100) but education has been a close second. The Report of 1927 (*Welsh in Education and Life*; see pp. 63–4) considered that education was the key to the well-being of the language, and the greater part of the energies of those concerned with its well-being has over the past fifty years been channelled into efforts to enhance its role in schools and in higher and adult education.

The Welsh language in primary and nursery schools

In the mid-1940s, Welsh was the main medium of instruction in those areas where Welsh was overwhelmingly the most widely spoken language. In the rest of Wales, efforts to teach the language to monoglot English-speaking pupils varied according to the policy of the local education authority, but there was little specific provision for the minority of children who came from Welsh-speaking homes. A highly significant step was taken in 1947, when the Carmarthenshire Education Committee designated one of its schools at Llanelli as a Welsh school, an option open to the committee following the passage of the Education Act of 1944. (Sir Ifan ab Owen Edwards, the founder of Urdd Gobaith Cymru, had established a Welsh school at Aberystwyth in 1939, but as it was a private institution its foundation was not as momentous as the step taken at Llanelli.) Another dozen schools were opened in the following four years, and in 1951 the private school at Aberystwyth came under local authority control. In the 1950s, two counties – Flintshire and Glamorgan – made a determined effort to ensure that Welsh-medium primary education was extensively available. The new schools were originally established to enable children of Welsh-speaking families to be educated in their mother tongue. However, they rapidly attracted the interest of non-Welsh-speaking parents, and by the late 1950s the majority of their pupils came from English-speaking homes. By 1974 there were sixty-one designated Welsh primary schools in Wales, attended by 8,500 pupils. Closely associated with their growth was the development of Welsh-medium nursery education. The first Welsh-medium nursery school was established soon after the war, in Maesteg. By the time Mudiad Ysgolion Meithrin (the nursery schools movement) was founded in 1971, there were sixty-eight schools with 950 pupils, a number which had grown to 577 schools with 9,338 pupils by 1998. In addition, there were, in 1998, 393 mother-and-child groups with 4,525 pupils. The rapid expansion of nursery schools created the need and demand for Welsh-medium primary schools. This was particularly the case in Cardiff where the original Welsh primary school, established with nineteen pupils in 1949, had expanded to become nine schools with 1,925 pupils by 1998. Another four schools will open by the turn of the century. The city had 2,190 Welsh-speakers under the age of fifteen in 1971, 4,685 in 1981 and 5,208 in 1991. In 1991, the ability to speak Welsh among Cardiffians was 153 per cent higher in the age groups from five to fifteen than it was among those over sixty-five. The contrast was equally marked in neighbouring areas such as Llantrisant, Pontypridd and Caerffili, and also in Mold in the north-east.

The growth of Welsh-medium education in places such as Cardiff brought into being considerable numbers of young Welsh-speakers whose experience of life was that of large towns and cities, thus greatly varying the social base of the language. The fear expressed in 1927 (see p. 64) that Welsh-speaking Wales was unable to develop its own urban middle class seemed allayed. The growth of the language in the Anglicized districts – the fact, for example, that a quarter of the pupils of the Taff-Ely district attend Welsh schools – together with the figures revealed in the census of 1991, created a sense of optimism, even of euphoria. Triumphalism is not however in order – not yet, at least. Those attending Welsh-medium primary schools constitute a small percentage of the number of pupils in Wales between the ages of five and fifteen – there are, after all, 110 primary schools in Cardiff – and their very existence may have caused indifference, even hostility, towards the language among those not attending them. On the other hand, hearing their friends and neighbours speaking Welsh can also have the effect of encouraging children attending English-medium schools to learn Welsh as a second lamguage. The pupils in Welsh schools in highly Anglicized areas live in an environment in which English is overwhelmingly the dominant language. In advocating English education for Wales, the authors of the Report of 1847 (see pp. 43–5) had their doubts whether 'the language of lessons can make head against the language of life' – a comment highly relevant to Welsh schools in places like Cardiff. A survey by Professors Carter and Aitchison, conducted in 1988, indicated that at least half the pupils receiving a Welsh-medium education rarely make use of the language outside school, although recent research on the Bridgend area suggests that Welsh is increasingly used in adult life by those who have learned the language at school. Carter and Aitchison came to the conclusion that, among the young people of Cardiff, 'Welsh is a plant which has been growing energetically but which has not as yet produced a deep and extensive root system.'

Initially, the specifically designated Welsh schools were in the largely English-speaking areas of the north-east and the south-east, or in western towns where considerable Anglicization had occurred. It was assumed that primary schools in the Welsh-speaking areas would be naturally Welsh. As pressures, caused in

Welsh in the primary classroom.

the main by in-migration, posed a threat to the natural Welshness of many rural schools, there were demands that those schools should also be designated Welsh schools. In the areas where designated Welsh schools had already been established, there was also a wide choice of English-medium schools. Offering a similar choice in rural areas was deemed to be fraught with difficulties. If schools which had been naturally Welsh were to become designated Welsh schools, there would be resistance from the large number of in-comers who were demanding English-medium education – and in their resistance they could expect to receive support from some at least of the Welsh-speaking parents. If their demands were met, Welsh would be squeezed out of schools over large areas in which it had been the dominant language only a few years previously. Thus, it was obvious that careful planning was needed in the field of education.

Welsh schools, whether designated or natural, are a minority of the schools of Wales. In the majority – the English-medium schools of the largely English-speaking areas – the degree to which Welsh is taught as a second language varies considerably. In the immediate post-war years it was taught in all the primary schools of Glamorgan but was rarely available in Monmouthshire. The effectiveness of second-language teaching was extremely uneven. For many pupils it was an exercise in futility, although there were some, even in the 1940s, whose schooling gave them a mastery of Welsh. Teaching methods improved in the 1950s and 1960s and attractive teaching materials multiplied, developments aided by the publication of *The Place of Welsh and English in the Schools of Wales* in 1952 and of *Primary Education in Wales* (the Gittins Report) in 1967.

Such developments did not occur without controversy. In the university towns of Aberystwyth and Bangor, groups of academics, imbued with the notion that they knew about education, established a movement called the Language Freedom Movement, which was active in resisting all moves to make Welsh an integral part of the curriculum. Opponents of the teaching of Welsh became more vocal in the late 1970s, following the reform of local government. On 1 April 1974, the thirteen counties and four county boroughs – the bodies responsible for education – were replaced by eight counties, some of which immediately set about devising a more consistent and forceful language policy. The most far-reaching was that of Gwynedd, which sought to make every child in the county fluent in Welsh and offered special facilities to incoming children to enable them to gain rapid fluency in the language. Dyfed, the county which in the 1970s and 1980s experienced the highest incidence of in-migration into traditional Welsh-speaking communities, divided its schools into categories. Category A schools, which included most of the county's rural schools outside south Pembrokeshire, gave precedence to Welsh, a decision which angered some parents, who established a movement called Education First. Clwyd, Powys and West Glamorgan, the other counties which included substantial Welsh-speaking communities, were rather less systematic in their approach. Mid Glamorgan and South Glamorgan continued to expand their network of Welsh-medium schools, although somewhat grudgingly on occasion. Gwent (the old Monmouthshire) – no longer a semi-detached county of Wales since the local government reforms of 1974 – warmed considerably towards Welsh-medium education and established three designated Welsh primary schools and a number of Welsh-language units. A further reorganization of local government took place in 1996, when the eight counties and the thirty-seven districts were replaced by twenty-two all-purpose county authorities. There are Welsh-medium primary schools within the confines of all the new authorities. The degree to which Welsh is available as a second language in primary schools varies from county to county, but the rules of the National Curriculum lay down that all pupils should have some Welsh lessons.

The Welsh language in secondary schools

In the 1940s, Welsh was available as a subject in most of the secondary schools of Wales. In the schools of the English-speaking areas, it was generally taught in the same manner as French, a major difficulty for those wishing to study the language for the Senior and Higher Certificates, as the papers set in the examinations were designed for those who spoke Welsh as their mother tongue. In Welsh-speaking areas, the language itself was the only subject taught through the medium of Welsh; the realization that teachers, who had spoken nothing but English in the classroom, were in fact fluent Welsh-speakers frequently came as a shock to their ex-pupils. By the early 1950s some secondary schools were using Welsh in teaching such subjects as Welsh history and religious instruction, but there were no secondary schools teaching largely through the medium of Welsh until Flintshire County Council established Ysgol Glan Clwyd near Rhyl in 1956 and Ysgol Maes Garmon in Mold in 1961. Glamorgan followed with Ysgol Rhydfelen near Pontypridd in 1962. By the mid-1980s there were fifteen such schools, largely in the Anglicized north-east and south-east, although some of them – those at Carmarthen, Aberystwyth and Bangor, for instance – were in towns which could draw upon a traditionally Welsh-speaking hinterland. The increase in their numbers was facilitated by the reorganization of secondary education in the wake of the establishment of comprehensive schools. Most of them were bilingual rather than exclusively Welsh-medium schools, for science subjects were generally taught through the medium of English. By the 1980s also, non-designated schools in Welsh-speaking areas, particularly in Gwynedd and Dyfed, were offering an increasing number of subjects through the medium of Welsh.

The Education Act of 1988 laid down that in Wales Welsh was to be a core subject in the new National Curriculum. From 1999 all secondary schools are obliged to offer Welsh as a second language to pupils up to sixteen years of age. The decision has had far-reaching implications in terms of the numbers of teachers and the range of resources needed. Special bursaries are now available for those wishing to train to teach Welsh, or through the medium of Welsh, and the Resources Centre at Aberystwyth has been active in producing a wide range of attractive teaching materials. These activities were initially co-ordinated by the Committee for the Development of Welsh Medium Education (usually known as PDAG, the acronym from its Welsh title); since 1994 PDAG's functions have been taken over by the Curriculum Council.

Welsh in Higher Education

In the early years of their existence, the colleges of the University of Wales made no use at all of Welsh as a medium of instruction. Members of the Department of Welsh at Cardiff began lecturing in Welsh in the 1920s and all such departments were operating almost exclusively in Welsh by the 1940s. Welsh was more widely used in teachers' training colleges but had virtually no status at all in technical colleges. In the 1950s, leading Nationalists argued that one of the university colleges should be designated as a college offering a full range of courses through the medium of Welsh, a notion which the university authorities considered undesirable and impractical. In 1955, however, the university promised to expand the use of Welsh hand in hand with the expansion of the number of secondary school pupils educated through the medium of Welsh. Over the years, about two dozen lecturers with a special responsibility for teaching through the medium of Welsh have been appointed, almost all of them in Arts departments. Although they represent a tiny proportion of the staff of the University, their appointment means that undergraduates studying through the medium of Welsh are no longer restricted to those actually studying the language itself. The University College of Wales, Aberystwyth launched its External Degree through the medium of Welsh in 1980, and the existence of groups of students following university courses through Welsh has proved to be a major stimulus to the production of scholarly works in the language. At Aberystwyth, the demand for a hall of residence in which Welsh would be the dominant language was met – after a ferocious controversy – in 1974, with the designation of Neuadd Pantycelyn as a mixed Welsh hall. Bangor followed with Neuadd John Morris-Jones in 1975. Welsh-medium courses have become increasingly available in colleges of education; technical and further

The Nant Gwrtheyrn language centre.

education colleges make fewer provisions, although secretarial courses in Welsh have expanded considerably.

Adult learners of Welsh

Over the centuries, many Welsh-speakers have taken perverse pride in their belief that their language could not be learned by those not brought up to speak it, and George Borrow noted in *Wild Wales* (1862) the suspicion with which adult learners of Welsh were regarded. Such notions lost ground in the second half of the twentieth century (although they did not vanish completely) and classes for Welsh learners proliferated. By the 1960s, the most ardent advocate of the teaching of Welsh to adults was R. M. Jones, who had himself learned the language at school in Cardiff. Also known as the poet Bobi Jones, R. M. Jones was from 1980 to 1989 Professor of Welsh at Aberystwyth, the first 'learner' to be appointed to a chair of Welsh; his *Cymraeg i Oedolion* (Welsh for Adults, 1965–6) was a landmark in the publication of material for teachers and learners of Welsh.

The increase in the use of Welsh by public bodies (see pp. 103–4) created a greater demand for employees fluent in the language. The demand was an added factor in fostering the growth of the adult learners movement, which also owed much to the desire of parents with children in Welsh schools to master the language which was the medium of their children's education. Cyngor y Dysgwyr (CYD – the Learners' Council), founded in 1984, has attracted considerable support. Courses organized by the University of Wales and other bodies, and language lessons on radio and television won a wide following.

Educationists developed a form of written Welsh which is closer to the spoken language than is the biblically based traditional written form. Known as *Cymraeg Byw* (Living Welsh), it has not found universal acceptance. The enthusiasts of the adult learning movement are inspired by the example of Israel, where Hebrew, once almost defunct, has became the chief language of the state; the Hebrew word *ulpan* has been adopted as the name of the intensive Welsh courses (*wlpan*), of which the eight-week residential course in Lampeter is an outstanding example. The growing number of learners who achieve fluency has provided a valuable boost to the Welsh-language community, despite the fact that native speakers are not always eager to assist them in their efforts to achieve proficiency. Many of the learners have a deeper interest in language as such than have those who have spoken Welsh from childhood; as a result, they frequently have a knowledge of a range of other languages and a richer understanding of sociolinguistics. One notable venture has been the refurbishment of the deserted village of Nant Gwrtheyrn, south-west of Caernarfon, as a year-round centre for language learning. Situated on the seashore in a deep ravine, it provides a captivating experience for those who visit it.

III Publishing and the press

The periodical press

Welsh-language publishing has known periods of great prosperity, particularly in the mid and late nineteenth century, but in the twentieth century it has become an increasingly precarious business. Old established periodicals suffered from declining circulations and by the 1950s *Baner ac Amserau Cymru* (see p. 42) was a shadow of its former self. Yet the Welsh press showed itself capable of versatility and innovation. The difficult years of the 1930s saw the launching of the lively illustrated weekly *Y Cymro*, the highly professional *Ford Gron* and the more radical journals *Tir Newydd* and *Heddiw*. From the 1950s onwards a plethora of new periodicals appeared, including the monthly magazine *Barn*, the literary journal *Taliesin* and the scientific periodical *Y Gwyddonydd*. Yet with the potential readership limited and the costs of publishing rising, most periodicals faced financial problems, to which *Y Faner* (as *Baner ac Amserau Cymru* had become) succumbed in 1992. The case for public subsidy was widely argued. The Arts Council, through its Welsh Committee, had assisted Welsh ventures since its inception in 1945. Such patronage increased greatly following the establishment of the largely autonomous Welsh Arts Council in 1967, and by the 1990s most Welsh-language periodicals came to rely at least in part upon public money. They include the general-interest weekly *Golwg* and magazines for, among others, women, naturalists, bibliophiles, anglers and devotees of the religious denominations.

One venture in the field of periodicals which – initially at least – owed nothing to subsidy, is the movement to publish *papurau bro*, or neighbourhood newspapers. The first of these was *Y Dinesydd*, launched at Cardiff in 1973; it was followed by scores of others, and although some have disappeared, most have survived and flourished. By 1998, there were fifty-six of them, with a combined circulation of about 52,000. Some of them – *Y Gadlas*, which serves the area around Llansannan in Conwy, for instance – are substantial publications; others, like *Yr Angor* at Aberystwyth, are on a more modest scale. Taken together, the *papurau bro* have a far greater readership than do nation-wide periodicals like *Y Cymro* and *Golwg* and are clear proof that the taste for reading Welsh exists on a significant scale. Most of them are monthlies and the effort – all of it voluntary and unpaid – involved in running them is considerable. Some of the groups responsible for them have branched out into other activities, such as drama festivals and the publication of books of local interest.

Books in Welsh

Ever since the appearance of the first printed book in Welsh in 1547 (see p. 23), the publication of Welsh books has been an uncertain business. As with periodicals, the Welsh book trade had its successes in the nineteenth century, the average annual number of Welsh books published rising from about forty in the 1820s to

Recent Welsh-language publications.

more than 120 in the 1880s. By the mid-twentieth century, however, the number had declined to little more than the early nineteenth-century figure. In 1950, the Cardiganshire Education Committee began subsidizing the publication of books for children, and its example was followed in subsequent years by other counties. From 1954 onwards, the Welsh Joint Education Committee gave grant-aid to the production of school-books in Welsh, and in 1956 the government began a scheme to assist publications in Welsh for adults. The Welsh Books Council was founded in 1961 and thereafter virtually every book published in Welsh has received some degree of state aid. In 1997, 636 books were published and distributed through the network of Welsh-language bookshops which had developed. Publishers of long standing, like Gwasg Gomer (founded in 1892) and the University of Wales Press, were joined by a number of newer ventures, such as Y Lolfa, which publishes, among other things, material considered too titillating or too extreme by other presses, Gwasg Carreg Gwalch and Gwasg Gwynedd.

Literature in Welsh

Of the books published in Welsh, at least a third are either children's books or school-books. Of those for adults, up to a third are books of verse, proof of the continuing appeal of poetry in Welsh-speaking Wales, an appeal to which the popularity of the programme *Talwrn y Beirdd* (the poets' cockpit) also bears witness. D. Gwenallt Jones, who wrote of industrial Glamorgan as well as rural Carmarthenshire, had emerged as a major poet by the mid-twentieth century, and Waldo Williams's *Dail Pren*, a work suffused with the poet's mystical awareness of the unity of nature and of universal brotherhood, was published in 1956. Fears that the erosion of Welsh-speaking communities would lead to the extinction of *y beirdd gwlad* (the country poets) were belied by the achievement of Dic Jones of Blaenporth in Ceredigion. The nostalgia for a lost utopia characteristic of much Welsh poetry was challenged by the work of Gwyn Thomas, a poet who delights in modernity. Experiments in concrete poetry and *vers libre* proliferate, but there is also an urge to return to older traditions. A marked revival of interest in *cynghanedd* (see p. 19) was apparent by the 1970s. It was encouraged by Cymdeithas Cerdd Dafod (literally, the society of the art of the tongue) and its journal *Barddas*, founded in 1976; the journal's editors, Alan Llwyd and Gerallt Lloyd Owen, proved themselves to be *cynganeddwyr* of astounding virtuosity. From the 1980s onwards, a succession of new, younger poets emerged to win the chief literary prizes of the National Eisteddfod, and the same period also witnessed the emergence of such notable female poets as Nesta Wyn Jones and Menna Elfyn.

While the major accolades are still given for poetry, Welsh prose literature has gained in prestige over the last few decades.

Actors from Brith Gof in their performance of the Gododdin.

The short story and the essay, the glories of Welsh prose in the days of Kate Roberts and T. H. Parry-Williams, have lost ground to the novel. The writing of novels, which had languished since the days of Daniel Owen, was stimulated by the work of T. Rowland Hughes, who produced a novel a year between 1943 and 1947. Islwyn Ffowc Elis created a new, young readership with *Cysgod y Cryman* (1956), and Caradog Prichard's semi-autobiographical and deeply moving novel *Un Nos Ola Leuad* was published in 1961. Historical novels have enjoyed a considerable vogue, particularly those of Marion Eames. T. Glynne Davies's *Marged* (1974) traces the life of a family over a century or more and Rhydwen Williams has published a cycle of novels set in the Rhondda. Those writing on contemporary themes have included John Rowlands, the first novelist writing in Welsh to include explicit descriptions of sexual scenes in his novels. Because of the geographical distribution of the language, Welsh novels with a city setting have been rare, although the growing strength of the Welsh-speaking community in Cardiff has already demonstrated its influence in the work of, amongst others, Harri Pritchard Jones, Siôn Eirian, Wiliam Owen Roberts and Mihangel Morgan. Wiliam Roberts's *Y Pla* (translated into English as *The Pestilence*), a remarkable picaresque novel set in the time of the Black Death, and an important post-modernist work, appeared in 1990, while Robin Llywelyn and Mihangel Morgan exploit different aspects of post-modernist development in their novels and short stories.

Welsh-language drama received a huge boost in the post-war period from the plays of Saunders Lewis; there were other playwrights of distinction too, including John Gwilym Jones, Huw Lloyd Edwards and Gwenlyn Parry. Much of the energy of the younger dramatists has been diverted to the writing of television soap operas and situation comedies, work which, although profitable, is highly ephemeral. Others have been involved in companies like Brith Gof and Dalier Sylw, in whose productions the script is usually an artefact jointly created by writers, actors and producers. Brith Gof in particular has won considerable renown, offering, all over the world, drama in Welsh which it has skilfully enabled its audience to understand.

Scholarship in Welsh

The tradition of Welsh linguistic scholarship initiated by Edward Lhuyd and revived in the late nineteenth century by John Rhŷs and John Morris-Jones continued to flourish in the twentieth century. Notable landmarks include D. Simon Evans's *Gramadeg Cymraeg Canol* (the Grammar of Middle Welsh, 1951), T. J. Morgan's *Y Treigladau a'u Cystrawen* (Mutations and Syntax, 1952), Stephen J. Williams's *Elfennau Gramadeg Cymraeg* (1959; English version, *A Welsh Grammar*, 1980), David A. Thorne's *A Comprehensive Welsh Grammar* (1993), Peter Wynn Thomas's *Gramadeg y Gymraeg* (the Grammar of Welsh, 1996) and the writings of Ellis Evans on Continental Celtic and Brittonic. This is a field of work with a marked international character and many articles on the subject have been published by scholars working in the United States, the countries of the European continent and Japan. The central role of the Bible in the evolution of the Welsh language was acknowledged with the publication of a revised version in 1988, 400 years after the appearance of William Morgan's masterpiece. The same year saw the translation of the Roman Catholic missal. Dialect has been the subject of considerable study; Alan R. Thomas's *Linguistic Geography of Wales* (1973), with its 288 maps, gave delight to a people much given to a discussion of their dialectical differences. Place-names are also of absorbing interest; Hywel Wyn Owen's *Pocket Guide to the Place-Names of Wales* was published in 1998 and more ambitious studies are in train. The statistical material available on the language has been analysed by Pryce, Carter, Aitchison and others, and Welsh sociolinguistics has begun to gain recognition as an academic study. In 1992, an exhaustive study of the social history of Welsh was initiated by the Centre for Advanced Welsh and Celtic Studies at Aberystwyth and four volumes on the subject will have been published by autumn 1999.

The institute at Aberystwyth was established in 1985; its first project was a thorough investigation of the work of the poets of the princes – y Gogynfeirdd. The earliest poets – y Cynfeirdd – had already been meticulously studied by Ifor Williams, John Morris-Jones's successor at Bangor; his stream of publications over fifty years and more represent a wholly remarkable contribution to Welsh literary and linguistic studies. The Welsh literary tradition up to 1900 was surveyed by Thomas Parry in his *Hanes Llenyddiaeth Gymraeg* (1945), an English version of which, by H. Idris Bell, was published under the title *A History of Welsh Literature* in 1955. Parry also established the definitive canon of the work of Dafydd ap Gwilym (1952) and edited the *Oxford Book of Welsh Verse* (1962, 9th edition 1994), a learned anthology of the highlights of the Welsh poetic tradition. Grants to research students have enabled the vast manuscript collections of Welsh medieval poetry to become available, at least in typescript, and Welsh medieval prose has attracted considerable scholarly attention. The works of the Renaissance writers, the early Puritans, the Methodists and the eisteddfod competitors and novelists of the nineteenth century have been the subjects of substantial monographs. Twentieth-century literature has been extensively surveyed and concepts of modern critical theory have received an airing in Welsh. Much of this scholarly work has been conveniently distilled in the University of Wales Press's series 'Writers of Wales', consisting of brief and elegantly produced studies of writers in both Welsh and English; the series now amounts to almost ninety volumes. The political and cultural context of modern Welsh literature was analysed by Ned Thomas in *The Welsh Extremist* (1971, new edition 1992), a work which did much to popularize a radical view of Welsh ethnicity. The relationship of the two literatures of Wales has been the subject of distinguished studies by M. Wynn Thomas.

The use of Welsh in literary and linguistic studies was largely the consequence of the fact that the language was the medium of instruction for university students in departments of Welsh. Its use in studies of other subjects – apart from theology – was unlikely as long as those subjects were taught solely through the medium of English. The expansion of the use of Welsh at university level, slight though it was, encouraged the production of academic works in fields such as education and philosophy. The expansion proved especially encouraging to Welsh historians, particularly those working at Aberystwyth. Notable among their works are J. Beverley Smith's study of Llywelyn ap Gruffydd, Prince of Wales (1996; English version 1998), *Cof Cenedl*, the annual volume of essays edited by Geraint H. Jenkins, and John Davies's comprehensive survey, *Hanes Cymru*, published by Penguin Books in 1990 (English version, *A History of Wales*, 1993).

New words and old

The coining of new words, widely practised in Wales in the late eighteenth and early nineteenth centuries, has been greatly stimulated by the needs of modern society. *Cyfrifiaduron* (computers) with their *meddalwedd* (software) and *caledwedd* (hardware) are one of the many fields in which a new Welsh terminology has been invented. Coinages such as *darllediad* (broadcast), *tonfedd* (wavelength) and *oriau brig* (peak hours) trip naturally off the tongues of broadcasters. Sports commentaries led to a wide range of neologisms, with those for rugby – the work of Eic Davies – being particularly apt and idiomatic. Words old and new have been collected in two of the most ambitious lexicographical projects yet undertaken in Wales. *Geiriadur Prifysgol Cymru* (the University of Wales Dictionary) has been appearing in parts since 1947; by early 1999 fifty instalments had appeared and the project had reached the word *rhywyr* (great or mighty man, hero). *Geiriadur yr Academi* (*The Welsh Academy English–Welsh Dictionary*), the hugely impressive work of Bruce Griffiths and Dafydd Glyn Jones, was published in 1995; this volume of 1,710 pages offers a full range of Welsh equivalents for English words and idioms.

IV Broadcasting

Radio

By the second half of the twentieth century, the printed word was increasingly supplemented by the broadcast word. The late 1940s and 1950s were the golden age of sound broadcasting in Welsh. The BBC producers, who included leading Welsh writers, were ambitious, offering their listeners Welsh translations of the works of the world's greatest dramatists, as well as literary talks of distinction. In attracting a substantial audience for radio in Welsh, however, the production of popular programmes was more significant. In the 1950s, *Galw Gari Tryfan*, a serial for children, won an extensive following, and variety programmes such as *Noson Lawen* and *Raligamps* enjoyed very high ratings.

In 1953, following the publication of the Beveridge Report on Broadcasting, Wales was given its own Broadcasting Council, some members of which constantly pressed for an increase in the number of hours devoted to broadcasting in Welsh. As the great majority of those receiving the Welsh Home Service could not understand Welsh, any substantial expansion in Welsh programmes aroused their antagonism. A solution became available in the 1970s with the development of VHF. In 1977, the decision was taken to offer a choice in Wales's opt-out from Radio Four, with English on the medium wave and Welsh on VHF. The division became complete in 1978 with the creation of Radio Wales and Radio Cymru. Initially, Radio Cymru did not broadcast exclusively in Welsh, but by the late 1990s it was offering an unbroken sequence of programmes in Welsh from 6 a.m. to 12 p.m. Radio

Cymru's development led to considerable controversy. A determined effort in the late 1990s to make it more populist led to accusations of 'dumbing down', and its use of slovenly Welsh and the broadcasting of English-language pop music has aroused much antagonism. Welsh programmes are also broadcast on commercial stations, in particular Swansea Sound and Radio Ceredigion.

Television

With an established tradition of sound broadcasting in Welsh, it seemed natural, with the coming of television, that Welsh-language programmes should be seen as well as heard. The BBC's transmitting station at Wenvoe was opened in 1952 and that of the commercial company Television Wales and West (TWW) at St Hilary in 1958. Both stations served much of the south-west of England as well as south-east Wales, a pattern similar to that of the initial and much criticized arrangements for sound broadcasting. Programmes from northern England could be received in parts of north-east Wales and those of the English Midlands in parts of central Wales. By 1960, 60 per cent of the households of Wales had a television set and, following the establishment of relay stations, the proportion had risen to 92 per cent by 1969.

Programmes in the Welsh language were included in the services from Wenvoe and St Hilary from the beginning; before the completion of the relay system, they were also broadcast from the BBC's transmitters at Sutton Coldfield and Holme Moss, and for a brief period Granada of Manchester produced and broadcast programmes in Welsh. Following the publication of the Pilkington Report, BBC Wales was established in 1964 with the obligation of initiating twelve hours of programmes a week, half of which were to be in Welsh. An attempt was made in 1961 to create a commercial television station for north and west Wales with the launching of WWN Television or Teledu Cymru. Its object was to offer a substantial number of programmes in Welsh. As its territory was thinly populated and its resources inadequate, it was taken over by TWW after broadcasting for ten months. TWW undertook to broadcast five and a half hours of Welsh a week, an obligation inherited by Harlech Television (HTV) when the licences were redistributed in 1968.

Thus, by the early 1960s, the BBC and ITV between them were broadcasting about eleven and a half hours of Welsh a week. The transition from sound to visual broadcasting had been successfully achieved and, under the guidance of brilliant producers like Hywel Davies, Welsh-language programmes of distinction were made. Yet, as the vast majority of those served by the main transmitters broadcasting in Welsh could not understand the language, the programmes were restricted to off-peak hours, often late at night. Furthermore, where an alternative service to that offering Welsh-language programmes was available – and this was the case in the most heavily populated areas of the north-east and the south-east – aerials were aligned to receive that service. That this occurred on an extensive scale is indicated by the fact that, in 1969, 70,000 copies of the BBC Wales edition of the *Radio Times* were sold in Wales, compared with 96,000 copies of other editions. Thus the existence of television programmes in Welsh led many people in Wales to avoid watching not only the Welsh-language programmes but also the English-language programmes emanating from Wales. In those areas where no alternative service was available, viewers unable to follow Welsh programmes became increasingly vocal in their opposition to them. Yet in those same areas the programmes in Welsh represented less than 10 per cent of the total output, while there was invariably an English programme on ITV when there was a Welsh one on BBC, and vice versa. As at least 90 per cent of broadcasting consisted of English-language programmes and as what was available at peak viewing hours was almost exclusively in English, those wishing to watch Welsh programmes also became increasingly vocal. By the late 1960s, broadcasting had become a highly divisive issue and polarization between the Welsh- and English-language communities was growing apace.

Sianel Pedwar Cymru

On 1 November 1982 Sianel Pedwar Cymru (S4C – the Welsh Fourth Channel) went on the air for the first time. The campaign which led to its launching is one of the most remarkable episodes in the recent history of the minority languages of Europe. By the early 1970s English monoglots, who did not want their viewing interrupted by programmes they did not understand, made common cause with those who wanted more Welsh programmes at more convenient hours. Both sides came to the conclusion that a separate channel for television broadcasts in Welsh was the only answer. Neither side was unanimous on the matter. On the English-language side, voices were heard doubting the need for any Welsh programmes at all, particularly in view of the fact that

Some of the cast of *Pam fi Duw?* (Why me God?), the popular television programme set in a Welsh-medium comprehensive school in the south Wales valleys.

the number of Welsh monoglots was so small. On the Welsh-language side, there were those who pointed out that a large number of people, who were not Welsh enthusiasts, watched programmes in Welsh when such programmes happened to be shown on their favourite channel; these viewers would be lost if all Welsh programmes were shown on a separate channel. This argument was forcefully put by Jac L. Williams, Professor of Education at Aberystwyth and a noted authority on bilingual schooling. There was also another group which believed that, if separate provision were made for programmes in Welsh, similar provision should be made for English-language programmes directly relating to Wales. This view was not widely canvassed in the early 1970s, but it has won an increasing number of adherents over the years.

The notion that the fourth television channel, when brought into service, should be used in Wales primarily to broadcast programmes in Welsh at peak hours was endorsed at a national conference convened by the Lord Mayor of Cardiff in 1973. It was enthusiastically supported by Charles Curran, the Director

General of the BBC, because it fitted in with his belief that the fourth channel, in Britain as a whole, should be devoted to minority interests. It also found support among leading figures in the broadcasting business in Wales, particularly those who felt that the existing situation was leading to a dangerous degree of polarization. The original plan was that the channel should be shared by the BBC and ITV, with each organization responsible for specific days but, in view of the demands for a role for independent producers, opinion warmed to the concept of a separate authority. In 1974 the Crawford Committee reported in favour of the Welsh fourth channel, and its report was accepted by the Labour government. By 1979, preparations for the channel were well advanced, and in that year, the Conservatives in their general election manifesto committed themselves to its establishment.

In May 1979 the Conservatives were returned to power. Four months later, in a speech at Cambridge, the Home Secretary, William Whitelaw, announced that the government would not be proceeding with the Welsh channel but would instead seek to improve the existing provision. The activists of Cymdeithas yr Iaith Gymraeg (see pp. 102–4), some of whom – Ffred Ffransis in particular – had suffered lengthy periods of imprisonment in their campaign to secure the channel, reacted angrily. So did many members of Plaid Cymru; 2,000 of them vowed not to pay the television licence fee and a number of leading figures in Welsh life made raids on transmitters. Then on 5 May 1980 Gwynfor Evans announced that he would undertake a fast to death unless the government adhered to its original commitment. His statement won wide publicity, and the mass rallies he addressed in the late summer led members of the government to believe that a mood of intransigence might well develop among a significant section of the Welsh population. With Gwilym Williams, the Archbishop of Wales, Lord Cledwyn, the leader of the Labour peers, and Sir Goronwy Daniel, the retired principal of the University College at Aberystwyth, acting as intermediaries, the government yielded on 17 September 1980.

Two years elapsed between the government's volte-face and the launching of Sianel Pedwar Cymru. Welsh became a 'television language'; of the languages of western Europe which are not the chief languages of sovereign states, the distinction of having their own channel is enjoyed only by Welsh, Catalan, Basque and Galician. (The Irish-language channel, launched in 1997, broadcasts in a language which is constitutionally considered to be the chief language of a sovereign state.) By British standards, S4C's viewing figures are low. However, its most popular programme, the soap opera *Pobol y Cwm*, attracts up to 250,000 viewers, 50 per cent of the total number of Welsh-speakers, a percentage which, if expressed in British terms, would represent viewing figures in excess of 25 million. Among the 250,000 there are probably many who do not consider themselves Welsh-speakers, for *Pobol y Cwm*, like most of S4C's other programmes, can be viewed with English subtitles. The channel's viewing figures relate only to the residents of Wales. S4C has, however, attracted numerous viewers in England and in Ireland. In early 1999 the service will be available throughout Europe by satellite. S4C is on the air for about 154 hours weekly. Of those hours, between thirty-five and forty, largely at peak viewing times, are in Welsh; the rest consist of a selection of the output of the British Channel Four. A new digital channel broadcasting in Welsh for twelve hours a day was launched in November 1998.

A number of S4C's programmes have been sold abroad; its animated programmes – *Gogs* and *SuperTed* for example – have attracted widespread attention. The BBC supplies at least twelve hours of S4C's programmes, *Pobol y Cwm* among them. The rest is bought from HTV and from independent production companies, for S4C is a commissioning, not a producing, channel. The growth of independent companies, not only in Cardiff but also in strongly Welsh-speaking areas, particularly around Caernarfon and in parts of Carmarthenshire, was one of the most striking developments in the cultural scene in Wales in the 1980s. Increasing employment in Welsh-language television was a marked feature of the early 1980s, a period when employment in other sectors of the Welsh economy slumped dramatically.

V Welsh in public life

In the mid-twentieth century, Welsh had virtually no public status. Although those who would be disadvantaged by using English in a court of law could use Welsh (see pp. 65–6), Welsh-speakers had no absolute right to use their language in court proceedings. Welsh was hardly ever seen on an official form, and public notices, apart from those on such buildings as Welsh chapels, were almost wholly in English. Awkwardly Anglicized versions of Welsh place-names abounded on road-signs, post offices rigorously

Saunders Lewis reading his radio lecture *Tynged yr Iaith* in 1962.

excluded the language and any suggestion that public servants such as telephone operators should use Welsh was greeted with hilarity. In the 1950s, some county councils – Carmarthenshire, for instance – erected bilingual notices on their boundaries and a few local authorities began to publish bilingual rate demands. Yet, when Eileen and Trefor Beasley of Llangennech asked the Llanelli Rural District Council in 1952 to send them a bilingual rate demand, they received a peremptory refusal. When the Beasleys refused to pay the rates, their property was seized; they continued the battle until the council yielded in 1960.

Cymdeithas yr Iaith Gymraeg – The Welsh Language Society

On 13 February 1962, Saunders Lewis, who had shunned public life since the war, gave the annual lecture of the BBC in Wales. Taking the theme 'Tynged yr Iaith' (the fate of the language), he urged his listeners to 'make it impossible to conduct local authority or central government business in Wales without the Welsh language'. 'To revive the Welsh language in Wales,' he declared, 'is nothing less than a revolution. Success can only come through revolutionary methods.' The challenge was taken up by a group of young nationalists who founded Cymdeithas yr Iaith Gymraeg (the Welsh Language Society, a title chosen out of respect for the similarly named society of the 1880s, see p. 50) in the summer of 1962. They began with a campaign to secure court summonses in Welsh, organizing a day of mass law-breaking in Aberystwyth on 2 February 1963. The society then turned its attention to the use of Welsh in the post office, on car licences and on road-signs. In the late 1960s, it conducted a large-scale campaign against monolingual road-signs, first painting them out and then removing them altogether. Its members were involved in a host of court cases, and periods of imprisonment became part of the experience of many Welsh-language campaigners. While they were almost exclusively young people, large numbers of older Welsh-speakers viewed their activities with tacit approval. In 1970 a group of magistrates, encouraged by the editor of the magazine *Barn*, Alwyn D. Rees, arranged to pay the fine of an imprisoned protester, indicating that members of the respectable middle class in Welsh-speaking Wales were prepared to condone law-breaking.

The activities of the society coincided with the granting to Wales of a significant degree of administrative autonomy. In 1964, the Welsh Office was established and a secretary of state for Wales with a seat in the British Cabinet was appointed, thus creating a new context for a discussion of the role of the Welsh language in the public life of Wales. The new arrangements also coincided with an upsurge in political nationalism. Gwynfor Evans, the president of Plaid Cymru from 1945 to 1981, captured the Carmarthen constituency in a by-election in 1966; although he lost the seat in 1970 – partly, he claimed, because of the un-popularity of some of the activities of Cymdeithas yr Iaith Gymraeg

– he recaptured it in the second General Election of 1974. In the first General Election of that year, Caernarfon and Meirionnydd were won by Plaid Cymru and have thereafter been safe seats for the party. Gwynfor Evans lost Carmarthen in 1979, but the party later won Anglesey, and Ceredigion and Pembroke North (now Ceredigion), victories which fuelled the belief that Wales had a future as a national community and which increased the confidence of Welsh-language activists. Another significant development was the entry of Britain into the European Community in 1972, a step which created in Wales a deeper awareness of the existence of linguistic minorities in mainland Europe and made possible new opportunies to co-operate with their members.

In the 1970s, the members of Cymdeithas yr Iaith Gymraeg were above all active in their campaign to win a Welsh television channel (see p. 99). They also expanded their activities to include protests against forces which they considered were undermining the viability of Welsh-speaking communities. They occupied holiday homes, demonstrated against estate agents and involved themselves in debates over planning policy. Pressure from the society, together with a heightened consciousness of the value of Welsh, led to an enhancement of the status of the language. This was particularly marked following the reorganization of local government in 1974. Gwynedd County Council adopted a bilingual policy for all aspects of its work. Instantaneous translation facilities were installed in its council chamber, where Welsh came to be more widely used than English. The district of Dwyfor went further and made Welsh the chief language of its activities. Dyfed County Council took tentative steps along the road trodden by Gwynedd, and some of its districts, Ceredigion in particular, made extensive use of Welsh. On the eve of the reorganization of local government in 1996, there were fears that Dwyfor's innovations would be cast aside, but the new Gwynedd (made up of Arfon, Dwyfor and Meirionnydd) has maintained many of them. The district of Ceredigion, now the county of Ceredigion, has also shown commitment, but elsewhere policies can be seen as little more than tokenism. The Welsh Language Board (see p. 105) has used its statutory right to review the linguistic plans of local authorities, but it is too early to assess the effectiveness of such schemes.

Other public bodies – the main utilities, the health service, social security offices and the university colleges – have gone in for varying degrees of bilingualism. There has also been some

Menna Elfyn, the Welsh poet, campaigning for a new Welsh Language Act,
outside the Welsh Office, Cardiff, early in 1993.

advance in the commercial field, with banks, building societies
and companies such as Boots, W. H. Smith and the main supermarket chains erecting Welsh signs, though again much of what
has been achieved hardly goes beyond tokenism. The private sector
is under pressure from the Welsh Language Board to increase the
use of Welsh but the Board's power to insist upon a coherent
policy is minimal.

The legal status of the Welsh language

The Welsh Courts Act of 1942 had long been seen as inadequate.
An incident at Ammanford in 1961, when a returning officer
refused to accept nomination papers because they had been completed in Welsh, publicized the imprecision of the legal standing
of the language. In 1963, the government established a committee
'to clarify the legal status of the Welsh language and to consider
whether any changes in the law ought to be made'. The main
recommendation of its report, published in 1965, was that anything done in Welsh should be as valid in the eyes of the law as if

it had been done in English. The committee also urged that more forms and official documents should be available in Welsh and that anyone wishing to use Welsh in a court of law should have an absolute right to do so. A rather watered-down version of its recommendations was incorporated in the Welsh Language Act of 1967, although the fundamental principle of the language clause of the Act of Union – that English should be the language of record in the courts – was retained.

In the 1970s and 1980s there was a growing demand for a new Welsh Language Act which would clarify and strengthen the provisions of the Act of 1967. The demand led to the Welsh Language Act of 1993, which gave statutory recognition to the Welsh Language Board and 'established the principle that in the conduct of public business and administration of justice in Wales the Welsh and English languages should be treated on a basis of equality'. The Board was charged with the duty of advising central government and all bodies providing services to the public on methods of giving substance to that principle, of investigating complaints and of instigating and overseeing the preparation and implementation of Welsh-language schemes. The Act fell short of acknowledging that Welsh was an official language and gave the Board no mandatory powers; indeed, where the private sector was concerned, its role could appear to be minimal. John Elfed Jones, the chairman of its precursor, the non-statutory Welsh Language Board established in 1988, considered that the Act fell far short of that Board's recommendations. Phrases in the Act such as 'reasonably practicable' and 'wherever appropriate' caused Cymdeithas yr Iaith to begin a campaign for stronger legislation. Nevertheless, the Board, under the chairmanship of Lord Elis-Thomas, has shown considerable vigour. The Board, and indeed all Welsh quangos, face a fascinating challenge as a result of the referendum of September 1997, when there was, by a tiny margin, a majority in favour of the establishment of a Welsh Assembly. The Assembly will take over the powers of the Secretary of State and will also have the right to pass secondary legislation. In a historic meeting between the architect of the referendum victory, the Secretary of State, Ron Davies, and Cymdeithas yr Iaith Gymraeg at the 1998 National Eisteddfod at Bridgend, Davies pledged that both languages would be equal in the Assembly. There are those, however, who wonder whether an Assembly representative of the entire population of Wales, and therefore necessarily representative of the country's large non-Welsh-speaking majority, will be as sympathetic to the Welsh language as was a British government more open, perhaps, to manipulation by a committed minority. However, decisions made by an all-Wales Assembly will have the approbation of the population of Wales as a whole; even if they fall short of the hopes of Welsh-language enthusiasts, they will have a validity and an endorsement which previous linguistic arrangements have lacked.

VI *Gwnewch bopeth yn Gymraeg*
   (Do everything in Welsh)

The proliferation of organizations concerned to involve people in activities through the medium of Welsh is one of the most marked features of the Welsh-speaking community over recent decades. Welsh is no longer kept for chapel-based social activities, a fact emphasized by the existence of Welsh-language licensed clubs. Nor is it exiled from business and professional life. There are associations for Welsh-speaking doctors and scientists; Welsh-speakers involved in public relations and in fostering commercial skills have their own organizations; several ventures seeking to encourage economic development in Welsh-speaking areas have been established, as have housing associations operating through the medium of Welsh.

The urge to extend the use of Welsh has been particularly marked in the field of the arts. The leading Welsh-language writers are members of Yr Academi Gymreig (the Welsh Academy), founded in 1959, an institution which since 1968 also has an English-language section. Undeb Awduron Cymru safeguards the interests of Welsh authors; Undeb Cyhoeddwyr a Llyfrwerthwyr Cymru represents publishers and booksellers; Cymdeithas Bob Owen with its magazine, *Y Casglwr*, caters for bibliophiles and book collectors. Welsh-speakers involved in the visual arts have their own society, Gweled. In the field of drama, Cwmni Theatr Cymru (and its English counterpart, the Welsh Theatre Company) founded in 1968, eventually collapsed under the weight of financial problems, but other companies – Dalier Sylw and Brith Gof, for instance – offer performances in many parts of Wales.

The musical scene, particularly in its pop aspects, has experienced remarkable developments. There are over a hundred Welsh-language pop groups, Anweledig, Y Tystion and Gorky's Zygotic Mynci prominent among them. Gŵyl Werin y Cnapan, a folk

Well-known Welsh-language band Gorky's Zygotic Mynci.

festival held at Ffostrasol in Ceredigion, is a highly convivial occasion, which attracts many visitors, especially from the other Celtic countries. A different aspect of Welsh folk music is represented by *cerdd dant* (literally, string music: the musician's art, as distinct from *cerdd dafod*). *Cerdd dant* is the singing of a counter melody to a tune played on a harp. A society to promote it was established in 1934, and the art has experienced a renaissance in recent years, as the enthusiasm of those attending its annual festival bears witness.

Other Welsh-language institutions include Merched y Wawr, a women's organization established in 1967 as a reaction to the refusal of the National Federation of Women's Institutes to permit the use of Welsh at an official level. They also include Cymdeithas

107

Mynydda Cymru for mountaineers, Cymdeithas Edward Lhuyd for naturalists, and a host of (largely male) dining clubs. Cefn has joined the battle to secure official status for the language, while Pont (Bridge) has sought to arouse an interest in things Welsh among recent immigrants to Wales. Urdd Gobaith Cymru (the Welsh League of Youth), which celebrated its seventieth birthday in 1992, continues to work among young people, in particular through its well-equipped camps at Llangrannog and Glan-llyn. Some trade unions have been persuaded to make more use of Welsh, and one of them, Undeb Cenedlaethol Athrawon Cymru (the National Union of Teachers of Wales), conducts its business almost entirely through the language. Also in the field of education, Mudiad Ysgolion Meithrin (see p. 80) is concerned with nursery education and Rhieni dros Addysg Gymraeg (Parents for Welsh education) has proved to be an effective pressure group. TAC (Teledwyr Annibynnol Cymru – the Independent Television Producers of Wales) represents the independent sector which has developed in the wake of the establishment of S4C, and television facilities companies, particularly Barcud (Kite) of Caernarfon, have come into existence. The increased use of Welsh has led to a demand for translation services; Welsh translators have their own professional association (Cymdeithas Cyfieithwyr Cymru) and there are a number of commercial translation companies.

The Eisteddfod

All these groups and many more have their stands at that mani-festation *par excellence* of Welshness, the National Eisteddfod. In addition to the National Eisteddfod, many towns and villages continue to hold their own local eisteddfodau, and large-scale eisteddfodau are held in Powys and in Anglesey and also at Cardigan and Lampeter. Urdd Gobaith Cymru's annual eisteddfod is on an even greater scale; indeed, it has been described as the largest youth festival in Europe.

For many Welsh-language loyalists, the National Eisteddfod is the highlight of the year. Apart from the crisis years of 1914 and 1940, it has been held annually since 1881, the location alternat-ing between north and south Wales. It attracts an attendance of about 150,000 on a site of about seventy acres. While the Welsh language has always had a leading role at the National Eisteddfod, the matter was placed beyond doubt in 1952 when the new constitution laid down that Welsh was to be the sole language of its activities, a rule which is now unequivocally observed. This provision has led to a certain amount of controversy, some county councils and individuals arguing that the non-Welsh-speaking majority are cut off from the Eisteddfod as a result. Such feelings, however, did not prevent the 1988 Eisteddfod at Newport or the 1998 Eisteddfod at Bridgend, towns in which Welsh-speakers are far from numerous, from being among the most successful ever.

The link between the Gorsedd and the Eisteddfod, forged by Iolo Morganwg, still holds firm. The ritual of the Gorsedd is undoubtedly the most widely known aspect of the National Eisteddfod, and the ceremonies hailing the achievement of the winners of the chief prizes are the responsibility of the Archdruid and his fellow Gorsedd officers. Traditionally, the Gorsedd only honoured the winners of the crown and the chair, both awarded for poetry, but at Aberystwyth in 1992 the honouring of the winner of the literature medal, awarded for prose, also came under its auspices. Although established as a cultural event, the National Eisteddfod is perhaps primarily a social event, the distinguished journalist, Trevor Fishlock, describing the experience of attending it as 'splashing about in the people bath'. While the competitions and ceremonies in the pavilion constitute the core of the eisteddfod's activities, many avid *eisteddfodwyr* find *y maes* (the field) far more fascinating. The hundreds of stands include that of the Welsh Office, proof of Wales's higher administrative profile. They also include those of political parties, philanthropic societies and book and craft shops. *Y Babell Lên* (the Literature Tent), where adjudications are delivered and poetry contests conducted, is the natural home of literature lovers, but devotees of drama, music and the visual arts also have their tents, while *Pabell y Cymdeithasau* (the Societies' Tent) offers a place for the annual meetings of many Welsh organizations. Indeed it is at the National Eisteddfod, above all, that the organizational vitality of Welsh-speaking Wales can best be appreciated.

Other developments apparent by the last decade of the twentieth century offer hope to those concerned with the future of the Welsh language but, as so often in its history, the hope is not unalloyed. The census of 1991 certainly gives grounds for some optimism, although the figures may not always mean what they seem. The re-emergence of submerged nationalities, such as the Baltic republics, is inspiring, but the conflicts – partly linguistic in origin – accompanying the collapse of the Soviet Union sound a warning note. To seek to preserve the Welsh language can be seen as an aspect of the conservation movement, which is certain to loom large in the years ahead. Yet conservationists are often strongly opposed to the strengthening of the economic infrastructure of Wales, which is central to the viability of Welsh-speaking communities. The general election of 1997 suggests that a large proportion – probably the majority – of Welsh-speakers in the most intensely Welsh-speaking constituencies of Wales now vote for Plaid Cymru. This may be a highly significant development, in that it involves an increasing resolve to reassert linguistic identity. On the other hand, if the party becomes exclusively identified with Welsh-speakers, it will be unable to become the party of Wales as a whole. Thus, dilemmas abound; they can be perplexing, but they can also add to that age-old fascination which holds the devotees of the Welsh language in thrall.

4 Welsh and other Non-state Languages in Europe

About 500 million people live in Europe west of the former Soviet Union. Of these, about 455 million have as their mother tongue the major language of the state in which they live. The remaining 45 million fall into three main categories. About twelve million are recent immigrants or the children of recent immigrants to the area in which they live. Some of them – the Arabic-speakers of France or the Urdu-speakers of Britain, for example – have come from outside Europe, while others, like the Portuguese-speakers in France or the Italian-speakers in Germany, are trans-frontier migrants within Europe itself. A further twelve million or so are members of old-established communities and speak languages which have full status elsewhere but are minority languages within the state in which they live. They include the Swedish-speakers of Finland, the Hungarian-speakers of Romania and the Albanian-speakers of Macedonia.

The rest – some 20 million in all – form the group which has immediate relevance to Welsh. They have as their mother tongue languages which are nowhere the major language of a sovereign state. The drawing up of a list of such languages is no simple matter. Should it not include Lallans, Piedmontese and Alsatian, which some consider to be languages rather than dialects? Should it include Irish, which is, after all, the first official language of the Irish Republic? The list of seventeen languages offered here is no more than tentative, and the statistics relating to the numbers and percentages speaking them vary wildly in their reliability. Some, such as those for Welsh and Scots Gaelic, are based upon official censuses, but others, the languages spoken in France in particular, are a matter of guesswork; the figures for Romany are even more speculative. Where official census statistics are available, they may offer little information about the degree to which those claiming a knowledge of a language actually use that language from day to day. This is an especially relevant consideration in the case of Irish; about a third of the population of the Irish Republic claim to be able to speak the language, but it is believed that less than one per cent make habitual use of it.

The seventeen languages differ enormously in their strength.

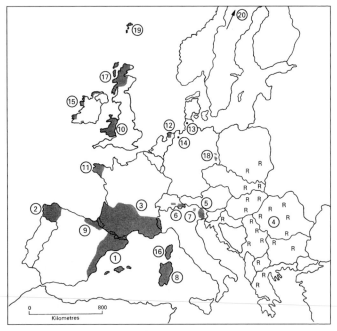

Areas of Europe west of the former Soviet Union inhabited by speakers of languages which are nowhere the major languages of sovereign states. R = Romany. (*See also list opposite.*)

Where their prospects are concerned, the chief determinants are total numbers, density and status. By far the strongest European language which is not the language of a sovereign state is Catalan. Although those who speak it argue that it has not yet achieved a state of complete normalization, it has full legal status in Catalonia, where it is also the major language in the schools and is sustained by several daily newspapers and by extensive use in broadcasting. It is spoken by over seven million people and is the powerful symbol of autonomist and nationalist movements. High levels in terms of numbers, intensity and status are also scored by Galician, which has the added advantage of being very close to Portuguese, one of the world's most widely-spoken languages. Catalan and Galician are Romance languages spoken in states in which the

112

NON-STATE LANGUAGES IN EUROPE

No. on map	Non-state language	Estimated Total No. of speakers	Percentage of population in main territory
1.	Catalan (Spain, France and Italy)	7,500,000	80% of Catalonia
2.	Galician (Spain)	2,200,000	80% of Galicia
3.	Occitan (France, Italy and Spain)	1,500,000	10% of Occitania
4.	Romany (most European countries)	1,000,000	n/a
	Rhaeto-Romansch	(810,000)	
5.	Friulan (Italy)	740,000	60% of Friuli-Venezia Giulia
6.	Romansch (Switzerland)	55,000	32% of Graubunden
7.	Ladin (Italy)	15,000	2% of Trentino Alto Adige
8.	Sard	800,000	55% of Sardinia
9.	Basque (Spain and France)	800,000	23% of Euskadi
10.	Welsh (United Kingdom)	550,000	18% of Wales
11.	Breton (France)	510,000	14% of Brittany
	Frisian	411,000	
12.	West Frisian (Netherlands)	400,000	67% of Friesland
13.	North Frisian (Germany)	10,000	n/a
14.	East Frisian (Germany)	1,000	n/a
15.	Irish (Irish Republic and United Kingdom)	1,000,000	32% of the Republic of Ireland
16.	Corsican (France)	117.000	45% of Corsica
17.	Scots Gaelic (United Kingdom)	80,000	1.3% of Scotland
18.	Sorb (Germany)	50,000	n/a
19.	Faroese (Denmark)	48,000	100% of Faroe Islands
20.	Sami (Norway, Sweden and Finland)	20,000	n/a

major language also belongs to the Romance group. This means that the difference between them and the major language is not great, and Catalonia and Galicia can therefore assimilate newcomers without great difficulty; conversely, there are few linguistic barriers to the absorption of Catalan and Galician speakers by Castilian-speaking, or in the case of the Catalans of France, by French-speaking communities.

Occitan, Sard and Friulan are also Romance languages spoken in states in which the major language belongs to the same linguistic group. Although they are quite widely spoken (assuming that the figures available are correct), their circumstances differ greatly from those of Catalan and Galician. Occitan, which includes Languedoçien, Provençal and Gascon, was once the leading literary language of Europe and the universally spoken language of southern France. Early in this century it was spoken by at least ten million people, but its speech area is now greatly fragmented and consists of some of the remoter districts of the Pyrenees, Gascony and the Alps, where it shades into Franco-Provençal, which may perhaps be considered a separate language. Occitan has no single literary form and no agreed system of spelling. It shares these drawbacks with Sard, a language which is much less widely spoken, but which has a less fragmented speech area. The speech area of Friulan is also cohesive, consisting as it does of a compact area north-east of Venice. Although all three languages score fairly highly in terms of numbers of speakers, and two score well in terms of density, all of them fare badly in terms of status. They have virtually no legal recognition, hardly more than a toehold in the education system, and the state broadcasting systems pay them scant attention. There are movements which seek to raise their status, and some important concessions have been won. Some Sard activists aim at full autonomy, if not independence, and there are fitful demands for autonomy among Occitan speakers, but there seems to be no overt nationalistic agitation among Friulan speakers.

Of the other Romance languages listed – Corsican, Romansch and Ladin – Corsican has no official status. It is taught sporadically in public schools and there are occasional broadcasts in the language. Corsica has a vigorous nationalist movement which sometimes resorts to violence. Romansch is recognized as a national but not as an official language of the Swiss Federation. It has a place in the schools, in broadcasting and in public life, and the decentralized nature of Switzerland allows linguistic tension to be defused. Romansch, nevertheless, faces many difficulties, arising from the small numbers of speakers, the fragmentation of its speech area, the lack of a single literary form and the destructive effect of tourism. Ladin, the central or Dolomitic version of Rhaeto-Romansch, has enjoyed a degree of public recognition since 1948, and it has been a beneficiary of the arrangements for giving official status to German in South Tyrol. The lack of a single literary language, however, and the smallness of the language base, make its situation highly precarious.

The most remarkable of the non-state languages is undoubtedly Romany. The Roma, commonly known as Gypsies, migrated from their Punjab homeland a thousand years ago and the persecution they suffered culminated in the murder of half a million of them by the Nazis. There are at least six million of them in Europe, but they are everywhere scattered and fragmented. The Romany language is extinct in most of western Europe, although it survived among a few families in Wales until the 1950s. It is extensively spoken in Serbia, Slovakia and Romania, and in each country it has absorbed words from the language of the dominant community. Romany receives some degree of recognition in Serbia and Slovakia, and Indian diplomats have shown an interest in its fate. As its speakers have been unable to consolidate themselves territorially, they offer virtually no parallels with other linguistic groups in Europe. The only group which has even slight similarities with them are the Sami. Like the Roma, the Sami (or Lapps) have semi-nomadic traditions, but whereas Romany-speakers are found in at least a dozen of the states of Europe, Sami-speakers are found in only four – Norway, Sweden, Finland and Russia. Compared with the Roma, they are a tiny group, but the self-awareness which has developed among them is leading to increasing cross-frontier co-operation, particularly in the field of broadcasting.

In terms of numbers, the linguistic groups closest to the Welsh-speakers are the speakers of Basque, Breton and Frisian. Frisian has close links with Dutch and German, the dominant languages of the states in which the Frisians live, though linguistically it is closer to English. Breton and Welsh are markedly different from French and English; Basque is entirely different from any of the other languages of Europe, representing as it does a speech which existed in western Europe before the coming of the speakers of Indo-European languages. Basque-speakers are situated on either side of the border between the Spanish and French states; about 696,000 live in the autonomous province of Euskadi and 53,000 in Navarre (both on the Spanish side of the border) and 78,000 in the northern Basque provinces, in south-west France. Basque has some status in Navarre, but virtually none in France, although the density factor is higher there than in Spain. In Euskadi, however, the autonomous government has launched an ambitious programme of language restoration, with schools adopting a determined scheme of language learning, television in Basque being broadcast for sixty-four hours a week and the language emphasized as the symbol of the renaissance of a people.

There is nothing comparable in Breton. In Brittany, the French government's traditional hostility towards all languages other than French has in recent years been modified slightly, but Breton still has no official status and only a minimal role in education and broadcasting. As a result, the numbers able to speak Breton decline rapidly by age group, the number of Breton-speaking parents transmitting the language to their children being small. Yet in some fields, particularly music, Breton culture shows considerable resilience.

The status of West Frisian is markedly higher. (East and North Frisian are in a much weaker position.) There are regulations governing its use in public life and the language is extensively taught in primary schools although it has only a limited role at secondary level. Radio programmes in Frisian are broadcast for about ten hours a week but there is virtually no television in the language. While there are a number of societies concerned to further Frisian, there is only slight evidence of anything resembling a Frisian nationalist movement.

The rest of the linguistic groups listed have less than 100,000 speakers. The strongest of them is undoubtedly Faroese, for all the inhabitants of the Faroe islands, apart from the Danish governor, have Faroese as their mother tongue. The survival of Sorb, a Slav language spoken in two areas of the former East Germany, is very remarkable. The Sorb community suffered grievously under the Nazis but received sympathetic treatment from the Communist regime. Whether it will survive in the circumstances created by the reunification of Germany is as yet uncertain.

As has been noted, Irish is an anomaly in that it is the first official language of a sovereign state, but is spoken by a minority of the citizens of that state. While the state is, in theory, concerned to advance Irish, in practice its support is fitful. However, an Irish-language television channel was launched in 1997, while Ráidio na Gaeltachta has provided a radio service since 1972. Many Irish-language enthusiasts are distressed by the fact that independence has not ensured the well-being of the language although, bearing in mind the parlous condition of Irish when independence was achieved, it would probably not have survived at all had it not received at least partial support from the state. Scots Gaelic, the sister language of Irish, was the dominant language of almost the whole of Scotland a thousand years ago, but it had retreated to the Highlands and Islands by the sixteenth century. It has declined markedly on the mainland and is now spoken by the majority only in parts of Skye and in the Western Isles. The establishment of the Western Isles authority in 1973 led to a considerable enlargement of its role in local government. Initiatives to strengthen its position in schools have been partially successful and there has been a considerable expansion in Gaelic television broadcasting.

A survey of the non-state languages of Europe leads inexorably to the conclusion that the situation of each one is unique. There is, however, a value in considering them together, if only to find areas of useful difference. It is also valuable for their speakers to co-operate, a process fostered by the establishment in 1983 of the European Bureau of Lesser-Used Languages. When the languages are listed, a clear hierarchy emerges. In terms of numbers and status, Catalan heads the list; indeed, it is difficult to see in what sense Catalan is a 'lesser-used' language, in view of the fact that it has far more speakers than some of the sovereign state languages of Europe. In terms of density, the winner is the modest Faroese.

Where does Welsh fit in? It could be claimed that its position is precisely in the centre, a point emphasized by Tom Nairn in his analysis of the non-state nationalities of Europe. Although the Welsh-speakers are by no means among the larger groups, Welsh has a far higher status than several of the more widely-spoken languages. Although the density factor is fairly low, Welsh-speakers live in a country, the other inhabitants of which recognize their kinship with the language, a bonus of immense importance. The centrality of Welsh is interesting in itself. It may also be important, for if Welsh can solve its problems, other languages can hope to do so too.

5 A Note on the Characteristics of Welsh

Languages, when they are described, always appear to be more complicated than they are in reality. Contrary to what many Welsh-speakers like to believe, Welsh is not a difficult language,

---

THE WELSH ALPHABET

a b c ch d dd e f ff g ng

h i ł ll m n o p ph

r rh s th u w y

---

as the thousands who have gained complete mastery of it in adulthood bear witness. In may ways, it is an easier language to learn than English. Unlike English, it has the inestimable advantage of being largely phonetic; that is, the words are pronounced as they are written, with none of the confusion which arises in English over such words as cough, bough, through, though and thorough. While English has several letters (*g*, *h*, and *k*, for example), which are often not pronounced at all, every letter in Welsh is pronounced.

PRONUNCIATION OF DIGRAPHS

ch	as in loch	ll	*ch* followed by *l*
dd	as in that	ph	as in pharmacy
ff	as in fair	rh	as in Rhine
ng	as in singing	th	as in thin

The Welsh alphabet consists of twenty simple letters and eight digraphs (two letters combining to produce a different sound, as with *ch* and *th*), an unusual feature to include in an alphabet. Welsh has no *j*, *k*, *q*, *v*, *x* or *z*. Most of the simple letters present no difficulties, but it should be noted that *c* is always pronounced to correspond with the English *k*, *f* with *v* and *s* with *ss*.

The most remarkable feature which Welsh shares with the other Celtic languages is the system of initial mutations. These changes in the initial consonants of some words have become an integral part of the language, and it has been suggested that they are the result of a fusion of the Celtic languages with the languages spoken by the pre-Celtic inhabitants of Britain and Ireland. There are three kinds of mutation: soft, nasal and aspirate. The most frequent instances of the soft mutation occur when the feminine noun is preceded by the definite article (*cath – y gath* [the cat]), when an adjective follows a feminine noun (*mawr – ystafell fawr* [large room]) and following *ei* (his) (*ci – ei gi* [his dog]). Nasal mutation occurs most frequently after *fy* (my) (*cadair – fy nghadair* [my chair]). Aspirate mutation follows *ei* (her) (*pen – ei phen* [her head]).

TABLE OF MUTATIONS			
Radical	*Soft*	*Nasal*	*Aspirate*
c	g	nhg	ch
p	b	mh	ph
t	d	nh	th
g	(disappears)	ng	
b	f	m	
d	dd	n	
ll	l		
m	f		
rh	r		

To the beginner, the whole matter can appear highly abstruse; yet it is comforting to know that a learner who ignores the mutations completely can be understood without much difficulty. A mastery of them is, however, the mark of the successful learner and is ultimately acquired naturally, as if the speaker unconsciously absorbs the inherent euphony of the language.

In almost all Welsh words, the stress falls on the last syllable but one: *gorýmdaith*; *áthro*; *amddiffýniad*. In those cases where the stress falls on the last syllable, it is usually the result of a contraction in the word: *Cymraég* was originally *Cym-ra-eg*, and *paratói* was *pa-ra-to-i*. Some words borrowed from English also retain the original accentuation: *apél*; *pólisi*; *páragraff.*

The noun has two genders, masculine and feminine. The 'it' of English does not exist. As in French, everything is either '*he*' or '*she*'. Some adjectives have masculine and feminine forms. Thus *gwyn* (white) is (*g*)*wen* when following a feminine noun. Some adjectives also have singular and plural forms (although adjectival plurals are used infrequently): *dyn tew* is a fat man, *dynion tewion* fat men. Where plurals are concerned, Welsh recognizes that some things come in pairs. Thus *llaw* (hand) has the plural *dwylaw* (*two* hands). To anyone used to English plurals, with the almost universal addition of *s*, the variety of Welsh plural forms can appear wilfully multifarious. There are seven ways of forming the plural.

PLURAL FORMS IN WELSH

adding a termination: *afal* (apple) *afalau*

vowel change: *bran* (crow) *brain*

adding a termination with a vowel change: *mab* (son) *meibion*

dropping a singular ending: *pluen* (feather) *plu*

dropping a singular ending with a vowel change: *hwyaden* (duck) *hwyaid*

substituting a plural for a singular ending: *cwningen* (rabbit) *cwningod*

substituting a plural ending for a singular with a vowel change: *miaren* (bramble) *mieri*

The numerals in Welsh also have distinctive features. Twenty is the basic unit in counting: *ugain* (twenty), *deugain* (two twenties – forty), *trigain* (three twenties – sixty), *pedwar ugain* (four twenties – eighty), followed by *cant* (a hundred) and sometimes by *chwe ugain* (six twenties – a hundred and twenty). The teens offer interesting complications: fourteen is *pedwar ar ddeg* (four on ten), but sixteen is *un ar bymtheg* (one on fifteen) and eighteen *deunaw* (two nines). There is now a growing tendency to adopt a decimal system – *un deg wyth* (one ten eight) for eighteen, *pedwar deg* (four tens) for forty and so on. The singular form of the noun is used after the numeral: *un afal* – one apple; *ugain afal* – twenty apples, which means that the complexities of plurals can often be avoided altogether.

In English, the order of the words in a sentence is subject, verb, object, indirect object. (The girl gave a book to her friend.) In Welsh it is verb, subject, object, indirect object:

> *Rhoddodd y ferch lyfr i'w chyfaill*
> Gave the girl a book to her friend

This order can be varied for the sake of emphasis or to ask a question:

> *Ceffyl a welodd y plentyn?*
> Horse saw the child?
> (Was it a horse the child saw?)

The adjective is almost always placed after the noun. When it is not, the meaning may be different. *Ci unig* means a lonely dog, but *unig gi* means the only dog; *hen gyfaill* means a friend of long standing, but *cyfaill hen* means an aged friend.

The genitive, expressed in English by an apostrophe s ('s), is expressed in Welsh by putting what is owned immediately before the owner: *ci Lowri* – Lowri's dog; *tŷ y dyn* – the man's house.

The tendency to the periphrastic, or more roundabout, form is very obvious in verb forms. 'I sing' in standard written Welsh is *canaf*, but the usual spoken form is *yr wyf i yn canu* (I am singing). This use of a part of the verb 'to be' (*yr wyf i*, I am) with the verb-noun (*canu*) may have been inherited by the incoming Celts from the pre-Celtic population. The construction has been copied in English to give the form 'I am singing', a construction not found in the other Germanic languages.

The existence of the written concise form and the spoken periphrastic form of the verb is an example of the considerable difference between formal and colloquial Welsh. Another example is the continued use in written Welsh of the ending *-nt* in the third person plural of the verb, as in *daethant* (they came), which in speech becomes *daethan.* Yet another example is *hwy,* which in speech becomes *nhw.* These differences are the result of the fact that written Welsh is based upon the forms employed by William Morgan in his translation of the Bible in 1588. Those forms were in turn based upon the usages of the classical poets, which were already archaic in Morgan's day. In preparing courses for learners, it is usual to employ more flexible colloquial forms. Thus, a learner is taught to say *Maen nhw'n dod* (they are coming), rather than *Y maent hwy yn dod.*

Welsh has no indefinite article. Thus, the dog is *y ci,* but a dog is simply *ci.* This is a feature Welsh shares with the other Celtic languages, as is the conjugation of prepositions and the absence of all-purpose words for yes and no.

CONJUGATION OF PREPOSITIONS

gan (with)	ar (on)
gennyf (with me)	arnaf (on me)
gennyt (with thee)	arnat (on thee)
ganddo (with him)	arno (on him)
ganddi (with her)	arni (on her)
gennym (with us)	arnom (on us)
gennych (with you)	arnoch (on you)
ganddynt (with them)	arnynt (on them)

Although Welsh has absorbed words from other languages, Latin, French and particularly English among them, its basic vocabulary is still largely of Celtic origin. This is also true of more technical words. Thus, while English words such as national, political, industrial and philosophical have equivalents in French, German and other European languages which are very similar, Welsh uses its own indigenous words – *cenedlaethol, gwleidyddol, diwydiannol* and *athronyddol.* Indeed, it has a very considerable ability to coin words from its own resources, although the sloppy speech of many Welsh-speakers, overloaded as it is with unnecessary English borrowings, can give the contrary impression.

Dialect

There is no 'Received Welsh' comparable with Received English; all Welsh-speakers speak in dialect to a greater or lesser extent. Even those whose speech is close to formal Welsh provide indicators through their intonation and through their pronunciation of certain letters – *u* in particular – as to the part of Wales to which their Welsh belongs. Most Welsh-speakers are fascinated by dialect and some claim to be able to identify the origins of a new acquaintance down even to parish level. Someone from Anglesey using a large number of words of local currency can present difficulties to someone from Glamorgan, and vice versa. The issue of unintelligibility, however, is often grossly exaggerated, for the difference between dialects in Wales is far less than it is in England.

There is a widespread assumption that there are only two forms of Welsh – northern and southern. The most familiar indicators are the words for 'now' and 'with'. 'Now' is *nawr* to the south and *rwan* to the north of the Rheidol valley; 'with' is *gyda* to the south and (*h*)*efo* to the north of the Dyfi valley. Other words – those for stallion, grandmother and liver, for example – also serve to emphasize the significance of the isogloss along the ancient border between the diocese of St David's and those of Bangor and St Asaph. Yet the pronunciations of some words link the north-west and the south-east; thus the word *perffaith* (perfect) is pronounced *perffath* in Gwynedd and Gwent, but *perffeth* in the rest of Wales. The tendency to turn *a* into *e* – *tên for tân* (fire), for example – occurs in Montgomeryshire and Meirionnydd, and also in the south-east. (It may explain the narrow *e* in the English dialect of Cardiff – 'a pint of dêk in Cêdiff Êms Pêk'.)

Dialectologists consider that Welsh has six major speech areas; within them there are a further sixteen minor speech areas. The differences between some of them are slight. The Welsh of the greater part of south-western Wales, for example, is broadly the same; a speaker of the dialect of the Ystwyth valley, moving to the lower Tywi valley, eighty kilometres away, would find only two or three unfamiliar words in regular use. If the whole of Wales were Welsh-speaking, by far the most commonly spoken dialect would be Gwenhwyseg, the speech of Gwent and east Glamorgan (the home of 45 per cent of the population of Wales), but the erosion of the language in that region has undermined the

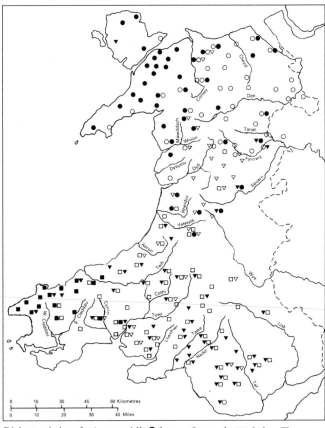

Dialect variations for 'young girl': ● *hogan*, ○ *geneth*, ▽ *lodes*, □ *croten*, ■ *rhoces*, ▼ *merch*.

dialect, which can now only be heard on the lips of the elderly in places such as Rhymni and Dowlais. As many of the teachers in Welsh-medium schools are natives of south-west Wales, their way of speaking has tended to become dominant among the new generation of Welsh-speakers in the south-east.

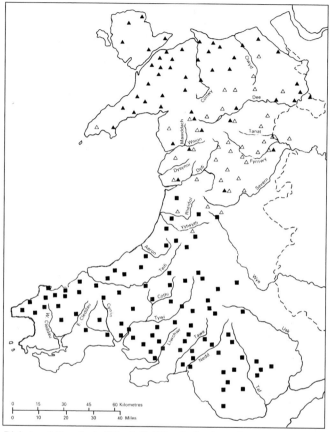

Dialect variations for 'milk': ▲ *llefrith*, △ *llaeth*, ■ *llâth*.

Postscript

I shall finish, as I began, on a personal note. I mentioned that in my childhood it seemed odd to me that there should be people who not only spoke Welsh effortlessly, but did so all the time. Now that I speak Welsh myself, this does not seem odd at all. What does seem peculiar, in view of the manifest vitality and innovativeness of Welsh-speaking Wales, is the constant lament that the end of the language is in sight. Perhaps I am fortunate in that, not having been brought up in a community in which Welsh was the dominant language, I cannot share the sense of despair felt by those who were brought up in such communities and who contemplate their erosion with something akin to panic. I am more aware of advances. In my native town, Bryn-mawr, there is now a Welsh-medium primary school with over two hundred pupils, and a few miles away over the hills stands a Welsh-medium secondary school. A great deal of the panic and despair stems, not so much from the erosion of the language in many of its former strongholds as from the realization that the way of life associated with the language in those strongholds has passed away. I did not know that way of life, and so its passing leaves me unmoved. Indeed, it could be argued that the association of Welsh with a vanishing way of life was detrimental to the language, and that its continuance is dependent upon its ability to anchor itself in modernity, an ability which it has, to some extent, shown.

Those distressed by the erosion of virtually monoglot Welsh communities point to the way in which the English language has burrowed itself into spheres of life which were formerly exclusively Welsh. Again, I and others like me cannot share in their distress. To those brought up as I was, in English-speaking communities, the English language was and is a part of the common experience, and I cannot conceive of Wales without it. The future of the Welsh language must depend upon the ability of those who speak it to come to terms with the existence of English in Wales. That Welsh has a future I do not doubt, for the vitality it has demonstrated over the past generation shows no sign of waning. That it should show such vitality is in itself a matter for wonder, when it is borne in mind that English, its nearest neighbour, has steamrollered into virtual extinction languages far distant from the shores of England. The prime necessity is to prove that a knowledge of Welsh is life-enhancing. A life-enhancing language will survive and flourish, as surely Welsh will.

Further Reading

Aitchison, J. W. and H. Carter, *A Geography of the Welsh Language 1961–1991*, University of Wales Press, 1993.

Davies, John, *A History of Wales*, Allen Lane, 1993.

Jenkins, Geraint H. (ed.), *The Welsh Language before the Industrial Revolution*, University of Wales Press, 1997.

Jenkins, Geraint H. (ed.), *Language and Community in the Nineteenth Century*, University of Wales Press, 1998.

Jones, Dot, *Statistical Evidence relating to the Welsh Language*, University of Wales Press, 1998.

Parry, Thomas, *A History of Welsh Literature*, Clarendon Press, 1955.

Stephens, Meic, *Linguistic Minorities in Western Europe*, Gomer, 1976.

Stephens, Meic (ed.), *The Welsh Language Today*, Gomer, 1973.

Stephens, Meic and R. Brinley Jones (series editors), *Writers of Wales* (a series of monographs on Welsh writers), University of Wales Press, 1970– .

Williams, Gwyn, *An Introduction to Welsh Literature*, University of Wales Press, 1992 (new edition).

Williams, Mari A. and Gwenfair Parry, *The Welsh Language and the 1891 Census*, University of Wales Press, Autumn 1999.

Williams, Stephen J., *A Welsh Grammar*, University of Wales Press, 1980.

Index

Morgan, Mihangel, 92
Morgan, Prys, 37
Morgan, T. J., 93
Morgan, William, 23–4, 93, 122
Morris, Lewis, 31, 42
Morris, Richard, 31
Morris-Jones, John, 11, 53, 92
Mudiad Ysgolion Meithrin, 80, 108
Mynydd Epynt, 67
Myvyrian Archalology, The, 39

Nant Gwrtheyrn, 87
National Assembly of Wales, 106
National Library of Wales, 46
National Museum of Wales, 46
National Society, 43
Neuadd John Morris-Jones, 85
Neuadd Pantycelyn, 85
Newport, 36, 109
Newtown, 75
Norse, 13
Noson Lawen, 95

Occitan, 114
Owen, Daniel, 37, 92
Owen, Gerallt Lloyd, 90
Owen, Hywel Wyn, 93
Oxford Book of Welsh Verse, 93

Parry, Gwenlyn, 92
Parry, R. Williams, 63
Parry, Thomas, 14, 93
Parry-Williams, T. H., 63, 92
Patagonia, 48, 54
Pembrokeshire, 17, 20, 35, 43, 83
Penllyn, 72, 77
Pentreath, Dorothy, 9
Penrith, 9
Pezron, Paul-Yves, 29
Pla, Y, 92
*Place of Welsh and English in the
    Schools of Wales, The*, 83
Plaid Genedlaethol Cymru, 63
Plaid Cymru, 99, 102–3, 110
Pobol y Cwm, 100
*Pocket Guide to the Place-Names of
    Wales, A*, 93

Pont, 108
Pontypool, 37, 55
Pontypridd, 81, 84
Port Talbot, 71
Powys, 11, 83, 108
Prestatyn, 78
Price, John, of Brecon, 22, 23
Price, Thomas (Carnhuanawc), 40
Prichard, Caradog, 92
Prichard, Rhys, 29
Primary Education in Wales (the
    Gittins Report), 83
Pryce, W. T. R., 93
Pughe, William Owen, 37–9
Puleston family, 20
Pwyllgor Amddiffyn Diwylliant
    Cymru, 67

Radio Ceredigion, 96
Radio Cymru, 95–6
Radio Wales, 95
Radnorshire, 35, 47, 54, 69
Raligamps, 95
Red Book of Hergest, the, 11
Rees, Alwyn D., 102
Rheged, 11
Rhieni dros Addysg Gymraeg, 108
Rhondda, 55, 59, 92
Rhondda Cynon Taf, 71
Rhos, 16
Rhys ap Gruffudd, 15, 28
Rhyl, 84
Rhŷs, John, 52, 92
Robert, Gruffydd, 25–7
Roberts, Kate, 63, 92
Roberts, Wiliam O., 92
Roman de la Rose, 15
Romansch, 114–15
Romany, 111, 115
Rowland, Daniel, 33
Rowlands, John, 92
Royal Commission on Elementary
    Education, 51–2

St David, 6
Salesbury family, 20
Salesbury, William, 23, 25, 33

134